The Second Chance Café

ALSO BY AMANDA PROWSE

Novels

Poppy Day
What Have I Done?
Clover's Child
A Little Love
Will You Remember Me?
Christmas for One
A Mother's Story
Perfect Daughter
The Second Chance Café
Three-and-a-Half Heartbeats
Another Love
My Husband's Wife
I Won't be Home for Christmas
The Food of Love
The Idea of You
The Art of Hiding
Anna
Theo
Kitty
The Coordinates of Loss
The Girl in the Corner

The Things I Know
The Light in the Hallway
The Day She Came Back
An Ordinary Life
Waiting to Begin
To Love and Be Loved
Picking Up the Pieces
All Good Things
Very Very Lucky
Swimming to Lundy
This One Life

Novellas

The Game
Something Quite Beautiful (collection)
A Christmas Wish
The Ten Pound Ticket
Imogen's Baby
Miss Potterton's Birthday Tea
Mr Portobello's Morning Paper
I Wish . . .
A Whole Heap of Wishes
A Wish for Forgiveness

Children's books

The Smile That Went a Mile (with Paul Ward Smith)
Today I'm In Charge! (with Paul Ward Smith)

Non-fiction

The Boy Between (with Josiah Hartley)
Women Like Us

The Second Chance Café

Amanda Prowse

An Aria Book

First published in the UK as *The Christmas Café* in 2015 by Head of Zeus Ltd

This edition first published in the UK in 2025 by Head of Zeus Ltd,
part of Bloomsbury Publishing Plc

Copyright © Amanda Prowse, 2015

The moral right of Amanda Prowse to be identified
as the author of this work has been asserted in accordance with
the Copyright, Designs and Patents Act of 1988.

All rights reserved. No part of this publication may be: i) reproduced or transmitted in
any form, electronic or mechanical, including photocopying, recording or by means of
any information storage or retrieval system without prior permission in writing from the
publishers; or ii) used or reproduced in any way for the training, development or operation
of artificial intelligence (AI) technologies, including generative AI technologies. The rights
holders expressly reserve this publication from the text and data mining exception as per
Article 4(3) of the Digital Single Market Directive (EU) 2019/790.

This is a work of fiction. All characters, organizations, and events portrayed
in this novel are either products of the author's imagination or are used fictitiously.

9 7 5 3 1 2 4 6 8

A catalogue record for this book is available from the British Library.

ISBN (PB): 9781035923502
ISBN (E): 9781784970369

Cover design: Rory Kee
Typeset by Adrian McLaughlin

Printed and bound in Great Britain by
CPI Group (UK) Ltd, Croydon CR0 4YY

Bloomsbury Publishing Plc
50 Bedford Square, London, WC1B 3DP, UK
Bloomsbury Publishing Ireland Limited,
29 Earlsfort Terrace, Dublin 2, D02 AY28, Ireland

HEAD OF ZEUS LTD
5–8 Hardwick Street
London, EC1R 4RG

To find out more about our authors and books
visit www.headofzeus.com
For product safety related questions contact productsafety@bloomsbury.com

For this I am truly indebted to my teams at Head of Zeus, Midas and PFD.

My colleagues, my friends.

I really, really, love you all.

Prologue

Bea stood in the early-evening light and let the warm New South Wales wind lift her long, layered grey hair and kiss her face. It was seasonably clement and the city had an air of expectation about it. As far as Sydney-siders were concerned, the warmer the better, allowing them to enjoy all that the outdoor life had to offer. She stared at the bronze boar in front of her; Il Porcellino stared back as her fingers twitched in the pocket of her funky grass-green linen smock. Commuters keen to get home and make the most of the evening sunshine, either with a trip to the beach or supper in the garden, rushed along Macquarie Street behind her, shedding jackets and rolling up sleeves. Groups of colleagues making an early start on the Christmas party season walked with arms across each other's shoulders, the booze-fuelled banter bringing them closer than any teambuilding around a boardroom table. Bea envied them the ordinariness of their preoccupations. Looking to the left and right, swallowing her shyness, she stepped forward and gingerly rubbed the shiny nose of the tusked creature.

'Please.' She mouthed the one word and closed her eyes briefly before tossing the little round coin with the square hole into the water at its feet. Throwing her head back, she took a deep breath and looked up at the grand arches and pretty green ironwork panels with terraces behind. It was a beautiful building in the city that they loved; that in itself was a comfort. There were far, far worse places for her husband to die.

'Ah, you're back. Did you have a little wander?' The kindly nurse flicked off the overhead strip-light, leaving the room dulled, with only a subdued glow coming from the side light above the sink. It was most fitting; cosy and calming.

'Not really, just went outside for a breather. It's warm tonight.' Bea pinched and pumped the front of her smock.

The nurse nodded. Her shift didn't finish until the morning; the weather outside was of little consequence. She placed her hooked fingers against Peter's wrist and swept her palm over his brow, smiling into his milky eyes. 'I'll be back in a wee while, Peter,' she said.

Bea greatly appreciated how civil the nurses were to her husband. He might or might not have been able to hear or comprehend them, but she was glad they assumed that he could.

She resumed her position in the vinyl chair by Peter's bedside, still in the clothes she had worn for the last seventy-two hours, crumpled and dappled with splashes of coffee and streaks of mascara that her tired arm had blotted from her tear-stained face.

'If you need anything, Mrs Greenstock, then you only have to buzz,' the nurse said as she made her way towards the door.

Bea nodded. 'Thank you, yes. Do you think he needs anything right now? Should we give him more medicine?'

The nurse smiled and spoke slowly as if addressing a child. 'No. No more medicine. Really, it's best we just let nature take its course.'

'How long, would you say, if you had to guess?' She spoke quietly, averting her eyes, guilty for asking.

The nurse shook her head, her voice equally soft. 'It's really hard to say. Sometimes, when the final decline starts, it can be quite quick; but other people hang on, literally for days. There's no way for us to know, but I would say that with Peter it will be sooner rather than later. It's good that you are here.' She crinkled her eyes in a smile as she shut the door behind her.

Bea was grateful for her honesty and her kindness. She sat forward in the chair with her elbows resting on her bony knees. 'Did you hear that, darling? It's good that I'm here. But actually, I'd rather neither of us was here. I'd rather we were on a little sailing boat in the Whitsundays catching fresh fish for lunch, washed down with a cold glass of wine. Then we could nap on the deck in the sunshine and when we woke up, we'd swim in that glorious sea, go ashore to walk on that fine, white sand and sit and watch the day pass overhead.' She smiled. 'Do you remember that wonderful Christmas? Just the two of us. It was paradise, wasn't it? The best ever.'

Bea held her husband's hand and leant over his face. His eyes seemed to have fogged, but his head moved slightly from side to side, as if seeking the face that he could no longer see.

'It's okay, my love, I'm right here. I'm not going anywhere.'

There was the slightest flicker around his mouth. She wanted to believe, in the half-light of this hospital side ward, that it was a final smile for her, but it could have been wishful thinking. He was preoccupied with his battle, bathed in a sickly sweet sweat as his body fought the inevitable. It was a cloying, unpleasant scent that she would smell in the future on certain flowers and on the breath of the ill and elderly and find herself immediately transported back to this room at this moment.

Bea thought of the many deathbed scenes that she had witnessed in movies and plays. The laborious last messages of love or confession as violins built to a crescendo. It was of course all utter, utter rubbish. She had seen one man die before, happening across a traffic accident one morning on the corner of Elizabeth Street and Park Street, and he had barely twitched an eyelid before passing. Peter fought for every last second, steely and determined till the end. She wished the movie scenes weren't rubbish, she wished he would sit up straight, look her in the eye, with his palm against her face and a bloom to his cheek, tell her that it was all going to be okay, that he had no regrets, that he had always loved her. This last fact she knew, but the thought of not hearing it again made her unbelievably sad.

She felt a rush of love and also gratitude for this man who had met the love of his life and been content to walk by her side, knowing that in her affections he came third, after her son and the memory of one she had loved long ago. Even now, in his final moments, he was self-contained, as if considering her needs until the last, making her experience as comfortable as he possibly could. She didn't need violins.

'I was so blessed to find you, Peter. You are a wonderful man, a wonderful friend, and I love you – you know that, don't you?' She sighed. 'What do I do now, my love? Where do I go from here?' She heard his words loud and clear, the mantra by which he had lived. *'Always remember, life is for the brave. This is our one time around the block!'*

'I know...' She nodded. Her many silver bangles jangled together, cracking open the silence with their noise. She squeezed his hand, hard, hoping for reciprocation.

'Oh, my love, your hand has gone cold.' She bent forward and kissed his nose, which was also cool against her lips, but his body was still hot, as though a furnace burning centrally was losing its ability to ignite anything out of immediate reach.

Peter turned his head a fraction and with every ounce of strength left in his body he reached up and past her, seeming to focus on the space to the right of her head. His thin legs twisted in the same direction, as if he was trying to leave his deathbed.

'Where are you off to?' She cried then, knowing where he was going and that she could not follow. 'You go, my darling; you go wherever you want to. It's okay. Just go to sleep and know that you are loved.'

Peter sank back against the shallow pillow and his breath faltered. He opened and closed his mouth as if trying to speak. She bent low and with her ear against his mouth, she heard the faintest whisper of his final words. 'It's been lovely.'

'Oh, it has, Peter! It really has!'

The gaps between each breath grew longer and longer, until there were no more.

Bea waited and watched, fixated on the waxy skin at the base of his throat, hoping for one more fluttering tremor that would mean he was still with her and she didn't have to start grieving. But there was none.

She'd been told to press the call button when the inevitable happened, or if she needed anything, but instead she sat holding his hand, with her other pressed in the nook of his elbow where warmth lingered. She wanted to stay just like that until the warmth disappeared, like singing a baby off to sleep, waiting for the right moment to shuffle backwards out of the room, leaving the door ajar.

It was way past midnight before she finally left her love and quietly closed the door behind her on nearly thirty years of marriage.

Second Chance Cafe

The hospital canteen was quiet, the silence shattered only by the occasional weary medic, wearing creased scrubs and with dark shadows beneath their eyes. They gave small nods in her direction, knowing it could not be happy circumstances that saw her lingering over a cup of scalding, weak, machine-issued coffee all alone at that ungodly hour. She was grateful for their lack of intervention, wanting to be alone with the images that were crystallising inside her mind. His last minutes, engraving themselves on her brain, there for perfect recall whenever she might need them in the future.

She looked around the walls of the canteen that had been her refuge for the last ten days, the place she'd crept to hourly, when nurses invaded the room to 'make him comfortable'. She always gave them ten minutes to complete the chores that she didn't want to witness; not for her sake, but for Peter's. It was strange to think that it would now be someone else's turn to sit on that plastic chair in the dead of night and figure out how to stop feeling numb. Women just like her, going through the same thing, would be scanning the panini menus, scooping chocolate bars from the shallow baskets and searching pockets for small change. She felt a wave of pity for them, because they didn't know what was coming and it was horrid.

'There you are!' Wyatt's voice jolted her from her musings. His short-sleeved white shirt was undone to reveal a little too much chest and his khaki board shorts had wisps of grass hanging off them; he looked like he had just come in from the garden. He sounded slightly cross, as if she had been hiding, his stance and tone indicating he had been mightily inconvenienced by the whole carry-on.

'I couldn't park the bloody car, even at this time of night. It's 2013, we can send shuttles up into space and we can fit more information than is held in the Canberra National Library on a digital postage stamp, but we can't work out how to allow entry to a locked car park after hours. It's a bloody ridiculous system.' He flipped the bunch of car keys back and forth until they nestled inside his clenched palm.

Bea nodded. It was. Bloody ridiculous.

'So, how's he doing?' Wyatt placed his knuckles on his hips; again, as if angry with her about something.

She stared at her son and twisted the bangles on her wrist. 'He died, Wyatt. He died a few hours ago.' It was the first time she had said it out loud. 'It was actually very peaceful. He just went to sleep. I was holding his hand. He seemed to reach across me, as though trying to head off somewhere. I told him it was okay to go; like giving him permission, I suppose. Permission to leave me. And he went.' She gave a brief smile.

'Oh, Mum,' he offered, neutrally.

She wondered what that meant. *'Oh, Mum, I'm so sorry,'* or *'I wish I'd got here sooner,'* or *'Please, Mother, less of the dramatics.'* It was hard to tell. Wyatt was a man who coped better with the practical than the emotional. He no doubt wanted her to start talking about funeral arrangements and finances, things to which he could relate, rather than how she was feeling. But that was simply tough shit.

'I didn't know what to do, so I called you.' She felt, awkwardly, that she had to justify the inconvenience.

'Of course.' He nodded. 'I'll take you home, when you're ready.' He placed his hand briefly on her shoulder, pulling away quickly.

She felt the imprint of his fingers on her skin, like a burn. She considered reminding him that neither heart disease nor in fact heartache were contagious. He was safe on both counts. She felt a mixture of disappointment and relief. Whilst it might have been nice to be swept up in an all-consuming hug, it would also have been acutely embarrassing; they were so out of practice.

Twenty minutes later, Wyatt's big, shiny Holden Storm, with its warm leather interior and startling spaceship-like display on the dashboard, swept up Elizabeth Street and turned into Reservoir Street, at the heart of the affluent Surry Hills district. Both streets were almost deserted. The car's headlights raked the walls and she winced, knowing they would wake several residents.

Pulling into the kerb, Wyatt turned to his mother. 'Are you sure you don't want me to come up?' The way he left his seatbelt fastened and the engine running told her all she needed to know.

'No, no, I'm fine. You get back to Sarah and Flora. Thank you for coming all this way, Wyatt, at this time of night.'

'If you're sure.'

'Absolutely. It's a good half-hour's drive back to Manly. You get yourself off, love.'

She sensed the easing of his tension and realised that she too had dreaded the prospect of small talk and long silences over a cup of tea.

Bea climbed the stairs and twisted her key in the lock; the apartment was dark and quiet. Peter had been in hospital for ten days and she had popped back twice for showers and a change of clothes, yet tonight the rooms felt emptier than they had before, as if the bricks and mortar sensed that he was not coming home. She slumped down on the sofa and sat in the shadows, finding solace in the peace and particular hush that night-time brings.

Peter's sandshoes sat side by side on the bathroom floor. His pyjamas were still in the laundry basket and his books were arranged in two small stacks on his bedside table. One pile waiting to be read and the other his favourites, which he liked to keep close. Rudyard Kipling's *The Jungle Book*, which he had loved since his teens, was among them. Bea's mind jumped back in time, to another Kipling book, another man, another life. A tall man with a green scarf, who had kept time on her heart with his palm. Thirty-four years ago now, and yet she remembered it like it was yesterday.

She picked up a green silk cushion and hugged it to her while she surveyed Peter's things, all now redundant, including the spectacles that sat on top of their case on the coffee table. She gingerly scooped them into her palm and held them against her chest. It was strange that these innocuous items now held such significance, vaulting the line from everyday thing to precious talisman. She wept, her loss and exhaustion sweeping over her like a wave that left her gulping for air. She was not just crying for the wonderful man she had lost but for the true, unconditional love that she had been unable to give him.

'I'm sorry, Peter. I'm so sorry.'

coffee-table top, hurriedly she piled them into her palm and held them against her chest. It was strange, if it felt tumultuous items now held such significance, wielding the power to overturn things or produce a ripple. She was at a loss and exhausted, weeping in a way her life as a wife and lover or mother, putting her life's work into meaning for the sake of someone, had made her forget. She'd never, not once, wondered that she had lost sight of the true, unconditional love that she had been unable to give him.

"Ign sorry Peter. I'm sorry."

One

Bea slowly opened one eye, peeking from her pillow at the new morning. The remnants of a dream lurked in her consciousness – she had been taken back in time, to the beat of a drum and the sound of a wide-decked, tall ship pushing through the waves. The wild torment of a younger body that yearned for the touch of her man, a memory of dancing under the stars on a swaying deck, the feel of his cotton shirt beneath her fingertips, his eyes, locked on hers, pulling her in. And his voice, deep and resolute, his words loud and clear, spoken on a still, hot, summer's night as the cicadas chirped and the black flying-fox bats circled overhead. *'I want to take you away. I want to make a home where you and I are free to love each other without judgement, without having to hide. I wish I could marry you, right here, right now. I won't ever let you go. I'll carry you with me, in here...'* His two fingers had patted his chest in the rhythm of a heartbeat.

She sighed. The sun streamed in through the open window, casting spiky shadows of the full-bloomed Queensland lacebark against the wooden floor. She instinctively put a hand out to the other side of the bed. It was hard to believe that it had been a full year since she had said goodbye to Peter in that dimly lit hospital ward; but the pain was easing, a little. What surprised her were moments like these, when she reached out but failed to find him lying next to her in his stripy blue pyjamas, or when she wanted to call him with some titbit of information.

Bea glanced guiltily at Peter's side of the bed. Even after all these years, an unsettling dream still had the power to do that to her: the flash of a memory, an image, a word. It could transport her back to a time before Peter, a time before her whole world had unravelled. And then, mercifully, he had swept in and saved her with his kindness.

She threw back the cool cotton bedspread and swung her legs onto the stripped wooden floor, letting her silk pyjamas unbunch themselves and slip crinkle-free down her legs, the sleeves falling in neat gaping triangles over her arms. She rather liked the contrast of the cream colour against the faint liver spots on the back of her hand. Deciding against her vintage silk kimono dressing gown, she left it on the bed and stood in front of the tall mirror, where she stretched her arms high above her head, turning sharply to the left as she waited for the familiar click of her neck. Next she bent forward with her hands clasped over her head and hung that way for a minute until her back, like her PJs, was kink-free. These were just a couple of the little rituals that she performed at the beginning of every day.

Second Chance Cafe

Bea held her breath and pulled the blind. She was, as ever, filled with joy and relief at the sight of Reservoir Street below, so very different from the dingy bedsit in Kings Cross she and Wyatt had shared for six years. Even after so many decades, the memory of that tiny hot room had the power to make her skin itch. She smiled as she took in the steep street with its pastel-coloured Victorian terraced properties and stunning wrought-iron balconies that sat proudly on either side of the thoroughfare. A runner laboured up the incline on the opposite side of the street, his headphones firmly in place. He raised his hand at the sight of her – funny how everyone knew her because of the business.

She sighed. It was a glorious day full of summer promise, and despite the loneliness that threatened there was something rather lovely about this early hour, the stillness of the place before the ensuing madness of the day. She had always been an early riser and this had proved most beneficial to the success of the Reservoir Street Kitchen. Up with the lark, she would have the lights on, ovens hungry and toasty, kettles filled, bread prepped and deliveries sorted and stowed before Kim and Tait made an appearance.

Bea took one last fond look at the slight dent on Peter's side of the bed, which would never, she hoped, regain its original shape, allowing her to imagine him only temporarily absent, sipping coffee down at The Rocks or fetching the morning paper. That made it easier somehow, kidding herself that he would be back sometime soon.

Radio 2GB babbled away in the background and Alan Jones' unmistakeable cadences filled the room, updating her on the state of the world. It was all she needed to lift her spirits. She still hadn't heard from Wyatt or Sarah with regard to Christmas and at that precise moment she hated her need of them. She tried to remain stoical, tried not to dwell on the fact that she only saw or heard from them once a month, but the truth was, she did mind, especially because this sparse, inadequate contact meant she was kept away from her granddaughter, Flora, a bubbly thirteen-year-old whom Bea adored. In recent years, on Flora's birthday she had made a point of going to the house in Manly twenty minutes early so as to catch a little time with Flora before she went out to play with her buddies. And each year, after Sarah's Christmas barbecue, they would sit together on the sand and chat. Bea would ask Flora what bands were 'in', and Flora would tease her for being an old granny, even though she'd only turned fifty-three this year. It wasn't much of an interaction, but as Bea reminded herself, they had busy, full lives and that little bit of contact was better than nothing.

She made herself a mug of Earl Grey with a large slice of lemon and stood in front of the open windows by the Juliet balcony as she looked out over the warm Sydney morning. The big sky was clear in its azure brilliance, and she allowed her mind to wander back to the same time last year, to a similarly perfect summer's day, which had seemed to spite her sadness. It was seven days after Peter had passed away and she'd sat on the sofa, resplendent in understated aubergine, remote and aloof, like a queen bee attended by a swarm of fluttering guests. Just like at weddings, everyone had wanted a small amount of time with her, the main attraction. The trick was not to monopolise or talk too much; funerals were all about short, meaningful sentences. 'So sorry for your loss...' 'It's a blessing...' 'A happy release...' 'He was a great bloke.' The offerings had all been pretty much identical in both content and the manner in which they were delivered, heads cocked to one side, doleful expressions, and the volume barely above a whisper.

The only original sentiment had come from Flora, who had seen it as more of a party and had been refreshingly oblivious as to why it might not be appropriate to laugh loudly, sing or throw snacks down to the disinterested little wattlebird resting in the tree below the balcony. Bea had watched Wyatt glare at his daughter from the other side of the room – probably more effective than actually engaging with her. She realised that Flora had always been that way, slightly out of kilter with what was expected by the rest of the pack. And, truthfully, she approved of Flora's attitude: funerals should be about celebrating a person's life. Peter's wake had been far too sedate; the delicate chink of glass against glass and the barely audible hum of conversation had been oppressive. She had watched Peter's sister and brother conversing in whispers behind cupped palms, covertly raising their eyebrows and shaking their heads between sips of wine, in a way that made everyone in the room feel really awkward, excluded.

It was no secret that they didn't like her and, truth be told, she wasn't overly fond of them; she still remembered the way they had cold-shouldered her when they'd first met, all those years ago. The conversation as to why they held Bea in such low regard had never been had, but she suspected it was because she fell way below the standard they would have expected for someone like Peter. She was his first bride and a lot younger than him – a mere twenty-five years old to his mature forty-seven, which they probably didn't approve of either. Arriving out of nowhere with a young son in tow and no respectable backstory – she had not been tragically widowed in her youth, nor forced to care for an abandoned child that was not her own – she was considered damaged goods. Now, having laid Peter to rest in a quiet grave in a sunny spot at South Head General Cemetery, overlooking the Tasman Sea, their dislike of her had morphed into resentment; this Bea knew was because the bulk of Peter's estate was going to her, the imposter! Not that it was a vast fortune, but it was certainly enough to keep the wolf from the door and to give her choices. This was yet another reason for her to be eternally grateful to her lovely husband.

She had looked around the room and knew that the Bea of her youth would have shouted to the assembled, *'Do you know what? I'd really rather be alone, and Peter didn't like half of you anyway. Please, make your way home via the nearest exit and when you have gone, I shall drink wine and dance in my bare feet until I fall asleep!'* But this wasn't the Bea of her youth; she was in her fifties and had learnt that sometimes it was best to observe the 'least said, soonest mended' rule. That was precisely how she got through the following hour of further platitudes about how time would heal all of her wounds. She knew from bitter experience that this was a lie. Thirty-five years on and her pulse still quickened as she remembered clinging to her beloved with her bare hands, begging, pleading not to be left alone. Time had not healed her wounds; it had merely placed a thin veneer of anaesthesia over them that dulled the pain, making them easier to live with.

Bea shook her head to clear the memory and lifted the cup of lemony tea to her lips as she wandered over to the sofa. Her wrist gave a familiar jangle. Twelve slim silver bracelets sat haphazardly on her left arm, each one bought by Peter for a particular birthday or anniversary; each one engraved on the inside with a declaration of love or a funny insight. The one he'd given her on her fiftieth birthday read: 'You are now officially old! Welcome to the club!'

She smiled at the memory of his wonderful humour and wished once again that she could have returned to him the same love that he'd given her. She had been happy with him, he had been a good father to Wyatt, and of course he'd helped her set up the Reservoir Street Kitchen, the café that was her pride and joy. But no matter how much she wished otherwise, her feelings for him were measured, a pale simulacrum of the way she had felt about her first love, her hand inside his as they glided over the wooden deck, the full moon providing the most perfect backdrop as her heart jumped and her foot tapped in time to the music, that night she'd wished would never end. Bea lightly stroked the dark green silk cushion, letting the fingers of her free hand linger on the fabric.

After showering and blow-drying her thick grey hair into its voluminous waves and fastening it into a haphazard knot with a barrette, she applied her scarlet lip stain and brushed a couple of coats of mascara onto her long lashes. As she accessorised her olive pedal pushers with a sleeveless tunic and chunky bone-coloured beads that hung around her neck in three strands, she reminded herself how very lucky she had been. If it hadn't been for Peter, life could have turned out very differently indeed. She then slipped her feet into her trademark petrol-blue Converse and pushed the memory of her dream to the very back of her mind.

Before going downstairs to open up the café, she glanced at the photo on the wall and spoke the same words out into the bright blue morning that she had for the past 364 days.

'I'm sorry, Peter. I'm sorry.'

Two

'Ah, Mr Giraldi. How are you today?' She waved from in front of the grand reclaimed bookshelf, where she was adjusting a miniature wooden rocking horse to sit just so, framed by battered copies of *Little Women* and *Moby Dick*, among others. She groomed the little horse with her fingertips, trying to make the most of his sparse mane and worn paintwork.

'Good, thank you, Bea, apart from the fact there is someone sitting at my table!' He removed the straw trilby that offered shade from the hot Sydney sun and lifted his walking cane, aiming it at the two tourists sitting beneath the bi-fold window. On sunny days the window was opened so that you were effectively dining al fresco, free to watch the goings-on of Surry Hills, one of the most vibrant of Sydney's inner-city suburbs. The couple, oblivious to their blunder, chattered and sipped at iced spiced chai latte. 'How long will they be? Have they asked for the bill yet?' he shouted in their direction.

'Not sure, but why don't you come take a seat over here? We can catch up and then you can always move later,' Bea suggested.

She hoped the enthusiastic couple, she English and he American, who had oohed and aahed as they walked into the Reservoir Street Kitchen for the first time, hadn't heard. 'We love delis and cafés,' the charming red-headed man had explained. 'We have history – it's where I met Megan, my wife.' He'd smiled. 'Shut up, Edd! No one cares how we met!' The woman had blushed and beamed. They were clearly very much in love.

'What's that you've found, more junk?' Mr Giraldi enquired, nodding at the rocking horse as he placed his hat on one of the other bleached and scrubbed wooden tables and took a seat.

The horse was the latest addition to the quirky decor, with Bea's objets d'art sitting in stark contrast to the polished cement floors, exposed steel joists and tempered glass of the premises. In its previous life the building on Reservoir Street had been a textile factory and Bea and Peter had been way ahead of their time in using the harsh industrial materials of the place to their advantage. Rather than dispose of the rusted pulleys that were strung like mini cable-cars across the high ceiling, or try to disguise the weathered brick and replace the chipped green enamelled lights that hung in low clusters, they had simply incorporated them into the design. One critic had described their new venture as 'wonderfully bohemian, daring and eclectic', which had made them chuckle over a bottle of red – they'd thought they were merely being thrifty! That had been twenty years ago.

Bea laughed. 'I keep telling you, Mr Giraldi: firstly, these things are not junk, they are pre-loved. And secondly, I don't find them, *they* find me. I'm like a magnet for these objects, and I think they make the place more beautiful, don't you?'

He simply tutted noncommittally as she ran her eyes over the unusual mix of items that sat on the industrial shelving units. The old European bakers' racks had been shipped over years ago – some still had blobs of flour encrusted on them, as hard as rock; the rusty wheels on each corner must have propelled them across tiled bakery floors, transporting rustic breads and baked goods of the sort that she would almost certainly be happy to serve today. There was an antique sewing machine on an ornate scrolled-iron trestle, nestled in a corner. Defunct brass fire extinguishers were used as doorstops and the vast, high walls were graced with everything from a stuffed kudu head to a child's chair covered in cartoon decoupage.

She smiled; each and every one of those things held a special memory or put her in mind of a happy time. 'Take these photos, for example.' She pointed at a wall, bare brick like two of the others, that held clusters of black and white vintage photographs in mismatched frames. They included a Victorian gentleman in a rather dandy hat, and a blurred shot of shoeless children gathered on the step of a building not five minutes from where she now stood; ironically, the price tag for that step and the house behind it was now in the millions. 'All of these pictures I have found on my wanderings, either in junk shops or on antiques stalls.'

'Same thing,' Mr Giraldi interjected.

Bea gave her little sideways nod. 'That's as maybe, but they amount to so many happy days spent wandering streets, strolling in the sunshine or sheltering from the rain. And the point is I salvage them, the photographs that nobody wants. These people who were someone's father, someone's daughter. I can't bear to think of them discarded, lost, these people who had lives, who mattered.'

'Don't think those scrawny, grubby kids mattered much!' Tait joined the conversation, indicating the picture with his eyebrows, his hands being preoccupied with a large round tray.

Bea watched as he dipped down to the table to deliver the goodies to a group of four girls. A sleek white teapot, white mugs, a 1950s-style glass sugar sifter with a natty chrome dispensing spout, and a shiny metal three-tiered cake stand filled with crayfish and lemon mayonnaise open sandwiches and four chunks of freshly frosted carrot cake. She observed the girls staring at Tait's tanned arms and broad chest. Peter had called her cynical for employing a very handsome young surfer to serve her clientele, who were almost all female; she, however, had thought it might be pure genius, and she was right. *I do miss you, Peter.* There were these moments, during each day, when she would look for him, think of him, want to share something with him, and at every realisation that he was gone her chest caved with a combination of guilt and grief that left her feeling hollow.

Second Chance Cafe

'Actually, Tait, I think every one of those little scraps mattered a lot. They were just little children, they didn't choose where they were born or who they were born to, and if you look at their faces, sure they're dirty, poor, a bit thin, but they actually look really happy.' She strolled over to her gallery of pictures – people long dead whom she had never known – and pointed at one about halfway up. A boy of no more than six or seven leant against a doorframe; he was smoking a clay pipe, his eyes peeking out from beneath his cloth cap. 'Look, look at the crinkles around the edge of his eyes. He looks older than his years, but he laughs a lot, I can tell.' *I hope he did. Poor little mite.*

'If you say so.' Tait smiled, revealing his perfect large white teeth that practically shimmered against his golden tan. He tucked the stray wisps of his long tawny hair behind his ears, as was his habit. Bea watched the girls follow him with their eyes as he disappeared through the saloon doors and into the kitchen.

'I don't have pictures of my own family, let alone someone else's!' Mr Giraldi growled.

'Are they all coming home for Christmas?' Bea placed her hands on her waist and her bangles jangled along her wrist, her signature noise. There were only four weeks to go until Christmas Day and plans were being made.

'Giovanni, his wife and their boys, yes, for a couple of hours. Claudia, Roberto and their kids are coming Christmas Eve, but Berta no. She's working, staying in Melbourne. I only have a small apartment and I don't want to travel. Besides, I like to stay where Angelica slept, and there's no space for everyone. It'd be nice to have everyone in one spot, but that's the way it is. I have nowhere to put them all. But we'll hook up on the computer thing – Gio can fix it up for me. I don't know how.' He batted his large hand across his chest, as if to dismiss the problem and the technology.

'I'm with you on that, can hardly switch my phone on and off, let alone work the computer. Peter used to do all that for me.'

'People still telling you it gets easier?' He leant on the top of his cane as he posed the question.

'Yes.' She nodded. She had marked the first anniversary of Peter's death by walking to the hospital and rubbing the nose of Il Porcellino before dropping a coin into the fountain.

'They're liars, all of them. And I should know, it's been seventeen years.' He pulled a large white handkerchief from his trouser pocket and wiped his eyes.

'You must miss her.'

'I do.' He took a stuttered breath as though even the recollection was painful. 'She was our translator – do you know what I mean?'

Bea wondered if he meant from Italian to English, but that seemed odd, his English was beautifully accented and faultless. 'I'm sorry, I don't,' she confessed.

Mr Giraldi looked skywards, as if that was from where the perfect explanation might be plucked. 'She got me. She got all of us! Berta is remote, quiet. I remember once asking Angelica, why is Berta so cold? And she clicked her tongue as though I was stupid and said, she is not cold! She is a furnace of passion, warmth and love, but she is so shy, private, that it tortures her, she puts up barriers.' He shook his head. 'I would never have known how to read my kids or they me without her translation. Gio is not angry all the time, he's afraid! Claudia's not as tough as she makes out, but only cries in private, hides any sadness. And me? She told them that no matter how fierce I might sound or how often I might dismiss their crazy ideas, I would die for them in a single heartbeat. And she was right, I would.' He nodded.

Bea considered his words. Maybe that was what she and Wyatt were missing, a translator. 'It sounds like you were a wonderful team.' She smiled.

'Oh, we were. She was our glue. I know if their mama were here, the kids wouldn't find it so hard to get home for Christmas. Space or not.' This he whispered. 'It's not only her wisdom I miss, but also the sight of her! Oh, Bea, she took my breath away. And to dance with her...' He tailed off, collecting himself. 'To hold her hand inside mine and sway with her to the music! I still dream of those moments.'

Bea heard the sound of a drumbeat inside her head, remembered the way her heart had thumped in time to the music.

'Life's just not the same.' He shrugged.

Bea nodded. She knew that for him this was true. 'What

can I get for you today, Mr Giraldi?' She rested her hands inside the navy and white butcher's pinny that she'd wrapped around her tiny frame. Peter had once admired her in her skinny jeans and Converse high-tops, saying that, side-on, she looked like a golf club. She had taken it as the compliment it was intended to be. Even now, she occasionally got sized up from behind by a young man who then found himself disappointed at the sight of her fifty-three-year-old face.

'I'll take a flat white coffee and some of that granola with honey and fruit.' He always ordered as though he were doing her a favour, like a kindly uncle finishing up the last of the cake to avoid waste.

'Coming right up. A flat white and granola for Mr Giraldi!' she called out as she entered the kitchen.

Kim nodded in response as she bent over three slices of granary bread and placed avocado in neat slices on top. Her tongue as ever poked from the side of her mouth as she concentrated. Her high ponytail swished behind her in rhythm with her body as it sashayed from the wooden counter-top to the fridge and back again.

'What are you doing for Christmas?' Tait asked Bea as he stacked plates into the sink. 'Off to your son's?'

Bea grabbed a coffee pot from the rack and thought how best to answer. It wasn't that they hadn't invited her exactly... It was always the same, in the run-up to any occasion, like when Flora's birthday came around: for weeks in advance she would mentally hover, waiting for an invite until finally she could stand it no longer and called them. Sarah would answer the phone, gushing graciously and laughing as though Bea was a silly old thing – '*Of course* you're invited! Please do come. Can you make it?' – leaving Bea in a quandary, wanting to go and see her granddaughter and spend time with her family, but painfully aware of having practically invited herself. The embarrassment would then linger like a cloud around her at the event itself.

'Yes, I expect so.' The words slipped from her mouth with a false brightness. 'Still four weeks to make a plan. We'll see.' She smiled as she scooped the coffee and filled the small blue tin cafetière, a rare find from the Paddo flea market.

'What about you, Kim?' Tait looked over at the young woman for whom food preparation was an art, her long, cellist's fingers working like a perfectionist.

'I... I... m-my...' She swallowed. 'My mum and dad are coming here and then g-going to my... my sister's on the G-Gold Coast.' She sighed, happy to have got the sentence out.

Tait nodded, tactfully refraining from asking another question, sparing them the minutes they didn't have to lose while she formed a response. He grabbed Mr Giraldi's coffee and swept from the kitchen.

'For God's sake, Bea, what is wrong with me? I just can't talk to him!' Kim threw the dishcloth on to the counter-top. 'I can't get my bloody words out. He thinks I've got a stutter!'

'Because you have when you talk to him,' Bea noted.

'Correction, when I *try* and talk to him! You are not helping, Bea! Jeez, he's just so beautiful; it does something to my brain. He's perfect, just perfect! It's not only that I can't talk to him, I can't think of anything to say.' Kim grabbed the pepper grinder and twisted it aggressively over the sandwiches. 'My friends think it's hysterical. I'm like the biggest chatterbox ever, they can't shut me up, and I'm funny! Really funny! But with him, it's different. Not only is he so out of my league looks-wise, he also thinks I have a bloody speech impediment! Grrr.'

Tait came back through the swing doors. 'Who are these for?' he picked up the sandwich plates and stared at Kim.

'Err... T-table... Table... err...'

'Table twelve.' Bea jumped in.

Tait nodded, smiled at Kim and left with the order.

Bea turned to see Kim bashing her head on the draining unit of the sink. She laughed.

Three

With her eyes closed, Bea let the warm, morning breeze flutter over her face. She was in one of her favourite places, sitting on her folded sweatshirt at the base of a plane tree in Prince Alfred Park. It was the best place to visit in the sunshine; if she looked to the right, she saw nothing but the manicured green spaces that led to the vast, popular pool and in the other direction sat the majestic cityscape, where the Sydney Tower rose high, reminding her of a spaceship that had landed on a maypole. From her home, it was a brisk walk along Elizabeth Street that brought her here. Bea used the time to clear her head and escape the kitchen before service began. Now, as she sat in peace, letting her hand caress the grass, the sound of children's laughter drifted on the breeze from the outdoor pool. It was one of the loveliest sounds she knew. Opening her eyes, she smiled, remembering when Wyatt was small and what it felt like to be woken by the slightest touch to her cheek. He would creep into her bedroom and place his tiny hand on her cheek. 'Wake up, Mummy!' he would breathe in her face. Time had proved there was no sweeter way to be roused from sleep. She watched a young mum run after her escapee toddler, catching her before scooping her up into her arms and showering her in kisses beneath her sun hat. The little girl squealed and wrapped her arms around her mum's neck. Bea felt her stomach bunch with longing at the memory of Wyatt at a similar age. Life had been hard, but in some ways it had been the very best time, when he was little and was content to do nothing more than sit in her company, playing cards or being read to.

She tried to remember when he had stopped wanting to touch her. As a child he had happily plonked himself in her lap and kissed her face. Even as a teen there were hugs on arrival and departure, and an arm had occasionally been cast over her shoulders as they walked side by side along Manly's promenade. She had loved those impromptu displays. It was as if he was proud of her, his young mum. Maybe it had stopped when he met Sarah, or when he'd had a daughter, as if he only had enough capacity to love two women properly. She couldn't recall exactly and it didn't really matter, the result was the same.

Bea glanced at her watch – it was time to be getting back, the lunch crowd would be arriving soon enough and she would be needed. As she trod the incline of Reservoir Street, feeling the pull on the back of her calves, she noticed that the vintage clothes shop opposite the café had strung Chinese lanterns in its window and placed a 'Happy Christmas' sign across the door. The sight of the decorations, as ever, put a smile on her face. Following their lead, she decided that later in the day she would dig out her own box of fairy lights from the basement, along with the one junk-shop find that only graced the café at Christmas time. This was a zinc-and-glass-framed photo of a white-capped Victorian maid lighting the thin candles on a rather sparse tree. The girl's expression was wistful, and to Bea it was as if she was wondering why it was that she had to do all the work, but couldn't enjoy the tree or the cluster of gifts placed around its base.

Bea bustled into the kitchen, where Kim was bent over the counter-top, concentrating on weighing out couscous for the roasted veg and pomegranate salad. Bea started washing a large bunch of peppery watercress under the cold tap, feeling the soft leaves beneath her fingers as she delicately brushed them, thinking of the flakes of chilli-smoked roasted salmon that would sit on top of them in today's sandwich special. She would whip up a spicy lemon-and-paprika aioli to accompany it, perfect for dunking chunky twice-cooked chips. The visualisation and mental preparation of the food she would serve bought her immense happiness.

Kim broke the silence. 'Hey, boss, did you know you got a letter today? A proper handwritten letter, from Scotland? I'm dying to know what's inside.' Kim waved the cream envelope in her direction and propped it on the counter-top. 'It arrived while you were out – I would have steamed it open and resealed it, if I thought I'd had the time.' She winked.

'From Scotland?' Bea asked quietly as she switched off the tap and swallowed, slowly drying the greens in her hand. Her fingers trembled.

'You all right there, Bea? You look a bit pale.'

She caught Kim's concerned look and rambled as she placed the watercress on the chopping board. 'Yes! Yes, of course! I was just, just thinking about... lunch,' she lied, 'whether salmon is a good idea, or whether to go for halloumi with onion jam or something else.' Her words sounded forced and unconvincing to them both.

'Come on! Open your letter! The suspense is killing me. I don't know anyone in Scotland – well, apart from Ewan McGregor, and if it's from him, give me his address. Please!' Kim laughed.

Bea dried her hands on a dishcloth, then wiped them down her pinny for good measure, before reaching for the envelope. She let her eyes rove over the spidery text and stroked the stamp with her thumb, hesitating before flipping it over and studying the back, which was blank. She wiggled her finger under the flap and eased it to the left and right, trying not to damage the envelope. She held her breath and twisted her body, so both the sheet and her face were averted.

She exhaled sharply, forcing a smile and letting her shoulders sag with something akin to relief. 'Well, it's from a lady who runs a coffee shop in Edinburgh.'

'What does Edinburgh Lady want? A job? Bit of a commute, isn't it?' Kim was on fire today.

'No.' Bea scanned the text with narrowed eyes. 'Not a job. Apparently she runs a sort of club, a society...'

'That sounds sordid and secretive, tell me more!' Kim leant over the tray of roasted veg that she was prepping and sprinkled the chunks of butternut squash, baby beetroots and shallots with black pepper and a little oregano.

Bea dug deep to find a laugh, trying to keep the tremor from her voice as she spoke. 'Sorry to disappoint, but it's nothing of the sort.' She read silently, mouthing some of the words as she concentrated. 'She runs a kind of little forum for owners of coffee shops, tea rooms and boutique cafés all over the world. They go online and swap recipes, send photos, that kind of thing.' Bea looked up. 'It might be nice, you know – having a café can feel like a lonely business.'

'None taken.' Kim held up her palm and laughed.

'I don't mean every day.' *I mean in the early hours or late at night when I am alone. I get lonely...* 'But, you know, when I'm wondering whether to expand or have to make business decisions, it might be good to talk to people in similar situations all over the world, get their perspective.'

'Ooh, a *global* little forum – that sounds like a hoot! Though I think you might struggle with the online bit!' Kim laughed.

'None taken,' Bea quipped, knowing Kim was right. But she was getting better and could now switch the machine on and off without help. 'And who knows, we might be able to introduce recipes from as far afield as Tokyo and Toulouse!'

'Toulouse? That'll be sausage recipes then. *Are* there members from Tokyo and Toulouse?'

'Well, I don't know, but possibly. They could be from anywhere. Florida or Berlin.'

'Berlin? So, more sausage recipes. I think it's a sausage club!' Kim chuckled.

Bea folded the paper and popped it back inside the envelope before stashing it in her pinny pocket. 'It's a lovely letter, actually. She sounds genuinely excited about the project. She says she read a review about us on the Tripthingy site, which is why she's invited me to join. She also said I should pop over to Edinburgh any time. Sweet, really, as though she is just around the corner and not over ten thousand miles away.'

'What's her name?'

Bea pulled the letter out again and distractedly ran her index finger to the bottom of the page. 'Alex. Alex McKay.'

Kim smiled. 'Ooh, Miss McKay! Love it! I'm picturing her now. I bet she's short and fat from all that sausage sampling, has a tight perm, wears gold-rimmed glasses, favours a pink sparkly mani-pedi and has a fondness for cats!'

'You don't know she's old or fat, she might be lithe and gorgeous!' Bea offered.

Kim shook her head. 'Uh-huh. I'm picturing her: she's incredibly fat and definitely loves cats! And clearly has no social life whatsoever if she has the time to contact people in Tokyo and Toulouse on a daily basis to discuss sausage-club business.'

'Well, that could be how she's describing me!' Bea stood with her palms splayed.

'Hardly! You are gorgeous! I'm actually a bit gutted that it's not from Ewan McGregor inviting you to tea. I was hoping that you might take me with you. He is delicious.'

Bea pursed her lips and stared at Kim. 'I thought you only had eyes for Tait?'

'Ssshh!' She waved her hand and peered towards the door. 'He might hear you!'

'Yes, and then he would know how you feel and maybe you could lose your stutter and my two favourite team members could move this thing forward.' Bea smiled.

'Firstly, we are your only team members, so that doesn't count for much. And secondly, there is no way he'd be interested in me! Did you see Janine, his last girlfriend? She was scorching hot, leggy and stunning. I'm not his type. Can you really see him meeting me from orchestra rehearsal or carrying my cello, with his board under the other arm?' Kim sighed. 'It ain't gonna happen.'

'Actually I *can* see it. You need to have more confidence, Kim. You are a lovely young woman. And you don't know until you dive in – you can't spend your life on the sidelines, hoping things will come to you. You've got to dig deep, find courage. Go for it!'

'I know. But it's not courage I need, it's another foot in height and boobs like Janine! That'd make it easier. I mean, can you imagine if I made my move and he rejected me outright – how could we work together after that? I'd want to drop through the floor every time I saw him!'

'And that's different from now, how?'

Kim sighed. 'Can we please change the subject? And I mean it, Bea, you are gorgeous, one of the coolest chicks I know – super stylish, super fab.'

Bea laughed. 'You have to say that; I'm your boss.'

'You're right I do, but luckily I mean it. You are one hot lady, even if you pretend to be a hundred and three.'

'Hundred and four actually.'

'What's a hundred and four?' Tait came in to collect the chalkboard with the day's specials written on it. A delicious summer greens vegetable soup and homemade cashew, lentil and quinoa loaf with spicy yoghurt dressing on the side.

'I was just... n-not... Bea's letter, only... she...' Kim blushed and waved the knife she was using in front of her face as though this might aid her speech.

Tait stared at her for a second before leaving with the board in his hands.

'Shit it!' Kim yelled.

'I may be a hundred and four, but I heard that okay!' Bea tutted.

During the mid-afternoon lull Bea took a deep breath, grabbed the box of Christmas decorations, gripped the sharp knife in her hand and sank to her knees. She ran the point around the tape that fastened the cardboard box, mindful that Peter had been the last one to seal it. She wound the tape around her fingers as she peeled it from the cardboard, thinking that it probably contained his fingerprints, a little bit of him still there in the place he'd loved. She was about to delve into the box when a sudden punch of sadness hit her stomach. *Once these are out of their box, it will be me that puts them away again and that will mean that I'll have been celebrating Christmas, properly celebrating it, without you. It didn't even cross my mind to put the decorations up last year, so soon after you'd passed. At the moment, they are still connected to you...*

'Need a hand?' Tait asked as he watched his boss contemplating the box labelled 'Christmas Lights' in black marker pen.

She blinked. 'I'm just wondering whether we should put these up?'

'Yes! Let's do it, let's get the Christmas spirit flowing here!' He clapped. 'Sure you don't want me to sort them? Kimmy's okay for the minute.'

'No, I'm good. I'll just prep them and then you can help me string them up. We can have a grand switch-on.'

Tait gave his ready smile. He was a good kid.

Bea folded back the wide flaps of the box and paused before placing her hands into the neatly wound spools of green wire. Peter had always been meticulous about his packing and methodical in his organisation. He had even placed a square of blue tape on the ends: as ever, trying to make her life as easy as possible.

Bea sorted the lights into two piles and stood, brushing the dust from her palms onto her apron. 'Right, Tait, ready when you are!'

She handed him the end of one of the strings of lights. He pulled out a chair and used it as a ladder, perching on the edge to hook the big fat bulb around the hook at the end of a girder, feeding the lights through his fingers. He dragged the chair across the floor and stood again in the middle of the room, securing the lights further along.

'This is going to look splendid!' Bea smiled as she reached for the next string. The two worked diligently for an hour, sorting the lights and fixing them in place, crisscrossing the strands until the whole ceiling was covered in a lattice of bulbs. She excitedly closed up the café, bolting the door and flipping the open sign. Then she called Kim for the big switch-on.

'Right, this is the beginning of Christmas, for me, right here. As soon as these lights go on, I know it's that special time of year. I think it appropriate we all make a wish, don't you?'

'Yes.' Tait nodded, flashing his white teeth.

Kim self-consciously wrapped her arms around her trunk, folded her lips under her teeth and looked at the floor.

'Close your eyes,' Bea instructed. 'We'll make our wishes and then open them after three, when it will officially be the start of the Reservoir Street Christmas!'

She shut her own eyes and clicked the switch on the

extension lead. She saw the flicker of light from behind her lids as she prepared to make her wish. She had decided to wish for a happy, independent widowhood, for a life in which she could honour Peter's memory. But in a flash her dream resurfaced, and it was as if her subconscious made the wish for her: *I want to see him, just once, to know he is happy. That's all I want, just to know he is happy and that I didn't imagine the whole thing. I want to know that he really did love me.*

Four

The front doorbell roused Bea from her musings. She was glad of the diversion; it was just in time to halt the uncomfortable cold creep of loneliness that threatened at the end of the day. It was always the same in that twilight gap between shutting up the doors of the Kitchen, waving goodbye to Kim and Tait and falling into bed. She pressed the off button on the laptop – she's wasn't sure how to shut things down properly and was still nervous of inadvertently deleting everything on the machine. It seemed easier to just make the screen go blank and close the lid before popping it in the kitchen.

She pulled her soft grey wrap from the 1930s chrome hallstand that she had picked up from Rozelle antiques market and threw it around her shoulders as she trod the narrow stairs to her private front door. Squinting, she gazed through the toughened glass, delighted and surprised by the face that smiled back.

'Flora! Oh my goodness!' she gushed as she loosened the bolt and turned the deadlock to allow her granddaughter entry.

Second Chance Cafe

'Hi, Gran,' Flora said nonchalantly, lifting her shoulder to reposition her backpack, which was clearly quite heavy.

'Flora, darling! What a lovely surprise. Is everything okay? Where's Daddy?'

Flora flung her thick hair over her shoulder and stared at Bea as though surprised that her sudden appearance might be cause for alarm. 'He's just parking the car and then he's coming up, worse luck.' She scowled. 'I said I could get the ferry and come over on my own, but they wouldn't even let me do that, even though I knew the way and everything! They treat me like a baby!'

Bea noted her clenched fists.

'They shouted at me for two hours without a break and then Dad carried on in the car, when there was no escape. I feel like I'm going mad! I just want some peace. They don't listen to me, they never listen, they just give me instructions or tell me what I'm doing wrong. Mum asked me what I wanted for Christmas and I said earplugs so I won't have to listen to them nagging me all day!'

'Oh.' Bea didn't know quite what to say next, but she felt a jolt of excitement as she always did at the thought of seeing her son. Surprise visits of this nature were extremely rare; she usually saw her family by appointment. She stood there trying to figure out what was going on. There was obviously some sort of discord with Flora, but what exactly she had yet to discover.

Bea held the door ajar and stared at her granddaughter. She looked beautiful in her denim cut-offs that showed off her long legs, and loose pink vest revealing her sports bra underneath. She was, at thirteen, on the cusp of womanhood, still with the rounded, cherubic beauty of childhood but with the clothes, trappings and stance of the older teenager she was impatient to become.

'Well, can I come in?' Flora pointed up the hallway.

'Yes, yes of course. Sorry, darling, I'm just a bit surprised to see you.'

'That's what Mum said and not to be surprised if you had plans.' Flora hovered on the spot. 'Do you have plans?'

'No, not at all. No plans and it is a lovely, lovely surprise!' She laughed, tutting at the idea of Sarah trying to dissuade her granddaughter from visiting.

'I haven't been here for ages!' Flora called from the top of the stairs.

'A whole year!' Bea confirmed.

'Hey, Mum.' Wyatt loped up the hill towards the front door. Bea as ever studied his face and physique, looking for signs of happiness, illness, fatigue, just as she had been doing since the day she first held him in her arms.

'Wyatt! How lovely to see you! Sarah not with you?' She looked behind him along the path.

'No.' He exhaled, trying to catch his breath, much less used to the steep incline than she was.

'Oh, well, come on up!' Bea buried the spike of happiness she felt at hearing that Sarah was not there; by default that meant she was temporarily one place higher up in the pecking order.

Second Chance Cafe

Wyatt walked past her and up the stairs towards the apartment. Bea watched as her son worked his long legs, taking the stairs two at a time. She followed him and straight away filled the kettle in her neat, minimalist kitchen.

'I was just saying to Flora that it's been a year since she was last here.'

'It hasn't been that long, has it?' Wyatt stood in the square hallway and stared at his mother, looking genuinely perplexed, confident she had made a mistake.

Bea knew that for Wyatt and Sarah – both of them still young, in her eyes, at thirty-four – life was full and busy and it was easy to lose track of time; for her, on the other hand, each day was mentally ticked off, getting closer and closer to what, she didn't know. She nodded her head. 'It really has. I've been out to see you twice in Manly, but you definitely haven't been here since November twentieth. I remember it rather well: it was a bright, blue-skied, sun-filled Wednesday and I can picture every minute of it. It was the day we buried Pappy.'

Wyatt looked down and Bea saw the blush of embarrassment that he hadn't remembered bloom on his cheeks.

'But, hey, you are here now and it's a lovely surprise,' she countered, trying not to taint the visit with guilt or accusation.

'I actually need to use the bathroom,' he said as he made his way along the hallway.

'Help yourself. You know where it is.'

Bea wandered into the lounge, where Flora stood at the window watching the comings and goings of Reservoir

Street below. Her bag had been dumped in the middle of the rug.

'It's noisy, isn't it?' Flora turned to her gran.

'I suppose it is a bit. But I'm used to it and I rather like it. I like knowing there are people around and I like listening to the conversations that float up to me – you wouldn't believe what I get to eavesdrop on!' Bea winked.

'Like what?' Flora tilted her head and stared at her gran, twisting her foot in her sneaker.

Bea tried to recall a conversation that wasn't salacious, outrageous or shocking, but all the mundane and therefore repeatable tales escaped her.

'Phew, that's better.' Wyatt strode into the room. Bea noted how Flora scowled in his direction. 'Sorry to descend on you like this, Mum. I didn't really know what else to do.' He ran his fingers through his thinning fringe, pushing the hair back off his face. Two determined strands flopped forward nonetheless, making a little heart shape on his tanned forehead.

'Don't be daft! You can come here any time. You know that.' Bea's mind raced, she had quite forgotten how it felt to be the 'go-to gal' in Wyatt's life, and it felt great! The questions raced through her mind. Had he and Sarah fallen out? Was one of them ill? Money problems?

'I told him that.' Flora stepped forwards and wrapped her gran in a hug.

'Oh, bless you.' Bea hugged her gently, quite taken aback, unused to such demonstrativeness. Holding the girl in her arms caused her tears to pool. She coughed and turned her attention to her son. 'I'm making tea.'

'Great.' Wyatt yawned.

'Have you eaten? I've got quinoa salad and some fat avocados that are lovely with lemon and black pepper. Are you hungry?' Her compulsion to feed her son hadn't waned since the time he was a newborn.

Wyatt raised his hand as though the mention of her food had caused him offence. 'Not for me. I'll give you a hand with that tea though.' He jerked his head towards the kitchen.

Bea gave an almost imperceptible nod and peeled Flora's arms from her waist. 'Daddy and I will go make the tea. Would you like to have a go on my computer?'

Flora shook her head and smiled as she ferreted in her backpack for her iPad.

In the kitchen, Wyatt leant on the sink with his arms across his chest. 'Sorry to barge in, Mum.'

'You're not barging in. As I said, you are all welcome here anytime. Of course.'

'Sarah's at her wits' end and I didn't really know what else to do, so…'

Bea placed her hand on the work surface as though she might need support. Her pulse raced at all the possibilities. 'What's going on?'

Wyatt hesitated, clearly thinking how best to phrase things. 'Flora has been suspended from school,' he whispered, shaking his head as if the facts were still too hard to comprehend. 'And they are considering excluding her permanently.'

'Why on earth would they suspend her?' Bea looked towards the sitting room, where the sweet child who had thrown her arms around her gran stood with her toffee-coloured hair falling down her back and an innocent smile playing on her lips.

Wyatt raised his arms and let them fall back to his sides. He obviously didn't know where to start. 'She's had warnings...'

'Warnings about what?'

'Disruptive behaviour, cheekiness. That kind of thing.' Wyatt kept his eyes on the floor.

'Surely not! I don't believe it. Not Flora! That doesn't sound like her at all.'

'That's what we thought, at first.' Wyatt looked up. 'But it's been going on for a while. And today, believe it or not, it came to a head when she attacked a boy.'

'Attacked a boy?' Bea echoed, a little louder than she had intended, as her hand flew to her chest.

'Yes. She drew blood,' he whispered, sounding ashamed and shocked. 'She's lucky they're not involving the police.'

'What? No! I don't believe it!'

Wyatt ran a hand over his stubbly chin. 'That was my reaction too, but then I read the letter they sent home. Sarah had to collect her at lunchtime today and things got a bit heated in the head's office. I came home and exploded. I'm so angry – not at her necessarily but at the whole bloody mess.' He placed his hands on his hips. 'Flora said she wanted to come and stay with you, and Sarah shouted at her, saying it was a good idea. I don't know what to do for the best, Mum, but I do think a cooling-off period is probably a good idea. Feels like I'm dumping her on you, but there's no obligation. I can take her home if you'd rather not...'

'No! I shall love having her and maybe I can get to the bottom of what's going on here. It doesn't sound like her, Wyatt. I'm sure every parent whose child is in the same position says the same thing, but we *know* Flora; she's sweet, kind.'

Wyatt grimaced. 'A couple of the parents have told Sarah they don't want Flora hanging out with their kids. To hear that...' He clenched his jaw, visibly choked. 'You always kept me on the straight and narrow, Mum.' This was a rare admission from him, a compliment of sorts.

'Well, you were easy to keep on the straight and narrow, never did anything wrong really, unless we are going to mention Mrs Dennis' hamster, poor thing.' She smiled at her son.

'As I said at the time, they can't prove a thing!' He gave a rare laugh, which faded as quickly as it had formed. 'Sarah and I are beside ourselves.'

'I can imagine. Go home and sleep on it, love. Everything feels better after a good night's sleep. I shall keep her here, put her to work and we can go from there.'

Flora appeared at the kitchen door. 'So, can I stay here?'

Bea was unsure how much she'd heard. 'Yes, love, for a night or so, but then your mum and dad will be wanting you back.'

'What if I don't want to go back, not ever?' Flora asked defiantly, holding her father's stare.

'Well, Flora, then it's a case of what we in the trade call tough bloody luck. Because you are thirteen and don't get to say what does and doesn't happen.' Bea looked fixedly at her son.

'I'm fourteen in a few weeks!'

'The rules would be the same if you were the grand old age of fifteen,' Bea stated.

'Don't let her take her phone and iPad to bed with her,' Wyatt interjected, 'or she'll be on them half the night.'

'God, people have more freedom in prison than I do living with you,' Flora whined.

'Well, that must be good for you to know because the way you're going you'll be able to compare the two.' Wyatt was sharp and sarcastic.

Bea nodded, looking at Flora as the tears welled in her granddaughter's eyes. 'It'll all turn out fine, darling. Don't cry!'

'I'm not crying!' Flora mumbled as the tears spilled down her cheeks. Wyatt stepped forward to hug her as she turned, made her way to the bathroom and locked the door.

Bea waved her son from the building and watched him slope off down Reservoir Street with his hands in his pockets. She returned to knock on the bathroom door.

'Would you like some hot chocolate, Flora?'

'Okay.' Flora sniffed.

Eventually she reappeared, loitering in the hallway, looking a little lost, her breathing still not yet calm. It twisted Bea's heart to see her only grandchild so upset.

'We'll have a nice mug of cocoa and sit on the sofa and have a good old chat, how does that sound?'

Flora nodded.

'Do you want to text Mum or Dad and say you're feeling a bit better? Dad will worry as you were quite upset when he left.' Bea, as ever, had Wyatt's well-being at the front of her mind, didn't want him to have a restless night.

'I'll text them in the morning. They treat me like I'm a baby, but I'm not six any more. It's my birthday at the end of December. I'm nearly fourteen.'

'Yes, I know, darling. But funnily enough, whether your kids are six, fourteen or thirty, you worry about them just the same; trust me.'

'All they do is worry about me or shout at me.' Flora's tone was softer now, less indignant, more aggrieved. Bea suspected she played the stroppy teen for Wyatt's benefit, because she thought that was required.

'They just love you.' Bea smiled as she reached into the fridge for slices of cherry shortbread to have with their cocoa.

'Did they tell you to say that?' Flora wrapped her arms around her slender trunk. Her thick hair fell in a blunt line, resting on her bare shoulders.

'No, but even if they had, I would have said it anyway, because it's the truth.'

'Were you this tough on my dad? I can't imagine it, you're too cool.'

'That's what Kim said! But it's the funniest thing, I think I'm the least cool person around. I'm a real technophobe and quite old-fashioned.'

'You're still cool, Gran. Plus you lived in London, that's very cool!'

'Gosh, that was a lifetime ago, and I was in Surrey, not London exactly; a whole other world.' Bea recalled the quiet pace of life on the Epsom Downs and the village atmosphere, where her parents knew everyone and every misdemeanour was reported back to them, leaving little room for mischief. She smiled, thinking of Diane, her big sister, who she had loved. They had been great friends as well as siblings. 'Taking the odd trip into the city to sit in a greasy, smoke-filled café didn't feel much like living it up, I can assure you! Sharing a round of toast with my sister in the freezing cold, wondering what to do with my life.'

'Did you ever see any famous bands?' Flora's eyes widened. She herself was a 5 Seconds of Summer fan, with a particular love of Ashton.

Bea placed the mugs and plates onto the tray and thought about it. 'No, they were never in our favourite café.' She winked. 'But I knew a tailor who fitted Mick Jagger for a suit on Savile Row – does that count?'

'Was Mick Jagger in the Beatles?' Flora asked.

'You are a funny little thing. No, he wasn't, but he was friends with them, I think.'

'A bit like 5SOS and 1D?'

'Maybe.' Bea plopped a generous pinch of mini marshmallows on to the top of each drink, having not the foggiest idea what Flora was talking about.

Flora laughed. Her giggle, however, quickly turned to tears that she muffled and swiped at with the back of her hand.

'Oh, darling! Whatever's the matter?'

'Nothing. I'm sorry.' Flora sniffed.

'Don't be sorry! Come on. Come and sit down.' Bea took her granddaughter's hand, steering her towards the sitting room.

It was a balmy evening with a warm wind blowing up from the harbour. The double doors in the corner of the room were open and the sounds of Surry Hills wafted up into the high rafters of the top-floor apartment. Bea smiled as she caught the lilting rhythms of a Spanish guitar and the buzz of girls laughing and men chatting as they strolled between the many artisan eateries that had sprung up in the neighbourhood. Everything from authentic Mexican and Vietnamese to organic handmade burgers was available within a short stroll of her front door – an incredible cornucopia. There was nowhere in Sydney she would rather live.

She had made few changes to the apartment since Peter had passed away, liking the fact that his eyes and hands had lingered on the objects within. It was a contemporary loft space that echoed the industrial feel of the business with its clean lines and decor. Kim had paid her the biggest compliment, saying that you couldn't guess the age of the person who lived there, they could be twenty or eighty. Bea had pointed out she was a good couple of decades off eighty, even though her joints needed reminding of this on a regular basis.

The living room floor was waxed oak, covered in dents and holes where in another era machinery and heavy office furniture had left their mark. A vast black leather sofa sat against a white wall on which hung an enormous oriental canvas; it reminded Bea of a bent willow but was in fact a random collection of lines and brushstrokes in sage green that gave the impression of a tree but close up was anything but. A scarlet leather Eames lounge chair and stool sat in front of the balcony window, topped with a furry white polar-bear-like throw; alongside was a natty-looking chrome telescope, perfect for star spotting. Despite the modern look and feel, the place was far from cold; the grey and mustard-coloured wool blankets on the arms of the sofa added texture, and the silver candle-lamps in the corners glowed softly. The glass-topped low table, whose legs were fashioned from chunks of girder, was piled with several large black-and-white books on subjects ranging from design to deep-sea fishing.

Three framed black-and-white photos sat on the brick wall in the nook between the log burner and the sofa. One of Wyatt and Sarah on their wedding day, with Sarah grinning like she had won a prize; one of Peter picnicking in the Botanical Gardens with a glass of wine, looking tanned and lovely; and one of Flora on her dad's boat a couple of years ago, when she was still gangly and less polished, still comfortable in her childish skin, wearing her dad's fishing hat, beaming proudly and showing off her braces, without the self-consciousness and doubt that now spilled from her. Bea liked the fact that every time she glanced up she saw a picture of the people she loved, placing them firmly in her thoughts. This despite the fact that Wyatt and Sarah seemed to be able to go for weeks, maybe even months, without giving her the slightest consideration, if their appalling record of contact was anything to go by. Except when she was needed, like now.

'I'll go grab our drinks. Make yourself comfy.' Bea smiled at Flora.

'Thanks, Gran.'

Bea hesitated in the doorway. 'Flora, one thing: do you have to call me Gran? It makes me sound ancient, can't you just call me Bea?'

'Sure.' Flora nodded. 'If you want me to.'

'I do.'

'Why have you never mentioned that before?'

'I haven't had the chance, not with your dad standing feet away, ready to shout down the suggestion, brand it one of my crazy, hippy ideas.'

Flora smiled, knowing this was true and liking the

fact that they shared a confidence. It made her feel quite grown-up.

Bea disappeared briefly into the small kitchen and returned with a white laminate tray bearing two white mugs and a plate of pale gold shortbread shot through with scarlet globes; their cherry scent was impossible to ignore. She set the tray on the coffee table.

'Come and sit down.' She patted the sofa next to her.

Flora sank down and exhaled. 'I like this room.'

'My little haven.' Bea smiled, holding the mug between her palms. 'Are you going to try Kim's shortbread?'

'No. I'm good.'

Bea noted the way Flora placed her hand on the flat of her stomach as if reminding herself why cakes were not a good idea. She couldn't remember when her own stomach had last been flat, taut. Not that she was fat, far from it, but her skin seemed to sag and crease with the creep of age, no longer clinging sharply to her muscles; it was more in league with gravity now than it ever had been. 'Maybe later then.' She smiled.

Flora rolled her eyes, as if this comment was reminiscent of her mother's nagging. 'Maybe.'

Bea sipped her drink. 'You can stay as long as you like, darling. You know that. As long as Mum and Dad are okay with it.'

Flora nodded. 'Thanks.' Her sweet, open smile was familiar to Bea. This was how she pictured her, not the scowling ball of angst she had encountered earlier.

'I'll open the skylight in the study, roll out the futon and pop the lamp on. You'll be snug as a bug in there.'

'It feels nice here, Gr— Bea. Cosy.' Flora kicked off her thongs and curled her feet under her on the sofa.

'Thank you. I like it very much too. Even after twenty years, there's nothing much I'd want to change.' Bea smiled as she stared across at the open window onto Reservoir Street. 'And to think it might never have happened – Pappy and I might have ended up in Mollymook, instead. Miles away.'

'When Pappy retired, you mean?'

'That's right. When your dad was a teenager, Pappy took early retirement and we sold the business, moved down the coast to Mollymook. You've not been there, have you?'

Flora shook her head. She hadn't been told much at all about her dad's youth.

'You'd like it, I think – there are whales and dolphins, and a lovely natural rock pool for swimming in called Bogey Hole. We were so excited. It was what we'd been working towards all those years. We couldn't wait to start living the beach life, playing lots of golf, eating fresh fish every night.' Bea's eyes twinkled as the memories flashed through her head. 'But after about a month, Pappy started getting antsy, couldn't relax, got bored of all that golf. Truth was, he was a city boy and he needed to get back to the bustle.'

'But what about you? Didn't you just want to stay on the beach?' Flora was curious, having only overheard her parents' version of events, retold at dinner parties of how her grandparents had retired to the beach and only lasted a few weeks. 'Threw the towel in,' her dad had smirked with a shake of his head, as though it was in some way a failure.

'I just wanted Peter to be happy. The day he gave up the lease on our Mollymook house, he had a spring in his step that I hadn't seen for a long time. But I remember worrying about where on earth we were going to live. We'd got rid of the house on Melville Terrace by then, so going back to Manly wasn't an option. But Pappy had it all worked out. He'd never sold this building.' Bea looked up at the high apex ceiling with its exposed steel beams. 'It seemed fitting to end up here, where we started, where we met.'

'That's so cool!' Flora stared at her gran with new respect. 'Making your own home almost from scratch. How would you even know where to start?'

'It was a great adventure, you're right, turning this place from offices and warehousing into the apartment. And then setting up the Kitchen...' Bea took another mouthful of cocoa, enjoying the feeling of the soft, melted marshmallows against the roof of her mouth. 'You know, a lot of people thought we were mad. Instead of sitting by the water or strolling around a golf course, taking it easy, we were donning bib 'n' brace overalls and picking up sledgehammers! Maybe we were a bit mad.' Bea laughed. 'In fact, there's no maybe about it!'

'Why did you guys open the café?' Flora asked.

There was the smallest flicker to Bea's eyelids. *Because I wanted to feed people around a table. Cooking for them with love and feeling their gratitude. I thought it might make up for the big, close family I craved.* 'Who doesn't want to run a café? It's great fun!'

'I guess. But it's hard work...' Flora blinked, giving Bea the impression that this too had been overhead on one of Wyatt's rants about the foolish ambitions of his mother, the only woman he knew who *chose* to slog her guts out every day.

'I think, Flora, that it's one of life's great privileges to do something because you want to and not because you have to. Don't you agree?'

'I suppose so.' Flora nodded, not entirely sure she understood. 'This apartment is awesome, even if it is a bit noisy with the doors open. It's cool.'

'Thank you, that's nice to hear. It's funny, my gran always seemed so old, even though I knew her when she was much younger than I am now!' She smiled, picturing her late grandmother back when they all lived in England. 'She had a little Edwardian house in Surrey, not far from the Epsom Downs—'

'So you came all the way from Surrey, England to Surry Hills, Australia – neat!'

Bea smiled at her funny, perceptive granddaughter. 'You couldn't imagine two more different places, darling!' She chuckled. 'Where my gran lived, on the Epsom Downs, was famous for horse-racing. They used to train the horses in the early morning and I used to love watching them galloping through the mist, heads down, steam rising from their bodies. Quite a sight. But I didn't like my gran's house so much: it was so old-fashioned, full of tasselled lamps, brass ornaments, chintzy cushions and embroidered pictures of dogs, if you can imagine that! And the whole place smelt of mothballs. I always wanted to fling open the windows, it was stifling.'

'Sounds gross.' Flora grinned.

Bea laughed; she liked the girl's honesty. The two sipped their drinks in amiable silence.

'It was just different and I believe it came into fashion a while back, all that vintage floral on just about everything, but personally I can think of nothing worse than being one of those women who wear frocks and mackintoshes that coordinate with their bread bins.'

Flora laughed; this sounded like her mother's friends for a start. 'Why did your parents leave Surrey and come out here in the first place? I mean, I'm glad you did, but I was just wondering why.'

'Well, I don't know how much Dad has told you, but my father was a minister. A man of God, at least that's what he told everyone.' *'You will leave and take your shame with you. You are not my daughter...'* His words were still crisp in her mind. 'He and my mum came to take over the running of a church in Byron Bay, up in northern New South Wales.'

'But you didn't stay with them?'

'No. I didn't.' Bea took a deep breath, not able to discuss this today; she needed to change the topic. 'I'm a bit worried about you, Flora. It *is* lovely to see you, but I'm worried about you. I hated seeing you so upset earlier. Dad said you were having a spot of bother at school. You don't have to talk to me, of course, but if you want to, then you can. Okay?'

Flora cupped her mug between her palms. 'Okay. I just didn't want to be at home...' She sipped at her drink, using it as a prop to avoid further explanation.

'Well, I'm glad you thought of coming to me. You look lovely, a bit skinny, but lovely.'

Flora looked up at her gran through her thick lashes. 'Do you ever wish, Gr— Bea, that you could rewind or fast-forward time?'

Bea stared at her granddaughter who was about to dive into life. An image filled her head from her own youth, when she was just a few years older than Flora: a narrow bed in a locked room, a plastic bowl in which to pee and a cold fear that hovered in her chest at what would happen when her time came. *I'd go back to then, I'd find him. I'd be stronger! I'd run as fast as I could around the world and I would cling to him and we would grow old side by side.* Bea sighed, knowing she would have done no such thing. She had had to let him go, and she did.

'I guess we all do,' she said quietly. 'When would you go back to?'

Flora looked up at the photos on the wall and swished

her long hair over her shoulder. 'I wouldn't go backwards. I'd fast-forward.'

'To when?'

'To when I'm older and I have my own money in the bank and I can get my own apartment and do what I want.' She jutted her chin.

'Oh! And what is it you'd want to do in your own apartment?' Bea asked nervously.

Flora considered this. 'I'd stay up late and go to bed whenever I wanted. I'd never eat any vegetables. I'd have a hot tub in my bedroom and put 5 Seconds of Summer posters over all the walls instead of wallpaper! Oh, and I'd get a dog.'

'Really? A dog?' Bea was touched by the innocence of her response. 'What kind of dog?'

'A French bulldog – they are so cute! And you can take them for walks or they just sit on your lap and watch TV with you. They're perfect.'

Bea watched as Flora's face lit up. 'They sound it.'

'And I think if you have a good dog, it's like having a best friend, isn't it?' The smile slipped from Flora's face.

'I guess it is.' Bea wondered if they were getting closer to the heart of the problem.

Flora picked at a thread on her cut-offs. 'I sometimes feel like I'm the only person in the world that feels like me, like there's this huge club of people that all know what's going on and I'm the only one that doesn't. Like I'm on my own.' And just like that her tears threatened again.

Bea squeezed her granddaughter's hand. 'You are not on your own, Flora. You are loved and if I can help fix things in any way, you know I will.' It was as close as she could come to prying.

'Thanks. I don't think anyone can fix things.' Flora blinked away her tears.

There was a second or two of awkward silence. 'Are you any good with computers?' Bea eventually asked.

'I guess.' She shrugged. 'Not bad.'

Bea stared at her. 'Do you know how to send an email and things?'

Flora threw her head back against the sofa and giggled loudly, reminding Bea of the thirteen-year-old girl she was. 'Gr— Bea! Who doesn't know how to send an email?'

'Well, me for starters! It's not that funny! I hardly even saw a computer until I was in my forties and Pappy used to look after everything electronic. I've been muddling through trying to teach myself, but I don't really know how to close anything down. I'm worried that if I press the wrong button, I'll delete everything.'

'It's quite hard to delete *everything*. Where's your laptop?' Flora sat forward on the sofa, flicked her hair over her shoulder and cracked her knuckles.

Bea retrieved the laptop from the kitchen and handed it to her granddaughter, who flipped the screen up and let her fingers dance competently over the keyboard before howling again. 'You've got like a million things open!' Flora shook her head, and looked skyward, reminding Bea very much of Wyatt, who often made the same gesture.

'I told you I was hopeless with technology.' Bea watched as Flora tutted and simultaneously clicked on the little flat square that made things happen.

'Okay – so that's closed a few screens down. It's easy, Gran – Bea. You just need to know where to click!' She nodded. 'The Christmas Café – you have a lot of their pages open. Not that they tell you much, it's a pretty basic website.'

'Ah, yes.' Bea gave a small cough to mask her embarrassment. 'The lady that owns it runs this club thing and asked me to join. I just kept clicking on different pictures and things.'

'Ooh, look at this!' Flora sounded excited as she pointed at a picture. 'It's the street in front of the café and it's covered in snow! I'd love to run up it and leave my footprints. It looks so pretty!'

Bea peered at the screen. 'Oh, it does! There's something about snow that makes everything look so Christmassy.'

'Oh, Gran! Look at the decorations in the window!' Flora pointed at the tartan swags that were strung from one side to the other, with tiny pine cones and sprigs of heather clustered in the upward loops.

'That's beautiful, isn't it? I think Miss McKay is far more creative than me. I thought Pappy's Christmas lights were a grand gesture, but look at that!'

Flora clicked on another page entitled 'The Perfect Christmas Cupcake'.

'Oh, wow! I could eat them all!'

The two oohed and aahed at the elegant display of Christmas-themed cupcakes, each one iced with a smooth puddle of white and adorned with either tiny green holly leaves and berries or miniature Santas fashioned out of sugar paste. Along the rim of the vast silver cake stand were little sugar-paste reindeer linked by gossamer strands of sugarwork that connected them to a sleigh bulging with gifts and parcels. The iced detail was breathtaking. It was the work of a Mr Guy Baudin, who was head of design at the café of the week, Plum Patisserie in Mayfair.

'Ooh, Mayfair, that's very posh!' Bea said. 'We're in good company.'

'You could be café of the week!' Flora enthused. 'What would you put on your page?'

Bea considered this. 'Mmm, not sure. Maybe my world-famous chocolate mousse?'

Flora wrinkled her nose and paused. 'I think we should get Kim to think about it.'

Bea laughed. 'Well, that told me!'

Flora scrolled through some of the featured cafés.

'Ooh, look at that one!' Bea pointed. 'Kaffeehaus Lohmann in Osnabrück, wherever that is! Look at that strawberry torte! I can smell it from here.'

'How long have you known about this club?' Flora asked.

'I didn't know anything about it until I received a letter from the lady that runs it. I was clicking on pages trying to find out about the forum she mentioned, but I couldn't figure out how to go backwards once I'd opened something. I've got her letter here somewhere.'

Bea popped on her glasses and reached into her soft leather rucksack. She pulled out the correspondence and passed it to Flora, who balanced the laptop on her knees and drew it from the envelope after scrutinising the postmark and stamp.

'Ooh, Scotland! That's a good stamp.'

'Yes it is; that's what I thought. Kim said the lady who wrote the letter sounded fat, and with a fondness for cats.'

Flora glanced up. 'That's funny. My teacher is a cat person, but I told her I like dogs—'

'French bulldogs, to be precise,' Bea interrupted.

'Exactly!' Flora beamed, happy that her gran had been paying attention. 'Maybe that's why she hates me.'

'Your teacher? Oh, I'm sure she doesn't hate you!'

'Is Edinburgh near London?' Flora changed the subject.

'No!' Bea chuckled. 'It's about six hundred and fifty kilometres away.'

'Not that far then.'

Bea smiled at her granddaughter: Aussie born and bred, with none of the small-island attitudes that she had grown up with. When your country was so big you could fit the UK into it more than thirty-one times, what was a seven-hour car journey up the motorway?

'Why do you think it's called the Christmas Café? D'you reckon they change the name when Christmas is over?

Maybe it becomes the Easter Café?' Flora's eyes lit up; she clearly liked this idea.

'Ooh, Easter Café would be good. Nothing but chocolate – can you imagine?' Bea drained the last of her mug. 'Could you send her an email from me?'

'Sure, do you have the address?'

'Yes, I've got her letter.' Bea pointed at the sheet.

'No!' Flora giggled. 'The email address? Don't worry, I'll get it from the website.'

Bea gathered the soft grey woollen wrap around her shoulders and watched as Flora tip-tapped her way dexterously across the keyboard. She found it amazing how tech-savvy this young girl was. She thought back to when she was thirteen, when she and her sister, Diane, would invent games that involved hiding objects in the garden for the other one to find, or writing plays they would then perform for their parents. Their favourite pastime had been singing along to the Top Forty every Sunday night and recording it on their radio-cassette player, trying to master the skill of hitting and releasing the pause button when the DJ was speaking between songs. That tape would then be played to death all week long, before the process was repeated the following Sunday. It was another world entirely.

'Okay, so you tell me what you want to say and I'll type it. My spelling isn't very good, but we can spellcheck it.'

'Ah, spelling, that I *can* do. We are a great team.' She winked. 'Right.' Bea considered what she wanted to say. 'Dear Alex...'

Flora snorted her laughter. 'That doesn't sound very friendly! You need to imagine that you are chatting to her on the phone – Mum told me that.'

'Oh, that's a good tip. Right...' Bea drew breath, ready to start again. 'Well, Alex, I have put your letter in my handbag...'

Flora laughed again and leant back with her arms folded across her chest.

Bea giggled too, happy that she could amuse her granddaughter so much. 'What's wrong with that?' she asked.

'I don't know! It just sounds funny.'

'I never realised it was going to be this tricky!' Bea pulled a face.

Flora straightened, pushed her hair behind her ears and levelled the laptop on her knees, looking much older than her thirteen years. 'I know, imagine Alex is standing over there and you are talking to her and I'll try and write what you say and then we can change it if we need to.'

Bea thought about what she wanted to say, slowly dictating the words that would link her to a café in Scotland. *Scotland*... She watched as Flora's fingers whizzed from side to side.

'Read it back to me, would you, Flora?'

Flora coughed. 'Hello, Alex. It was so lovely to get your letter. It caused much excitement here, so rare to receive a proper letter written in ink, and the Scottish stamp has been much admired. I had a look at your café forum online and am quite enamoured with the cupcakes from Plum

Patisserie. I must admit my mouth watered at the sight of the strawberry torte in Osnabrück – is that Austria? Our café is very different. The Reservoir Street Kitchen, named after the street in which we live, is a neighbourhood café which I set up twenty years ago with my husband. We serve fresh food made with love. It's the kind of place where everyone feels like they have family and friends even if they don't. I'd love to know what inspired you to set up the Christmas Café. Yours sincerely, Bea Greenstock.' Flora made a face at the rather formal sign-off. 'Shall I mention her cats?'

'No!' Bea shouted. The pair of them laughed again. 'I like you being here, Flora Greenstock.'

'I like being here too.' Flora gave a long, slow yawn. The day's events had taken their toll.

'Come on then, missy, it's bedtime for you. You've had quite a day.' Bea patted her leg. 'There are clean towels in the linen cupboard on the landing.'

'Thanks, Bea.' Flora stood up.

'And don't forget: no phone or iPad, that's what Dad said.'

Flora rolled her eyes and sloped off into the hall, placing both items on the counter-top in the kitchen.

Bea watched her disappear, then turned to the photograph of Peter on the wall. 'Well, this is a turn-up for the books. Lovely to see her, Peter, but what's this all about, eh?'

She stretched her legs and placed her green silk cushion on her lap, before reaching for the letter, a letter from far,

far away. Her fingers drummed on the Edinburgh postmark as her head filled with a lilting Scottish burr. It was the voice that had lulled her to sleep with stories of lochs shimmering in the sun and winding paths up mountainsides abundant with flowers. *'The white heather is the rarest; they say it grows only on soil where no blood has been shed. It's lucky...'* She remembered every word he had spoken, as if it was yesterday.

Five

Bea had slept more soundly than she'd expected. There was something quite comforting about having someone else under her roof; it made her feel protected in some way, like she used to when she lay next to Peter night after night. Thinking about him made her tears gather. She sniffed them away, not wanting to give them the satisfaction.

Bea was surprised to find Flora awake and alert at 5.30 a.m. She had tiptoed past the study door and into the sitting room, not wanting to disturb her granddaughter, but she needn't have worried: there she was in the kitchen, in her short cotton sleepsuit, holding a half-eaten banana.

Bea took up position in the middle of the sitting room and stood with her arms outstretched and her knees bent. 'Morning, Flora. You're up nice and early. How did you sleep?'

'Good, thanks, though I didn't know where I was when I woke up. I got my phone back – that's okay, isn't it?'

Bea couldn't decide if this was said with sincerity or a hint of sarcasm. 'Sure.' She smiled, then closed her eyes and flopped forward.

'What are you doing?'

'A few stretching exercises: my own mix. I do them every morning. Keeps me supple.'

Bea could see Flora didn't know whether to laugh or join in. She realised how little they actually knew about each other, their knowledge restricted to just the outline facts about each other's lives. Apart from what they had each gleaned second-hand from Wyatt and Sarah, the details were sketchy.

Flora grunted noncommittally. 'Can I have a shower?'

Bea closed her eyes and nodded. She didn't want to be disturbed. As she went through her exercise routine, she tried to ignore the sounds of Flora nosing through the bathroom cupboards, the water jets hitting the shower tray and the catchy chorus she sang as she washed.

Twenty minutes later, Flora returned with two glasses of orange juice on a vintage black lacquered tray. 'I got you one too, Gran— Bea.'

'Oh, well thank you, how lovely.' They both took up their previous night's positions on the sofa. 'You remembered I like ice in my juice – top marks!'

Flora sighed. 'It's about the only thing I've got top marks in recently. School is really rubbish. I'm not even allowed to go at the moment. I suppose Dad told you I've been suspended?' She looked up at her gran, who gave a brief nod. 'They're so mad at me, but it's not even my fault!' Flora stared into the middle distance.

Bea swallowed the temptation to ask whose fault it was.

'They only want what's best for you, darling.' She was aware of how quickly she jumped to their defence without knowing the facts. She felt a slight shiver along her spine as her own mother's words sprang into her head. *'Sydney? Well, good luck. You're going to need it. What in God's name will you do there with no money, no husband and a bastard baby? Not that it's any concern of mine.'*

'I guess.' Flora shrugged. 'I don't even want to go back. I don't care!' The wobble of her lip implied the opposite. 'They've suspended me, and then it's the summer holidays, so they've only given me a longer holiday – some punishment!' she scoffed, but her composure was rattled.

'I think it's more a chance to sort out what's going on with you, Flora, rather than a punishment. At least that's how I'd look at it.' She tried to sound encouraging. 'Can I ask you a question?'

'Sure.' Flora sat back on the sofa.

'Why *are* you so fed up? What's making you so mad?' Bea nudged her with her elbow.

'Everything!' Flora huffed, crossing her arms across her chest.

'Could you be a bit more specific? I mean, when you say "everything", do you mean things like global warming, world hunger? Which, while they are undoubtedly important issues, are very hard to solve. Or by "everything" do you mean things a bit closer to home?'

Flora considered her gran's words. 'I do get mad about the big stuff, particularly people that hunt animals.

I did a project on that and it makes me cry to think about it!'

'I understand that, darling,' Bea said soothingly. *Kind, kind girl...*

'But I guess, yes, what makes me really mad are more things about me.' Her voice was quiet.

'What things about you?'

Flora kicked her bare foot against the floor, 'Lori Frankoli has got big boobs, proper boobs, and she wears a bra, not a sports top.' Whether inadvertently or not, Flora pinched her sleepsuit and pulled it away from her chest.

Bea wasn't sure how to respond. 'And do you want big boobs?' She considered her own rather flat chest, her boyish figure, and hoped that, if that was Flora's overriding wish, she would take after her mum, who was more blessed in that department.

'I don't know.' She shrugged. 'Marcus Jordan said he'd only go out with a girl who wore a bra.'

'I see. Do you want to go out with Marcus Jordan?' Bea asked tentatively.

'No! I don't want to go out with Marcus Jordan. I hate him!' Flora practically shouted.

'Right.' Bea swallowed. 'Why do you hate him?' She hoped she was getting closer to the source of Flora's angst.

'He told Craig Dawson that I was having a period.' Her cheeks reddened at the mention of this very adult term.

'Oh.' Bea hadn't expected this. 'And were you?'

'No! I don't have periods yet, but Katie Phipps said she

had hers and I didn't want to feel left out so I kind of said I was too and she told Lori…'

'With the big boobs?'

'Uh-huh.' Flora nodded. 'I carry tampons around with me all the time just in case, and she told Marcus and everyone was laughing at me because Craig's mum and my mum are friends and my mum told her that actually I hadn't started yet and they knew I had Tampax in my bag…' Her bottom lip wobbled as her tears gathered once again.

'Oh, darling!' Bea placed her arm around the girl's slender back.

'I just don't know why Mum said anything! She's such a cow.' She pushed the heels of her hands into her eyes.

'No she isn't. She's your mum and she loves you. You mustn't talk about her like that. She probably didn't understand why it was important. It was probably a conversation between her and her friend, something she mentioned in passing and she didn't know how it would affect you.'

'So then I yelled at her, and Dad yelled at me and said I'll have to wait a whole year until I can get my ears pierced just because I yelled at Mum, even though he told me I could get it done when I was fourteen, and I told Lori I was getting it done and she said I bet you don't, turns out she was right! Because now I've got to wait till I'm fifteen! And she's had hers done for ages. It's so unfair! And then Lori and Marcus were laughing at me in the dining hall, asking me if I had a tampon and stuff like that and I flipped. I don't really know how it happened. He was trying to get the Tampax out of my bag and I swung my arm out to get the bag back and kind of punched him in the mouth.' She looked up at her gran to gauge her reaction. 'He was bleeding and then everything went crazy. They took me to the headmaster and called Mum and...' Flora's tears fell as the words tumbled out.

'Oh, darling girl. It's okay. Take your time.' Bea pulled her into her arms and caressed her head while she spoke. 'It feels like a terrible mess, but in the scheme of things it's a mere blip.'

'Doesn't feel like a blip. Lori's supposed to be my friend, but she was shouting that I'd attacked him! I didn't attack him: it was one punch and I didn't even mean to do it! It was an accident. But everyone started repeating it, saying, "She's attacked him! She hit him!" And now that's what everyone thinks because that's what everyone was saying.'

'Even one punch isn't the answer, love.' *No matter how tempting...* Bea buried the thought.

'I'd never attack Marcus, not really.'

'Marcus who you hate? And don't want to go out with?' Bea confirmed.

Flora nodded. 'I just got so mad and they were laughing at me and Lori was leaning on his shoulder like she owns him. And she was looking at me and kind of winding me up and winding him up too, like she does when he answers questions in class – he's smart. And she'd already said that I had Woolworths tennis shoes and that had made Marcus and Craig laugh. And Mum said just get cheapies and then if I liked school tennis, she'd get me some good ones.' Her speech was fast and garbled.

'Ssshh... It's okay, Flora. Take deep breaths.'

'I hate Lori and her stupid boobs.'

'She sounds mean,' Bea admitted.

'She's my only proper friend and so I'm st-stuck with her,' Flora stuttered through her tears.

'It's not always easy being young. Things can feel like the end of the world, but I promise you it is just a blip. Ask your dad! He thought he was going to prison when he was eleven.'

Flora pulled away and stared at her gran, wide-eyed. 'What did he do?'

'Well, it's for him to tell you the detail, but there was a mishap with a hamster and our neighbour Mrs Dennis chased him down the street with a cricket bat. I had to tell her that violence wasn't the answer too.'

Bea's laptop gave a loud ping.

'That's your email alert.' Flora sat upright, glad of the distraction. 'You might have a reply from Alex!' She wiped her eyes and sniffed.

'Oh, how exciting!' Bea reached for the computer.

Flora leant across. 'So you move that little arrow by catching it with your finger on the pad, then steer it to the email icon – the envelope – and tap it twice.'

Bea tried and failed, twice. Her third attempt was successful. 'I did it!' She was delighted.

'You did!'

'Well, I had a very good teacher.' Bea smiled at her granddaughter, who rubbed the rest of the tears from her lashes and forced herself to smile.

Bea reached for her glasses and read the text aloud. 'Thank you for your email, glad you got the letter. I rather enjoyed putting pen to paper, a skill I need to hone. In answer to your questions, yes, I do have a cat, a very proud white Persian called Professor Richards. He's named after an old teacher of mine who had just the same knack of looking at me with withering disdain when I failed to grasp a concept and would also only talk to me when in the mood!'

Bea looked up from the computer and shook her head at Flora. 'I can't believe you asked her if she had a cat!'

Flora smirked but didn't say anything, and Bea continued reading.

'Secondly, Osnabrück is in Germany, I have been reliably informed, and they were delighted to hear how much you admired their torte. The forum has been running for four years or so and keeps me busy. I like the idea that lone café owners like myself have an outlet, and how wonderful to share experiences across the ether.

'I set up the Christmas Café because, to me, Christmas is the one time of the year when people come together; it's a time for sharing and giving a warm welcome to strangers, and I wanted to capture that. Business is good here, and that leads to the old dilemma of whether to dilute my profits and take on another member of staff, or whether to get up earlier and work later. The Scottish winters are not conducive to early starts! I should think the Sydney winters are much kinder; it's on my list of places to visit. One day.

'Do you have a cat? Is that where your interest springs? We have light rain and drizzle here today. Hope the weather is being kinder to you. VBW, Alex.'

'She admits she talks to her cat!' Flora said, raising her eyebrows. 'That's a bit weird.'

'Oh, Flora, it's not the weirdest thing. I talk to the toaster, asking about how the toast is coming along, the washing machine, photographs. Talking to a cat sounds positively sane by comparison.'

'You have a point. Are you going to reply?'

Bea paused. She wanted to reply to the kind woman with the white cat, but some instinct made her wait. She was quite a private person usually, and even if it was just small talk about cafés, she didn't really want her granddaughter being privy to all her correspondence with this lady.

'I'm not sure. I'll have a little think. By the way, I forgot to mention your phone was making a buzzy whirring noise. I didn't know what to do with it so I put it under a cushion. Doesn't it irritate you, that dreadful intrusion?'

Flora retrieved her phone, then held it out to her gran. 'It's an Instagram from Lori. She sent me a photo of her new swimsuit.'

'Fascinating.' *The little moo...* 'I know Kim and Tait do Instagram, but I don't really know what it is, that and Chapter Face are all alien to me.'

'Chapter Face?' Flora snorted her laughter. 'It's Facebook! And Instagram would be good for the business, you could send out food pictures and messages.'

'What kind of messages?'

Flora leant closer and showed Bea the screen. 'Look, here's one just come in from a guy I follow at Bondi. He's having breakfast and he's put "Banana on toast, yum..." and then he's included a picture.'

Bea held the phone out at arm's length and squinted, intrigued. 'So it's a food thing, like a log of who is eating what, when...'

Flora laughed. 'No! Not always, but sometimes, yes. That was just a food example, but it can be about anything, anything at all. It's a way of telling people what you are up to at any time!'

'So it could be random things like "I am playing Scrabble" or "My cat's ignoring me"?' she said, thinking of Alex McKay.

'Yes.'

'How interesting, but I guess what I don't understand is why? Why there is a need for people to tell everyone what they are up to and why anyone would be remotely interested in what anyone else is doing. So what that some random chap in Bondi is having his breakfast?'

Flora looked at her gran and gave it some thought. 'I have no idea!'

The two sipped at their juice.

'Shall I pop the TV on?' It was how Flora started her day, when up early enough.

Second Chance Cafe

Bea laughed. 'You can try, but I don't have a television.'

'You don't?'

'No. I've never had one and so don't see the need.'

'Do you never have moments when you get bored and just want to veg out?'

'Not really. I listen to music, I do the crossword, I cook and I sleep.'

'I love TV. I can't imagine not having one. Think I'd go crazy!'

Bea stared at her granddaughter and tutted.

When Flora went off to get dressed, Bea once again tapped on the keyboard and studied the words of Alex's email. *To me, Christmas is the one time of the year when people come together; it's a time for sharing and giving a warm welcome to strangers, and I wanted to capture that.* She turned to Peter's photograph. 'What a lovely thing.' She smiled.

Six

Bea watched as Kim did a double-take, lifting her eyes from the chopping board where she was peeling mangoes for the fruit salad and scanning Flora from head to toe.

'Kim, you remember Flora, don't you?' she asked.

'Sure I do. Hey! How you doing, Flora?' Kim smiled sweetly at the girl, who looked more than a little awkward. Flora raised her hand in greeting.

'She's a bit nervous about her first day at work, but I've told her it'll be a breeze.' Bea winked at Kim.

'It certainly will. I could do with a hand over here if you're free?'

Flora tightened the pinny around her middle and sidled up to Kim.

'If I halve all these pomegranates, can you remove the seeds and put them in here for me?' She moved the shiny stainless steel bowl in front of Flora.

'Sure.' Flora smiled tentatively. 'Shall I wash my hands?'

'Ah, see, you're a natural! You'd be surprised how many people forget that very important step.' Kim smiled at her.

'Let me give you some advice, Flora. If you turn the cut fruit upside down and knock the rounded side with a heavy spoon, the seeds should fall out undamaged.'

Flora nodded and commenced her task. 'I love the Christmas lights, Bea!' she enthused. 'Mum and Dad aren't really brothering with decorations this year.'

'Ah, that's a shame.' Bea sighed. 'Your house usually looks so lovely at Christmas time – it always puts me in a festive mood, seeing the deck covered in lights when I pull up to your driveway, and all those twinkling bulbs in nets around the tree trunks. Your mum always does such a good job, it's beautiful.'

Flora huffed. 'I guess, but there's not much point this year, with them being away until a couple of days before Christmas.' She turned her attention to the pomegranate in her palm, bashing the hard skin and watching as the glossy pips tumbled into the bowl.

Bea felt the dart of Kim's eyes in her direction and concentrated on avoiding her gaze. 'No, well, that would be a waste of their time. And they're so busy,' she added, feeling a stab of disappointment at this news, embarrassed that she didn't know of their plans, plans that evidently excluded her. She felt her neck turn crimson.

'Where are they going?' Kim asked.

'Bali. They're going with friends. They've rented a house on the beach with its own swim-up bar. It looks lovely.'

'Right.' Kim cocked her head. 'Are you going too?'

Bea was all ears.

Flora shrugged. 'Well, I was, but I'm not sure now. I've been in a bit of trouble at school and stuff.' She rolled her hand as if this gesture might fill in the gaps.

Bea blinked away her awkwardness. 'Yes, Bali does sound lovely.' She tried to imagine what she might have done to offend Wyatt and Sarah, particularly as this was her first proper Christmas without Peter. The previous Christmas, so close to his passing, had been a blur, but this year she had assumed they would be there for her through the build-up. Bali, however, didn't sound much like Christmas to her, especially not with Wyatt and Sarah's friends. Even after four decades in Australia, she still hankered for the cold, wintry Christmases of her English childhood. She had vivid memories of presents piled under the tree, embroidered stockings on the mantelpiece, a roaring fire in the grate. One year, when she was about ten, it had snowed and after church she and Diane had tobogganed down Box Hill on homemade sledges that didn't last the hour.

In Sydney, Christmas was all about sunshine, busy beaches, fireworks, fine dining and chilled wine with friends on the terrace. When the temperature outside was a balmy twenty-two degrees, she couldn't bring herself to send cards showing fat Santas surrounded by snow. The inflatable Santas on the water at Darling Harbour were much more appropriate.

'What will you do if you don't go with them?' Kim asked Flora as she reached for the brioche dough and began to shape it, sprinkling it with cinnamon as she did so.

'Dunno. Thought I'd come stay with Gran – I mean Bea.' She smiled over her shoulder at her gran, who beamed back at her.

'Morning! Morning!' Tait shouted as he swung into the kitchen and grabbed his apron from the hook. 'Hi, Flora, how are ya?'

'Good, thanks. I'm helping Kim with the fruit salad.' She raised the red-skinned pomegranate in her hand.

'So I can see. Haven't seen you in a wee while.' He smiled.

'I've been at school.'

'Oh, well, good on ya. What's your favourite subject?'

'Art.' Flora smiled. 'I like painting.'

'Right.' He nodded. 'Beauty and brains, lucky girl.'

'Shit it!' Kim shouted from the corner of the kitchen, where she'd just dropped the dough in a greasy lump on the floor. 'Sorry, Flora!'

'S'okay. I've heard all the swear words. My friends and I wrote them down in a list,' Flora said without irony, head down, concentrating on retrieving the pips.

Kim raised her shoulders and grinned at Bea.

'So, why no school today? Have you broken up already?' Tait asked as he grabbed an artisan sourdough loaf from the delivery basket and began slicing it.

'I've been suspended.' Flora caught her gran's eye, unsure if it was supposed to be a secret.

Kim looked up and Tait paused from the task in hand. 'Is that right? What did you do? Set the school on fire?'

Flora sighed. 'No. I punched Marcus Jordan in the

mouth and his tooth went into his lip and he was bleeding.' She concentrated on her pip removal.

'Well, get you, Little Klitschko! Hope he deserved it!' Tait roared.

'No one deserves to be punched, Tait.' Bea glared at him. 'It's not the way to resolve anything.' She tried to emphasise with her eyes and the tilt of her head that they were not to encourage that sort of behaviour.

'Well, no, of course not, not unless they really, really deserve it. What do you think, Kim?'

Bea rolled her eyes. He had missed the point somewhat.

'I. I think... he, well... it depends,' Kim mumbled.

'See, Kim agrees with me. If someone is really mean, they might sometimes deserve the old one-two.' He jabbed his fists, then swept back out into the café.

'Ignore him, Flora. Violence is never the answer,' Bea directed.

'I've finished the pomegranates.' Flora lifted the bowl to show Kim her efforts, then picked up a pineapple and held it out towards her tutor. 'Do you have any more advice?'

'Yes.' Kim sighed and placed her hands on her hips, pushing out her bottom lip to blow her fringe from her eyes. 'Never, ever work with the object of your desire. It will only cause you stress and mean you spend ridiculous amounts of money on getting your hair done and buying expensive mascara that promises you luscious lashes but actually gives you nothing of the sort. Okay?'

'Okay.' Flora nodded, wondering exactly what 'object of your desire' meant.

It broke Bea's heart to see Kim so flustered. If only she were more confident, more aware of her wonderfully magnetic personality and natural beauty. For the rest of the day, Tait was on form, and with Flora to chat to he was jovial and chatty. But Kim retreated into the detail of her chores, not wanting her nerves to get the better of her in front of Flora.

Bea climbed the stairs feeling happy. It had been a busy day and having Flora to share it with had made it extra special. She had relished the gentle ribbing that had flown back and forth, both Tait and Kim showering Flora with love and attention, just the diversion she needed. Several customers had commented on the Christmas lights and she now pictured the chilled bottle of Marsanne that awaited her in the fridge.

Flora was wrapped in a towel on the sofa, her hair wet from the shower, the sun-kissed freckles on her back and shoulders exposed. She looked tired, unused to the physical demands of working in the Kitchen. And she had clearly been crying.

Bea sat down by her side. 'Don't get cold sitting there like that.' She placed a wool throw over Flora's bare legs.

Flora ignored her and carried on stabbing away at the screen on her phone.

'Have you thought about what you might want for Christmas – apart from your earplugs, of course?' Bea asked.

Flora laughed. 'Don't know really. I'm saving up for Uggs so I don't mind if you want to give me money.'

'Okay, that's what we'll do. Uggs sound good.' Bea drew a deep breath. 'Flora, I love having you here; it's smashing to have your company. And I've loved working with you today—'

'I've loved it too.' Flora wiped her eyes.

'But I think you need to go and see your mum and dad. I really do. You can't hide out here forever, and the longer you don't talk to them, the more it will eat away at you, like an unpaid bill.'

'I've never had an unpaid bill.' Flora blinked at her gran.

'Well, let's hope you never do!' Bea laughed.

It felt alien to be suggesting that Flora go home. The last twenty-four hours had been such a lovely opportunity to get to know her better and she desperately wanted to wrap up her young granddaughter and keep her with her forever. But Bea could see she needed to go home, home to her mum and dad so they could start to unpick the things that were troubling her.

Flora sighed and tucked the blanket around her body. She picked up a mustard-coloured wool cushion and folded it into herself. 'I guess. I'm a bit scared. I don't want them shouting at me any more and I know I can say horrid things, but I don't really mean them.' Her voice was small, her eyes downcast. Bea thought she looked like she had when she was a toddler.

'You should tell them that,' she urged.

'I can't. They're always arguing and I can't tell them anything, like how much I hate being in Year 8.'

'Why are they always arguing?' Bea couldn't think beyond that comment, worried that their marriage might be in trouble, or more specifically that Wyatt might be unhappy.

Flora looked at her gran and hesitated. 'Don't know really.'

'Well, what do they argue about?' Bea was aware that this was prying, but she couldn't help herself.

'Lots of things. Me. Money. You.' She sniffed up her tears.

Me? Bea gasped. Why would they be arguing about *her*?

Flora continued. 'It all started when I told them I was staying at Jen's one night, but instead Lori and I slept out on the beach.'

'What? Flora, that's crazy! Anything could have happened to you! Don't ever do that again, promise me!' Bea was aware she had raised her voice. It was often like that with children, she remembered: you got angry when you were scared for them.

'I won't.' Her voice was small. 'Mum phoned Jen's and when she heard I wasn't there, she went nuts.'

'I don't blame her. That's crazy! Why did you do that?'

Flora shrugged. 'Cos some of the older kids were having a party and Lori's brother said we could go with him and I knew Mum and Dad wouldn't let me, so I made out I was going to Jen's for a sleepover.'

'The only way Mum and Dad can keep you safe is if they know where you are. You know that, don't you?'

Flora nodded. 'They treat me like a baby.'

'Oh, darling, you are still a baby in so many ways. I want you not to be in such a rush; everything will come to you.'

'I guess, but Mum and Dad...' Fat tears rolled down her cheeks, which she scooted away with the back of her arm. 'They don't understand.'

'Well, help them understand. Tell them how you feel, tell them all of it. It seems to me, Flora, that there are lots of little things going on and it all feels a bit overwhelming, understandably, but by talking about it, you can sort it bit by bit. It'll make you feel better.'

'Suppose so. Lori isn't even talking to me because I punched Marcus and it was kind of her fault I did it.' She stared dejectedly at the floor. 'I wish I wasn't me.'

'What a very odd thing to say. How can you even begin to wish that you were someone else? You are beautiful and funny and quirky and confident – you always have been. And I am the best authority. I've watched how you've changed from year to year, from when you were a big fat baby to how you are today. I'm like one of those people that takes the same photo every day for a year and then makes it into a little flick-book movie. You have a glow about you, Flora, and I am many things, but I do not lie.'

'Thank you.' Flora sniffed and composed herself. Her sadness turned to anger as she recalled the events of the previous day. 'I can't believe that school have made a such a big deal out of it – everyone was talking about it. And then I got back and Mum and Dad were screaming at me! Dad said I couldn't go to Bali, and that's a good thing, it'll be crappy anyway. I'd rather not go! I'd rather not go anywhere. At least here no one knows me, apart from Kim and Tait, but in Manly everyone will be looking at me or teasing me about Marcus. I don't care if Lori isn't my friend.' Her chest heaved, making a mockery of her strong words. 'I'd rather be lonely than hang out with her.'

'Lonely? Don't be ridiculous. You are at the threshold, about to jump in. Take it from one who knows about loneliness, you are just starting out, Flora, you have your whole life ahead of you. And if Lori is as mean as she seems, you've had a very lucky escape. Things will work themselves out. You'll see.' She squeezed her granddaughter's arm.

'I hope so.' Flora's face crumpled.

'Life is full of amazing twists and turns, darling. And it's quite incredible how quickly things change and become normal when you live them.'

Bea saw an image in her mind: she was staring at a certificate on a table, there was a dark smudge of an inky thumbprint in the corner, the woman's hand was poised ready to write in a slanting italic hand. *'And the father's name?'*

'And Mum and Dad will come around, just you wait and see!' She smiled, relieved that her own dark memories were just that: memories.

'Do you really think I should go home then?' Flora looked up at her gran.

Bea sighed. 'I would love nothing more than to keep you here for ever and ever. But yes, I think you should go home. Don't sleep another night without fixing things with Mum and Dad. They love you very much, even if their ideas are very different to yours.'

Flora nodded, trying to be brave, but her tears fell nonetheless.

'Come on, darling, nothing is that bad.' She patted her granddaughter's hand.

'Can I come back if I need to?' Flora picked at the hem of her towel.

'Oh, you silly thing, you don't have to ask! Of course you can, any time. But I expect they will be so pleased to see you that the whole thing will be forgotten. That's usually how these things work.'

Flora wandered off to the study to get dressed and Bea picked up the phone to Wyatt. She heard him grabbing his car keys even before the conversation was finished.

Once Flora had left, the apartment felt empty and deafeningly quiet. Bea went to lie on the sofa, pulling the soft grey wool throw over her legs and placing her favourite green cushion under her cheek. The fabric, made from the scarf of someone very dear, gave her comfort, as it always did. A memory rose up suddenly: *'Please, please stay with me! Please! If you want me to beg, I will. I will beg until you promise me you won't go!'* She had been desperate. He had stared at her, gripping her arms, supporting her, his eyes imploring her to understand as tears snaked down his face. *'If I could, I would, you know I would. But it's not my choice to make. I cannot... cannot grab happiness at the expense of another. But you have to know that my heart, my spirit, will be here, wrapped around you, holding you tight, keeping you close...'*

Bea sat up sharply, looking for something to distract her from the pain of her memories. Her laptop was open and humming faintly in the corner. She pulled it to her and clicked on 'Reply' just like Flora had shown her.

From: BeaG

Subject: Hello Again

This is the firstemail I have sent you are honoured. My granddaughter wrote lastbutshe is no longer here and the flatfeels rather empty. No I don't have a cat, not really a cat fan. Winterhere is lovely I have never been toscotland but would very much like to go. I once knew someone who spoke veryhighly of it. It's on my list. My team are marvellous Tait and Kim both brilliant. I'm fiftythree, my husbandied about a year ago so it's a sad time of year for me what does vbw mean. I seem to have missed some gaps, sorry. Still getting used to keyboard, nothing like a typewriter, my husband used to deal with all technostuff for me.

Bea x

With her tongue lodged between her teeth in concentration, she clicked on the little arrow, which she now knew meant 'Send', and heard a very satisfying whoosh as her letter travelled out from the screen and across to the other side of the world. Like magic.

Seven

Having Flora stay with her in Surry Hills had reminded Bea of when Wyatt was the same age, an adventurous teenager who'd brought joy and a different perspective to her world. Peter had parented him at arm's length, seemingly always wary of the fact that he was not his father; perhaps because he was so much older, he'd been unwilling to intrude on the special bond that she shared with her son, forged in their six years of living hand-to-mouth, just the two of them.

She glanced out of the balcony door, drinking in the bustle of Reservoir Street below, still fearing that one day she might look out and find herself staring at the dingy streets of Kings Cross instead, as if she had dreamt her lovely life and was still stuck in the bedsit she'd shared with Wyatt all those years ago. It was hard to shake the memory of the slum-like room, the many unsavoury characters that worked the streets around them, how she used to wake at the slightest noise, always on the alert, before Peter had saved them.

When she had first arrived in Sydney from Byron Bay, evicted from the family home, pregnant, single, lonely and broken-hearted, everything had been a struggle. It felt as if she was on a permanent hunt, a never-ending quest to find enough food and work just to get by. Wyatt had been the golden ray of light in a dark world: he was the reason she never gave up, never submitted to the despair that threatened to engulf her. He was her focus, her reason for living, and for him she wanted a better future. For six years she stoically made her way from job to job, taking whatever she could, reluctantly leaving Wyatt with her neighbour, Ginny, who worked in the cigarette kiosk outside the train station and was Bea's only friend in the city.

The big turnaround had come one day not long after Wyatt's sixth birthday. The instruction from the temping agency had been brief: turn up on Monday, look smart, don't mention the kid and report to the second floor of Greenstock and Greenstock, the cloth manufacturer.

As she made her way to the Surry Hills address that morning, Bea had surveyed the other girls walking in the same direction, heading for the typing pools and secretarial desks of the bankers, solicitors and advertising agencies that were springing up all over Sydney. They looked similar, wearing bright jackets with shoulder pads, sporting bouffant hair and too much eyeliner, all trying to catch the eye of a particular boss. She might have looked like them, but she wasn't like them. They chattered about boyfriends and music, fashion and films, but her experiences set her apart, made it hard to make friends. How could she gossip about Midnight Oil when her head was preoccupied with worries about the landlord's latest rent increase? How could she bear to discuss boyfriends when the man she craved was gone for good?

At the top of the Greenstock and Greenstock stairway, Bea found herself in a tiled floored hallway with an incredible view over Surry Hills. The streets wound their way to the water behind her and the whole scene looked strikingly beautiful. She pulled the creases from her tweed skirt, borrowed from a girl who lived with her mother across the landing from them. She ran a hand over the navy, pussy-bow blouse and twisted her large gold-hoop earrings before stepping out onto the second floor as per her instructions. She continued down the corridor, taking in the wood-panelled doors and trendy chrome detailing, until she came to an open door.

Behind it sat a bespectacled man in his late forties, relaxed in a leather chair, reading a document and smoking a big fat cigar. A triangular chrome ashtray on a stand was within ash-flicking distance. He had short dark hair that sat on his head like a cap and his white shirt was immaculate against his sharp navy suit and tanned skin.

'Can I help you?' He looked, looked away and looked again, this time holding her stare. His voice was gravelly and still bore the faintest trace of his childhood in Germany. The leaves of paper twitched in his palm, which remained poised. She had clearly interrupted him.

'Yes, hello, I'm Bea!' she said with more gusto than she felt, hoping that her bright smile might hide the quiver in her voice. She badly needed this job.

'Well, good for you. I'm Peter!' His quip was made pleasant by his open smile.

'I'm your new person,' she added.

'My new person? What happened to my old person?' He looked behind his chair to see if they might be hiding.

'I don't know, maybe she quit because of your sarcasm?'

'Or maybe I fired her because she was too damn cheeky?' He was quick.

'Maybe. Or maybe she just scared easily.'

'Maybe she did. And what about you, do you scare easily?' He drew on his cigar and blew the smoke out into the room.

Tempted though she was to tell him the truth, she held his gaze and fronted it out. 'No, no I don't. In fact you'll find I'm quite hard to get rid of.'

'Right. Well, that told me. If you're sticking around, how about a cup of coffee?'

'I'd love one, thank you,' she fired back with a lot more confidence than she felt. 'Milk, no sugar.'

The two had laughed about their auspicious meeting over the years. Stick around she did, quickly learning that Peter's acerbic wit and dour delivery hid a heart that groaned with love and a nature that was gentle, generous and kind. She continued to work with him in the family textile business for many years, until he sold up and experimented with retirement. And then in its place rose the Reservoir Street Kitchen, which was her domain, with Peter pottering supportively alongside.

Second Chance Cafe

In the early days she had felt torn, secretly pining for the man she had lost, while daily reminding herself that she had made the right choice in not tracking him down. The older she got and the more established she and Peter grew, the better she understood the devastation that her contact and revelation could bring to that other family far away. She kept the information from her young son too, not wanting him to be burdened with such a big secret. And as time went on, it got harder to broach the subject that had lain dormant for so many years.

Wyatt was only a young boy when she and Peter had married in a simple no-frills ceremony at the Registry Office on Regent Street. Peter's brother and sister were reluctant witnesses, making their excuses before the ink had dried on the page and scampering off to gossip over a cup of tea, no doubt. Bea had worn a lemon-coloured shift dress and Peter his best suit with a yellow rose in the lapel. Afterwards they had supper in Chinatown, where they ate noodles with plastic chopsticks in the street.

Wyatt seemed happy as the three stood under the swaying red lanterns, eating their chop suey and joking about it being the cheapest wedding reception in history. He had been a little scrap really, but at nearly seven already a determined character. His childhood on the tough streets of Kings Cross had taught him how to hold his own and rebuff any comments designed to hurt or undermine, but despite his cool delivery and streetwise stance, what Wyatt actually needed was a father figure.

Peter, however, found it hard to pierce the steely shell Wyatt had acquired. He had no experience of children and behaved with the self-consciousness of an older single man desperate not to get it wrong. The result was that he often came across as aloof, remote. Keen not to presume on Wyatt's affections, he waited for Wyatt to come to him. Wyatt, on the other hand, felt that Peter didn't make enough of an effort with him. It was almost like a stand-off, a no-win situation with Bea caught in the middle.

Peter wanted to give the boy the best education possible and so, once he turned ten, Wyatt was sent away to Scotch College up in Melbourne. Bea had been very conflicted about allowing him to board. The two of them had been so close for the first, difficult years in Sydney and she was desperate for him not to feel excluded now that Peter was part of their family too. But she couldn't deny that their relationship had become much more difficult, with Wyatt increasingly closed and self-contained. Peter had been adamant that sending Wyatt away to school would be good for all of them, and especially for Wyatt. He needed to be able to do his own thing, away from the intensity of Bea's attentions, Peter had said. Now, years later, with Wyatt grown up and a parent himself, Bea wasn't so sure it had been the right decision. The distance between them had only got greater, she felt, and the problem was never really fixed.

There had been some special moments in Peter's relationship with Wyatt, though. Moments that stuck in her mind and that she rolled around her brain like treasure in her palm. In particular she liked to think about the day she came home to find Peter reading to Wyatt from one of his favourite books. The house had been unnaturally silent, with no TV spewing cartoon sound-effects into the room. Tiptoeing in unseen, she'd watched them: Peter sitting in the armchair and Wyatt lying on the sofa on his tummy, his bare legs kicking up, his face resting on his palms, flexing back on planted elbows, listening intently as Peter read. 'Then, if you had been watching, you would have seen the most wonderful thing in the world – the wolf checked in mid spring. He made his bound before he saw what it was he was jumping at, and then he tried to stop himself. The result was that he shot up straight into the air for four or five feet, landing almost where he left ground. "Man!" he snapped. "A man's cub. Look!"'

It was a scene she had stored away, treasuring always. It brought her comfort at the oddest of times. Like the night Peter had died, when Bea had cradled his glasses to her chest and, unable to face their bed alone, had decided to sleep where she lay. Her eyes were gritty and tired, yet the sight of that book and the memory of that day had lifted her.

She had sleepwalked through the few days until the funeral. The day had been difficult for Wyatt – he hadn't really known how to act, his manner and body language making it clear that he would rather be somewhere else, anywhere else. He kept poking his finger inside his stiff white shirt collar and pulling, as if to release some unseen pressure. Towards the end of the wake she could tell that he was mentally rehearsing his getaway story. He hovered, with Sarah at his elbow, looking anxious, then strolled towards her, unblinking, like he did when he wasn't being truthful.

'We'd better be pushing off, Mum. It's been a good day, but Sarah needs to get back and I've got to sort some... err... stuff, anyway. Call if you need anything.'

She smiled as he bent and grazed her cheek with the touch of a kiss. They weren't the first to leave, but probably the second.

'Just one second, Wyatt, before you dash off. I have something for you.' She stood and gathered up her embroidered pashmina, flinging it over her shoulder before disappearing into the bedroom.

'Wyatt?' she called a few seconds later, having expected him to shadow her.

He rather awkwardly abandoned his wife and followed his mother's voice along the corridor.

'Close the door, love,' she instructed. As he did so, she heard the faintest sigh of irritation. 'I know you're in a hurry to get back to your... err... "stuff", but Peter wanted me to give you this. He was quite adamant. And his wishes are important to me, as they were to him.' She smiled and handed him the book. Its khaki cover was fraying slightly along the spine and at the corners.

Wyatt ran his finger over the faded gold embossed elephant on the front and then the simple gold lettering. It was Peter's favourite book, Rudyard Kipling's *The Jungle Book*; his most prized possession.

Wyatt sank down onto the bed and let the book fall open in his hands. '"We be of one blood, ye and I,"' he read out loud. He smiled at his mum and then looked back at the tiny type crammed onto the yellowing page. It was beautiful. 'I don't know what to say! He... he wanted me to have it?'

She saw his Adam's apple rise and fall in a huge swallow of emotion. 'Yes. He loved you. He loved you very much.'

Wyatt exhaled through bloated cheeks, taken aback, embarrassed, ashamed. 'Blimey.' He shook his head, had clearly not been expecting it. 'And I, y'know, I...'

She had nodded. 'Yes, Wyatt, I know.'

'He used to read it to me.'

Again she nodded. 'Yes, Wyatt, I know.'

Bea smiled at the recollection as she flipped open her laptop. A little envelope blinked at her in the corner. She concentrated, doing as Flora had instructed, gathering the little remote arrow via the pad with her finger and clicking. To her amazement, the email opened. 'I did it!' Bea announced rather proudly, glancing at Peter's photograph on the wall and taking his smile as congratulations.

From: Christmas Café

Subject: Re: Hello Again

Bea, your first email, really? I am indeed honoured! Don't worry, I think gapsaregreatlyoverrated. Oh and VBW stands for Very Best Wishes!

The team at Christmas Café consists of Elsie, as miserable as the day is long and with a demeanour that could curdle milk, but as loyal as you could wish for.

You are an insomniac's dream: I can't sleep and up pinged your message, marvellous! I am sorry to hear about your husband. I know what that feels like, we are in similar boats; for me it's been ten years. Walking is my escape, my passion and my solace. And Scotland is a beautiful, beautiful country. Unique. I can truly say that standing alone on a rugged, misty moor, looking across the mossy dips and tranquil lochs, with smoke hovering over the water and blue sky beckoning from the horizon, there is no place that I feel as close to God. And all that practically on my doorstep! Compared to Australia, it's far easier to navigate. I would be more than happy to be your guide and your translator.

VBW! Alex x

PS – I think you might be my new e-penfriend.

PPS – I told Professor Richards you weren't a cat fan. He didn't seem too offended.

Bea laughed out loud. This woman was funny. How wonderful to be chatting to someone on the other side of the world as though they were in the next room. She envied Alex her tranquillity, wishing she could stroll on that misty moor and find such peace. She rather liked having an e-penfriend, whatever that was. She skipped to the kitchen, willing the kettle to boil quicker as she plopped the Earl Grey tea bag and lemon slice into her mug, composing in her head the email she would send in reply.

Second Chance Cafe

From: BeaG

Subject: Re: Hello Again

Well, Alex, that sounds beautiful; I envy you having that special place to wander in. We have the Blue Mountains, and standing at Echo Point to watch the sun rise over the Three Sisters is one of the most stunning things I have ever witnessed. Peter took me there many times, but I remember the first more than any other. We were with a gaggle of noisy tourists all eager to get a good photograph, but as the first rays peeked over the rocks, everyone fell silent, totally awestruck by the experience. I'm ashamed to say it's been a year or two since I last visited and in truth I feel a little scared of going there without him.

    I did actually live in England, in Surrey, until I was fourteen, but I never made it to Scotland. I've not been back since. The memories of that early life are precious to me. I'm estranged from my family, a story far too long to go into right now, but I think fondly of those years, when I had no idea of how my life would change. I remember laughing a lot.

Bea paused and thought of her sister, remembered again the Epsom Downs horses she'd told Flora about, and the white Christmases. She sighed and returned to the keyboard.

    As you can see, I'm concentrating now and the gaps are sorted. I'm not too good with the keyboard, take an age to type – used to be much faster. I must get better.

I'm sorry for your loss too. Ten years is a long time. I don't like being on my own, not really. I sometimes feel too vulnerable and lonely to be happy. There are days when the world feels like it's spinning too fast and I want to get off. Do you ever feel that way?

Bea x

Thinking of her sister and those happy childhood years had unnerved her. At fourteen she'd been a mere baby, blissfully unaware that in just a few years her world would unravel in ways she couldn't have begun to imagine. She thought about the many jaunts she and Peter had taken, exploring the vast, beautiful country that they called home. *I miss that...* Her laptop buzzed, drawing her from her thoughts.

From: Christmas Café

Subject: Re: Hello Again

The Three Sisters sound quite majestic, I will google them.

In answer to your question, yes, I feel that way most days; everything moves too quickly and I find myself longing for a gentler pace. Truth is, I'm afraid that if I slow down, I might forget why I need to get up every day, lose my purpose. I haven't told anyone that before. I think it's maybe easier to open up to you, my e-penfriend, with this screen between us!

Right, time is marching on and I'm finally feeling sleepy. I have thoroughly enjoyed our chat. And don't worry, Bea, you are not alone. Christmas is a difficult time for lots of us.

Very best wishes,

Alex x

Eight

'Santa Maria! Christmas lights in here too? Are you kidding me? They are everywhere! I was at Paddy's Market earlier; it's full of sparkly trash, bits of bloody tinsel on every pole and dancing Santa Clauses holding candy canes. And now in here too. I can't escape it!' Mr Giraldi shook his head in disdain as he took a seat at his preferred table.

Tait smiled. 'Ah, come on, Mr Giraldi, don't go all bah humbug on us. You've got to get into the swing!'

Kim walked in with the specials board ready to go outside.

'Hey, Kim,' Tait said, 'I'm just saying, we've got the Christmas spirit flowing here, we can't have Mr Giraldi spoiling our vibe, can we? He doesn't even like tinsel!'

Kim stared at him and nodded. 'I... I think... I...' she managed, before rushing back into the kitchen and busying herself with stacking the dishwasher.

'Cat's got her tongue again.' Mr Giraldi chuckled, tapping his walking stick on the floor in time with his wheezing. 'I got so many grandkids, Christmas almost bankrupts me. They only want money! Can you believe it! Money! What does a kid need money for? In my day we were grateful for a satsuma, a walnut and a blessing!'

Tait was about to respond when out of the corner of his eye he spotted Wyatt striding up the hill with Flora following closely behind. Her thick shock of auburn hair made her instantly recognisable.

A minute later, Wyatt swept through the door. 'Is Mum here?'

'Sure.' Tait pointed his thumb towards the kitchen. 'She's out back.'

'Hi, Tait.' Flora's voice caught in her throat. Her eyes were red and swollen from crying.

'You okay, Little Klitschko?' he whispered.

Flora gave the briefest nod and followed her dad into the kitchen, rushing through the swing doors.

'Wyatt! What on earth...?' Bea looked up from the counter-top and wiped her floury hands on her pinny. 'Flora? What's going on?'

'Oh, Gran!' Flora fell into Bea's arms.

'Sorry to barge in like this, Mum.' Wyatt glanced at Kim, not wanting to give details in front of this stranger and especially not with everyone in the café poised to listen.

'Can you hold the fort here, Kim?' Bea asked over her granddaughter's shoulder.

'Sure.' Kim nodded, trying not to stare at the trio, who all stood there awkwardly, emotion tumbling from them in waves. It made her sad to see Flora so tearful.

Second Chance Cafe

'Let's get you upstairs,' Bea cooed. She released her granddaughter, ran her hands under the hot tap and trod the stairs to her apartment. 'Wyatt, can you put the kettle on?'

Flora dumped her bag on the sitting room floor and flopped down on the sofa.

Bea stood watching her cry for a few moments then walked over to the balcony doors and threw them open, hoping a breeze would whip round the room and take the edge off the frayed tempers. 'Flora, what's all this about? What happened? You seemed quite sparky when you left here yesterday.'

'I'm sure she was,' Wyatt interjected, walking past his mum so that they both stood facing Flora on the sofa. 'Are you going to tell your gran what you've been up to?' His tone was level, stern.

Flora shrugged, her face sullen, and looked at the floor.

Wyatt sighed. 'After you called and I set off to pick her up last night, Sarah decided to freshen up her room, change her bed linen and make it nice.' He paused. 'Under her bed she found a carrier bag full of make-up.'

'She can wear a little make-up, can't she, love? I mean, she's nearly fourteen,' Bea said soothingly, wondering what the fuss was about and thinking how hard it must be for a dad to recognise that his little girl was growing up.

'She's had her own make-up since she was little; we've always let her experiment, you know that. But this was a bit different. It wasn't the usual bits she gets from the store, it was expensive brands, all wrapped and sealed. Stolen.'

'Stolen?' Bea looked at Flora.

'It wasn't me! I didn't steal it. I told you, I was just looking after it!' Flora banged the sofa with tightly clenched fists and shouted, as though extra volume might give her case added weight.

'Who stole it then?' Bea asked.

Flora shrugged.

'Flora, whoever you're covering for would most definitely not cover for you. No one with any decency would have asked you to look after stolen goods. That's a fact.' Bea sighed. *Bloody Lori big boobs, no doubt.*

'I'm not going back with Dad, no way!' Flora shouted.

'Okay, okay.' Bea patted the air. 'Let's keep calm and find a solution.'

'There is no solution. They don't even listen to me. I fucking hate them!' she shouted towards her dad.

Bea gasped and Wyatt visibly flinched.

'You cannot speak like that! I won't have it, not under my roof and certainly not to your dad. Do you understand me?' Bea was as stern as she could manage, but she was on the verge of tears herself. She was dismayed to see the transformation of her sweet girl into someone quite unrecognisable.

'This is what we have to put up with.' Wyatt held his palm up towards his daughter and spoke to Bea as though Flora wasn't there.

'Why don't you just go then!' Flora screamed through her tears. 'I hate you!'

Wyatt stared at his mum. 'Do you think I should go? I don't want to abandon her and I don't want it to become your problem, but nor do I want her to get more agitated. I don't know what's best.' He kept his level tone, despite his unease.

Bea raised her arms and let them fall, equally at a loss. 'I really don't know what to suggest.' She chewed her lip and stared at her granddaughter, who had curled into a foetal position on the sofa. 'Maybe you should go, let things calm down a bit, and I'll call you later?'

Wyatt nodded. 'I'm going, Flora. I'll speak to you later.' He bent down and tried to stroke away the hair that had fallen in a curtain over her face. She didn't react, kept her eyes firmly closed.

Bea watched Wyatt walk down Reservoir Street towards his car, chatting on his phone, no doubt filling Sarah in on the latest developments. He cut a forlorn figure and she felt anger flare on his behalf. She loved her granddaughter, of course, but causing her son this level of upset was unacceptable.

Bea took a seat at the end of the sofa and waited for her granddaughter's anger to dissipate, hoping the stillness of the room might bring a sense of calm.

If you can wait and not be tired by waiting,
Or being lied about, don't deal in lies,
Or being hated, don't give way to hating,
And yet don't look too good, nor talk too wise...

As she sat, she repeated the lines in her head, over and over, hearing his voice still. It was her poem for troubled times, a poem from when she was young – a bit older than Flora but just as much at odds with the world. Maybe Flora would find it reassuring too.

Bea remembered the perfect quiet of the night she'd first heard those lines as if it were yesterday. They were on a boat, bobbing on the ocean, the deck rough beneath their outstretched legs as they'd stared up at the fading stars and then, later, at the purple dawn, which had crept in to steal away the night. It was the night she met her love; her parents and the other passengers had retreated below deck, leaving the two of them there in the half light. Sneaking the opportunity, she'd rested her head on his shoulder and with her eyes closed she'd listened as he'd recited his favourite poetry, his voice cutting through the darkness. *'If you can wait and not be tired by waiting...'* Oh, thought Bea resignedly, *that should be the line to go on my headstone.*

It was half an hour before Flora looked up, flipping her hair over her shoulder and propping herself up into a semi-seated position. Her body language was softer, her voice steady. 'I didn't steal it.'

Bea noted her bloodshot eyes and puffy cheeks. 'I believe you. But you did know it was stolen?'

Flora nodded.

'Right. I have to say that at this very moment I'm more upset at how you spoke to your dad than a bag of bloody make-up.'

'They wouldn't let me talk. I tried to tell them it wasn't me, but they just kept saying if it wasn't me then I had to say who had done it and that they were going to the police, and if they did that...' Her chest heaved again. She closed her eyes.

'They won't do that, Flora,' Bea said, hoping she spoke the truth. 'Try and take deep breaths and keep calm.'

'I hate them!' she muttered.

'No you don't, love. Trust me. They would be so upset to hear you say that. Did you see your dad's face? He was so shocked, and I can understand why. It really isn't any way to talk to or about your parents.'

'You don't understand.' Flora shook her head.

'Well, tell me then, give me all the missing pieces. I'm not getting any more involved if I don't know what I'm getting involved in.'

Flora sighed. 'There's this club.'

'A nightclub?' Bea ventured, wondering if this had something to do with Flora's night on the beach.

'No!' Flora gave a small hiccupping laugh. 'It's just a thing at school where people do dares and stuff.'

'What kind of stuff?'

Flora gave her usual shrug. 'I don't know, things like hiding behind the wall and shouting things out.'

'What things?'

'Things like... fuck off.' Flora's cheeks flared at having said the word twice within the last hour.

'Oh my goodness, Flora! Why would you think that's a good idea?'

Flora kept her eyes downcast and shrugged again. 'I hate being in Year 8! Maisie moved away.'

'I didn't know that.' Bea pictured the sweet girl, a neighbour who'd been a constant in Flora's life since kindergarten, always there at her parties and in stories about what she'd been up to.

'Her dad got a job in Darwin.'

'You must miss her.'

'I do,' Flora whispered. 'I don't have any friends and then Lori and Katie said I could hang out with them, but I had to do the dares and then the whole thing with Marcus happened and I don't want to go back to school after Christmas. I don't.'

Bea gathered her granddaughter into her arms and held her tightly. 'You've got yourself into a bit of a pickle, but it will all work out, you wait and see.'

'I'm sorry, Bea.' Flora whispered her apology.

'What for, darling?'

'For saying "fuck" in front of you, twice.'

Bea held her granddaughter's beautiful hair and let it fall through her fingers. 'Oh, sweet girl, it's actually three times if we count your apology.' She kissed Flora's scalp and smiled at Peter's picture on the wall. She knew he would be smiling at the terrible farce of it all.

As Flora slept, exhausted from all the drama, Bea considered the best course of action. She decided she'd call Sarah later, make sure their approaches were in sync; the last thing they wanted was to present a fractured front. She pondered the complex relationships within families, recalled the evening well over a decade ago when Wyatt had marched her from the kitchen, saying eagerly, 'Come on, Mum!' as he held her hand and led her to the dining room table to be introduced to his new friend Sarah.

When it got to dessert, Bea had brought in her famous chocolate mousse with pride, holding the bowl high, knowing it was Wyatt's favourite.

'Oh, wow!' Peter had laughed. 'The pièce de resistance, and entirely meat-free, as far as I'm aware!'

Sarah had given him a sideways glance and kept quiet, unwilling to be subjected to any more ribbing. Earlier, while Peter had been carving the roast beef, she'd told them that she was a pescatarian, and Peter had been genuinely bemused. 'What's that?' he'd asked. 'Does it come after Gemini?'

'So, what are your plans, Sarah?' Bea tried to engage the girl as she set the mousse down on the table. 'Wyatt tells me you studied history.'

'Yes, I did, but I'm not working right now.'

'What would you like to do?' Bea asked keenly, trying to show interest in the guest who had uttered barely more than a few syllables during the entire evening.

'I don't know really, possibly work in a gallery or museum, but I'm not sure. I'm waiting for the right opportunity; I don't want to get stuck in any old job. My mother says it's better to hold out for my dream than get trapped in something that isn't going to make me happy.'

'No, quite.' Bea swallowed the many phrases that spun through her head. *How will you know when your dream comes along if you have no idea what you're bloody waiting for? And I'd say to your mother that it's better that you do something, anything, rather than sit around and expect Wyatt to provide for you. Show some backbone, have some pride!*

'Before you serve the pud, Mum, there's something I'd like to say.'

Peter flashed his wife a look; she kept her eyes fixed on her son.

Wyatt reached out and took Sarah's tiny hand into his. 'Wow, well, where to begin?'

Bea considered shouting out, feigning cramp or knocking the dessert on to the floor, causing a diversion in any way she could, in the faint hope that she could create enough of a distraction for the whole thing to be forgotten. Knowing this was extremely unlikely, she braced herself for what was coming next.

Wyatt picked up his glass and exhaled. 'The thing is, I've asked Sarah to marry me and I'm delighted to say that she's said yes!'

Peter rose from the table and clapped his hands together. 'Bravo! Bravo, Wyatt! That's wonderful. I think I might have a couple of bottles of fizz chilling somewhere – this calls for a celebration!' He winked at his wife and gently squeezed her shoulder as he ambled from the room.

Bea was aware that her smile was a little fixed and her

reaction delayed. Sarah was so very far from what she had in her mind when she considered a bride for her son; it was all she could do not to scream. But Peter had predicted it, before they'd even arrived.

'She could be the one,' he'd said, smiling, and had promptly stashed two bottles of fizz in the fridge just in case.

'Oh, listen to you – *the one*!' Bea had retorted. 'You're so old-fashioned. And no, I don't think for a moment that there will be any announcement – he's only known her for five minutes!' In truth, she disliked conversations like that and avoided phrases like 'the one' and 'the love of her life' whenever possible. Even after thirteen years of marriage, it was another face that popped into her head on such occasions, making her feel disloyal and sad in equal measure.

'Well, you can say that, but when you know, you know. Look at me – a confirmed bachelor knocking fifty and in you walked and that was that. I was floored!'

'You were only a bachelor because you were a workaholic and the chances of meeting *the one* are considerably slimmer when you don't ever lift your head up from your desk!'

'I beg to differ! It worked for me and I think you'll find I got you by doing just that!' Peter chuckled.

Bea kissed his hand. 'I got very lucky that day.'

'We both did.'

'But surely Wyatt isn't thinking along those lines? He's fresh out of university; he's too young to be settling down.'

Peter laughed. 'When you were his age you already had a son. If anything, he's lagging behind.'

'Oh God, I know you're right, but I can't help it. Whenever I picture him, it's him when he was little, in his cap and short trousers, waving at the car as we dropped him off at school, with that trying-to-be-brave look on his face, smiling but petrified. I guess I'll always think of him in that way.'

'It's understandable. I think all mothers like to feel that they're needed, even when they're not.'

'And I'm not, am I?'

He shook his head. 'No, my love. But that's a good thing.'

Bea smiled, recalling Peter's words and the knack he had of reassuring her while simultaneously steering her mood.

She let Flora sleep for an hour, then glanced at her watch and saw that it was nearly eleven. 'Come on, Miss Sleepy Head. I can't let you mope and sob the day away on the sofa. Why don't you come and help in the kitchen and then when the lunch rush is over we could go for a wander, maybe take a stroll out to Woolloomooloo or we could go up around by the lido and back down via Mrs Macquarie's Chair. A good old-fashioned stroll to clear your head and maybe an ice cream on the way back. How about it?'

Flora sat up, blew her nose and nodded. She felt better already. 'Yes, please. I'd like that.'

Tait and Kim were sweet, making a fuss of her and keeping her occupied with chores like napkin folding and spoon polishing, all designed to distract. When lunch service was drawing to an end, Bea and Flora donned their sunnies and hats and set off up Reservoir Street's steep hill, welcoming the breeze that ruffled the eucalypt trees that lined the route.

Flora was surprised by her gran's pace. She was nimble on her feet the way keen walkers are.

'I reckon if I put my Converse out by the front door, they could do this route by themselves!' Bea laughed.

She stepped to the kerb to let a man in sporty attire pass by. His toddler son sat on his shoulders, stretching up into the dappled light to grab overhead branches, trying to reach at the sky.

'Cheers!' The man smiled and the little boy squealed.

His wife jogged up behind them. She was pushing a double stroller with adorable twin girls in matching sunnies and hats strapped into it. 'Thanks, we're trying to catch up, but it's not so easy with this!' She nodded at the bulky stroller.

'They're adorable!' Bea admired the cute little girls.

'Thanks. We've another two at school!'

'Oh, you lucky thing!'

'See ya!' The Lycra-clad woman raced ahead and accelerated up the hill, nearly catching her husband.

'I bet they have a grand old time – imagine the tea table in their house.' Bea laughed, knowing she would have loved the chaos.

'I wish I had brothers and sisters or cousins,' Flora said.

'You do? Why's that, love?'

'Cos then Mum and Dad wouldn't be so obsessed with me. They'd have to share their nosying around a bit and that would give me a break!'

'There are some advantages, though. You get your mum and dad all to yourself, you don't have to share them – that's a nice thing too.'

'Is it? I don't think so.'

'Your dad was an only child, obviously, so any spare cash I could scrape together went entirely on him.' Bea remembered getting her first proper pay packet and finally having enough money to get him a new T-shirt and jeans. She'd folded some notes into his palm: *'A few dollars, love, to get whatever you like!'* It had felt good. 'I don't know how I'd have coped with more than one.'

Flora shrugged. 'Yeah, but we've got the space.'

'True.'

'Especially at birthdays and Christmas, wouldn't it be great to have a whole crowd instead of just us? Y'know, people to play games with or chat to. I'd love that. It'd be like a proper party.'

Bea thought of Mr Giraldi. 'It would, love.'

'I sometimes need some space, a bit of freedom, but they're constantly asking what I'm up to – it's like a million questions the moment I walk through the door, it drives me nuts! And if I'm quiet, they want to know what's wrong, but what's wrong is that I want them to shut up and leave me alone!'

Second Chance Cafe

Bea remembered the weekends when Wyatt was home from school. *'Can I get you something to eat? Do you have laundry? What would you like for tea? Do you need a lift? Can I get you a blanket?'* His frequent sighs of irritation. It was hard not to bombard him: she missed him so much, loved him so much. She hadn't considered until now that that kind of attention might be a pressure.

They turned left, walking fast along Crown Street, then dropping down to reach Bourke Street. Twisting through the back lanes, they covered the couple of kilometres with ease, crossing the main road via the metal footbridge until finally they had the iconic pale green wooden buildings of Woolloomooloo Pier in their sights. The restaurants that lined the dockside were packed with well-dressed diners who were busy sipping chilled white wine, feasting on fresh seafood and sumptuous salads and admiring the expensive yachts moored in the private marina. Harry's Café de Wheels was also doing a brisk trade, handing out its famous pies to the snaking queue and serving iced coffees to the yummy mummies whose babies dozed in their hooded strollers.

They stopped for a breather, staring into the murky water by the dock, which was teeming with jellyfish.

'I hate being thirteen,' Flora said, kicking her feet against the low wall.

'Why, darling?'

Flora shrugged. 'Because I don't count. I'm not old enough to do anything and I don't know what's going to happen to me and that makes me feel really wobbly.'

Bea thought of all the things she wanted to say to her granddaughter, the advice she wanted to offer, the words of comfort and reassurance that were on the tip of her tongue. She chose her words carefully, wary of piling on meaningless sentiment when she was already feeling disenfranchised.

'Yes, you're right, the world can seem scary when you feel that way. But you're not alone. All of us feel that way sometimes. I'm in my fifties and I still feel wobbly because I don't know what's around the corner. But you know what? It might be great things! And you're wrong about not counting: right now you're the only thing that three adults are thinking about, worrying about – in fact five, as we can probably include Kim and Tait as well.'

'Do you think I should text Mum and Dad?' she whispered, closing one eye as she looked up into the sunshine.

'I think you should do what you think is right. If I was you, I would want to make contact because worrying about it only makes things feel worse.'

Flora nodded as she fished in her pocket for her phone. As she did so, her fingers pulled out a slender cream envelope. 'Oh, I forgot, Dad asked me to give you this. Said he found it in a book about a jungle or something that Pappy had given him.'

Bea stood on the Woolloomooloo Pier, took the thin package into her hands and smiled at the unexpected sight of Peter's italic script, written in the black ink he favoured. What on earth could it be?

While Flora was engrossed in her phone, Bea peeled the sheet from the envelope and devoured its words. It comprised one simple paragraph written in the middle of the page. He must have hidden it in the book intended for Wyatt, knowing that Wyatt would discover it quite by chance and then pass it on to her.

> You are so young, Bea, and you still have a whole other life ahead of you. Always remember, life is for the brave. So go find happiness and let yourself love!
> You were my greatest joy. You made me so happy, always. What greater gift is there than that?

She smiled at the wonderful message. Even from beyond the grave, he had the power to revive her flagging spirits; to be kind, generous and thoughtful. As ever, he had put her needs first. Like magic, his words began to salve the guilty rip in her heart. She read them again and again, engraving them on her mind. *Oh, Peter! Thank you. Thank you, darling!*

Seeing her gran's teary smile, Flora gave Bea a quizzical look. Bea just shook her head, not ready to share her feelings quite yet. 'It's an emotional time for both of us, darling,' she said. 'Like I told you, you never know what's around the corner. But don't fret: it's a lovely letter. Let's carry on with our walk, shall we?'

The two continued their circuit via the Botanic Gardens and paused at the viewing point near Mrs Macquarie's

Chair to look at the Opera House glinting in the sun. Bea ran her hand over the sandstone rock that had been hand-carved by convicts into the shape of a bench, all so that the Governor's wife, Mrs Elizabeth Macquarie, could sit on the peninsula in Sydney Harbour and watch for ships sailing in from Great Britain. Bea tried to imagine the woman perched there in her empire-line Regency frock, sweating beneath her petticoats and all that intricate lace and silk. Images of Great Britain, the country of her birth, flashed through Bea's mind. And alongside them came Peter's words. *A whole other life ahead of you... Life is for the brave ... Go find happiness!* Maybe she should set sail for the land of misty moors and tranquil lochs, the land through which her heart and mind had wandered on many a lonely night.

Back on Reservoir Street, Kim beamed at the reappearance of Flora, made even better when Tait emerged from the dining area laughing, sharing a joke with the young girl, showing himself to be the great guy she knew he was. 'You feeling a bit better there, little scrapper?' His concern was sincere.

'Yes.' Flora sighed. 'I had ice cream on the way home.'

'Well, there is no situation in the whole wide world that ice cream doesn't fix. Isn't that right, Kim?' he said over his shoulder.

'Uh-huh.' She nodded.

Bea didn't know whose smile was the widest: Flora's at the attention she was getting from the Reservoir Street

Kitchen staff or Kim's, whose face split from ear to ear as she glanced at the blond and beautiful Tait.

Bea's phone rang. She flipped the lid and laboriously pressed the button, still uncomfortable with her mobile phone, as she took the call outside. 'Yes, hello?'

'Mum?'

'Hey, Wyatt! How are you?'

His hesitation told her he was nervous. 'Good, I guess. Flora texted us to say she was sorry, which is a step in the right direction, I suppose. I'm worried she thinks this is all some kind of game, but she's messing up her life – this gang she's got herself in with... it's worrying.'

'They're not really a gang, love. They're just kids, and I suspect kids without as much guidance as Flora. She's a smart girl, she just needs a bit of steering.'

'You are not to encourage her, Mum, not to make this all into some kind of joke. Because it's not funny. We're at our wits' end.'

Bea was staggered at how quickly his anger had flared. 'Wyatt, if you're phoning to thank me for putting my business aside, taking Flora in and looking after her, then you are most welcome, but I do not expect to be lambasted for it.'

Bea was proud of her assertiveness – she usually just let Wyatt go unchallenged. She heard him take a deep breath.

'Sarah is beside herself,' he offered by way of explanation.

Bea pictured Sarah, nursing a large gin on the smoked glass terrace, dipping her toe in the infinity pool and hoping the sun didn't melt her forehead.

'I'm sure she is, but tell Sarah worse things happen at sea.' As she spoke she could smell the salty air, saw herself strolling around the deck in the moonlight, strangled by her high collar, bored by the boat ride and the company of her parents. And then, *'Miss Gerraty, this is Dr Brodie...'* She felt her eyes crinkle in an involuntary smile at the memory of that moment, when her stomach had knotted, her pulse had quickened and she'd fallen.

'This isn't the time to be flippant, Mum!'

His tone brought her back to the present. She had evidently made him cross again; it was a skill she seemed to have. 'You're right, no time for flippancy, but please remember that your daughter is a clever, healthy girl who is only thirteen. She's not messing up her life, she's trying to figure things out and she *is* only thirteen! It's a horrible age between childhood and womanhood. She's lovely, a lovely soul, and that's what every parent wants. She just needs space, maybe some time away.'

She heard his sigh. 'I am grateful that she's with you, but please, please don't encourage her with any of your silliness,' he snapped.

Bea snorted her laughter. 'My silliness? Listen how you talk to me, Wyatt! You think me advocating space and some time away will make things worse for Flora? Or maybe it's my liberal tendencies that give you cause for concern?'

'Please don't trivialise this.'

'Why not, Wyatt? It is trivial. In the grand scheme of things.'

Second Chance Cafe

'I might have guessed that would be your stance.'

Bea pictured his scalp reddening beneath his thinning hair. 'I tell you what, love, I'm going back to work. I'll keep Flora here for as long as she needs, but I suggest you and Sarah take a good hard look at what's going on under your roof. Flora said she can't talk to you because you're arguing all the time.' She cringed the moment the words left her mouth; she had never meddled in this way.

'If you're suggesting that my daughter steals and fights because of how we parent her, that would be a bit rich!' he spluttered.

'If that is in some way a dig at how I parented you,' Bea shot back, 'then please remind yourself that it was me that gave you the best education, me that dragged you from the bloody gutter to a seat at a university table... me! And if you think that parenting is what causes these situations, may I also remind you that my child was never in a fight or felt the need to fence stolen goods under his bloody bed!'

She ended the call and felt a sense of elation at having stood up to her son, quickly followed by a quake in her stomach, weakened by the exchange.

'Give me strength!' she said to the blue sky above.

Nine

In the still of the late afternoon the sun had danced across the sitting room and come to rest on the far wall. Bea wanted to talk to a friend; her new e-penfriend was just the person. She could chat to Alex from the comfort of her bed if she so chose, didn't need to apply make-up or leave the house and could end the conversation whenever she felt like it. Plus Alex was remote enough in her life not to judge or intrude. Perfect.

> From: BeaG
>
> Subject: Re: Hello Again
>
> Hey Alex,
>
> Goodness me, what a day. Hope yours was less eventful! My granddaughter has suggested you might change the name of the café for different events – Valentine's, Easter... although, thinking about it, I'm sure that would cost you a fortune in neon. Christmas Café sounds perfect. Do you serve Christmas food every day?
>
> I was thinking about what you said in your last mail, that Christmas is a difficult time. It really is, isn't it? I feel

particularly alone at this time of year. Hard to admit, but I do very much wish that I had a man by my side. I loved being half of a couple. Celebrating without him makes the joy a little thin, the fun a little forced. I never minded being in a crowd if he was close by, but now, the prospect of attending a social event without him to call upon leaves me feeling nervous and a little afraid, which is ridiculous. I'm fifty-three!

As I was reminded only recently, I have a whole other life ahead of me. What am I supposed to do? Sit quietly through the coming years? Watch more TV? Learn to knit? Hardly. I long for company – and not necessarily a love interest. I would in fact settle for a better relationship with my son. That doesn't feel like too much to ask. I wanted to end on something light and witty, but my brain's gone a bit blank, sorry.

Bea x

Bea sat staring at the screen, thinking about the truth behind her words. She wished she was the kind of person that could nap, knowing that twenty minutes of escape would be just the thing to reset her whirring mind. She closed her eyes and listened to the laughter coming from the café below: someone was chuckling and it made her smile. She loved how happiness could be infectious, like a yawn.

It was a pleasant surprise as her laptop buzzed her into action. She sat up straight and wriggled back against the sofa cushions.

From: Christmas Café

Subject: Re: Hello Again

Hello Bea,

I know what you mean about Christmas. It comes with expectations, doesn't it? A certain pressure. And yes, we only serve Christmas fare: turkey and Christmas pudding every day, that's the whole menu!

It's been a long time since I was comfortable at a social event. I prefer to be walking or settled with a good book! It's a great testament to your marriage that you miss being half of a couple, a wonderful compliment to your husband. Are you not close to your son? And why such an eventful day? If you don't mind me asking...

Ax

Bea replied immediately. It was as if the two of them were in conversation, not typing emails across ten thousand miles.

From: BeaG

Subject: Re: Hello Again

I don't mind at all. Eventful because my granddaughter, Flora, is having a bit of a tough time. She's staying with me, desperate for a change of scene. Being a teenager isn't easy, is it?

As for my son, that's a bit harder to explain. Things weren't the easiest for him when he was small and I guess we didn't address issues that maybe we should have. I hardly ever see him. I receive a monthly telephone call, which I sometimes confuse with one of those sales calls, the type where they tell me I've been selected at random to have a free and fabulous kitchen installed or that I've won a time-share in Phuket. His calls are a bit like that, scripted and formulaic. We exchange pleasantries, swap our views on the forthcoming weather and then he says, 'I must go...', as though he's running out of time. Truth is, it's not time he's running out of, it's things to say to me.

Bea stopped typing and gave a wry smile as she steeled herself to continue.

I have to confess that after I've set the receiver down, I often sit and remember the hours and hours of conversation that we used to have about cricket, travel, space. Nothing was off limits. We were very good friends – I was lucky. But things change, don't they? That's the one constant, change.

Bx

PS Turkey and Christmas pudding every day? Really?

There was a pause in communication. Bea pictured Alex reading her email; she swallowed the ripple of embarrassment, hoping she hadn't over-shared.

From: Christmas Café

Subject: Re: Hello Again

Flora? Now there's a good Scottish name. To be honest, I'm trying to remember what being a teenager felt like; it's been a while. I'd swap with her, though: no aching joints, dwindling prospects or constant discussions with my peers about health. I'm sorry to hear that you and your son are distant. It happens; life can be too busy and sometimes we prioritise wrongly. Have you told him how you feel? He might be unaware?

Ax

PS No! Of course not! We have a full and varied menu of wholesome, home-cooked food.

From: BeaG

Subject: Re: Hello Again

You'd swap? Urgh, tell me about it! I'd give anything to run my hand over a flat stomach instead of the crêpey old pouch I'm now saddled with!

I'm really enjoying our chats, it's like I've found a new mate – always a good thing, you can never have too many! And no, I haven't told my son how I feel. I guess that's the nub of the problem right there: lots of chat about things that don't really matter and little discussion about the big stuff.

Bx

From: Christmas Café

Subject: Re: Hello Again

Agreed, you can never have too many friends! Your comment made me laugh; a toned stomach is indeed a dim and distant memory for me too. Not sure what the correct response is to make you feel better... And as for the big stuff, it's not too late until it's too late.

'What are you doing?'

Bea abandoned her email and looked up to find Flora standing in the doorway. She was spooning large mouthfuls of muesli into her mouth as she talked, positioning the food in the centre of her tongue and jutting her chin to make sure none spilled.

'Oh, just swapping emails with Alex. She's got a good sense of humour.' Bea smiled. 'I'm her e-penfriend apparently.'

'Cool!' was Flora's succinct summary. 'Did you speak to my dad today?'

'Yes. Yes, he called earlier.' Bea closed the screen and looked at her granddaughter.

'What did he say?' Flora stopped shovelling the cereal.

'He was a bit upset; wants to put everything right and doesn't really know where to start. I think he's a bit afraid.' *And I shouldn't have shouted at him. This isn't about us.* She hated the way he addressed her with such impatience; it made her feel stupid or, worse still, like an inconvenience that had to be tolerated. She had always hidden this from Peter, not wanting to encourage discord between the two of them and knowing that Peter would have taken him to task.

'It's all my fault, isn't it?' Flora looked doleful.

'Not everything, no. Don't you worry about Daddy and me. I seem to irritate him no matter what the issue. I don't think I noticed it as much when Peter was around – or maybe it didn't bother me as much because I was distracted.' She sighed, remembered it was Flora she was speaking to and smiled to compensate for the over-sharing.

'I miss him, he was a great pappy. He used to let me puff on his cigar when no one was looking and he even gave me my own once. I still have it in my drawer. And although he was quiet, he was really noisy when we were on our own. He used to make me laugh.'

'He was only quiet in front of your dad; at home he was very different.'

'They didn't really get on, did they?' Flora braced herself for the reply, aware that this was unchartered water.

'It's not that they didn't get on, they were just very different. They both found it hard.'

'That must have made you sad. Must have made you all sad.' Flora slurped up her milk.

Bea smiled at the smart, insightful child. 'It did a bit.'

The front doorbell rang. Bea hopped off the sofa and trod the stairs.

It was Kim looking back at her through the glass.

'You don't need to ring, honey, just come on up!'

'Didn't like to, in case you and Flora were chatting. Hey, Flora!' Kim stuck her head round the sitting room door and waved at her.

'Cup of tea?' Bea was already in the kitchen, filling the kettle.

'Why not. It's funny how I work with food and drink all

day but often forget to take either myself.' Kim refastened her ponytail, scraping up the stray tendrils that had fallen loose through the day. 'Not interrupting, am I?'

'No, not at all.' Bea lowered her voice a bit, mindful that Flora was in the next room. 'We were just talking about Wyatt's childhood. The trials of parenthood! It's reminded me that you can only do what you think is right at the time and then pray that you don't end up being proved wrong.'

'Seems like sound advice. My mum and dad were always far too busy; even when we were on holiday it felt more like a school trip. I wish they'd relaxed more with us, just chatted.'

'That's exactly what I'm talking about.' Bea pulled mugs from the shelf. 'Maybe your mum and dad didn't want to waste a single opportunity to teach you something – maybe that was their goal. And you *have* turned out super smart.'

Kim blushed. 'I don't know about that.'

'But *you* see it as them not relaxing, not spending quality time!' Bea opened her palms to the sky. 'I think Mr Giraldi hit the nail on the head when he said that all families need a translator!'

'Sign me up! I'd love to know what my parents are on about. Wyatt was lucky to have you.' Kim sighed.

'Don't think he'd see it that way, especially at the moment. He gets so mad at me, I suppose because he can. It's always been that way. He wasn't happy about sharing his mum and when he was home from school he used to dream up any number of situations that excluded Peter.

I always went along with it, of course. I figured if he was happy then I was happy and that made Peter happy! Peter thought he was doing the right thing by paying for Wyatt's very expensive education and Wyatt thought he was being shipped off and ignored. Which was a shame, a great shame. Both of them were hamstrung by convention and expectation. It all seems a little silly now and, as Flora put it, rather sad. If they had managed to get over the first hurdle of awkwardness, they might have been good friends. It would have been good for both of them.'

'You must miss him.'

'Peter or Wyatt?' Bea levelled.

'Well, Peter, obviously, as Wyatt is still around!' Kim laughed.

'Do you know, Kimmy, I miss them both, actually. Peter was my good companion and he made me feel safe, and Wyatt was my little rock.'

'What happened?' Kim sank back against the countertop and gripped her mug of peppermint tea.

'Oh, a few things. Flora's mother for one,' she whispered, sticking her head out of the kitchen, reassured to see Flora on the sofa, absorbed in her iPad and laughing at some clip that sounded like a cartoon. She kept her voice low. 'I'm not blaming her. Wyatt wanted to stretch his wings, rebel in some small way, which is quite natural. If anything, I encouraged him. But then, while he was stretching his wings, he got to thinking about how I'd let him down and those thoughts became paramount and turned to anger.

I guess he's been punishing me ever since, in one way or another.'

'How did you let him down?'

'Oh, goodness, it's a long and boring story.' Bea fussed with her beads, rearranging them on her chest, glad of the distraction. Liking the familiar jangle of her bangles. 'And I'm not sure that I did. It's more that he thought I did, which for him makes it the same thing.'

'God, now I'm curious.' Kim smiled.

'Well, you know what they say about curiosity...'

Bea pictured Wyatt lying on the sofa in his school uniform with his feet on her lap; he must have been about seven. *'I'm glad you're my mummy...'*

'Did you like Flora's mum more when you first met her than you do now?'

'Oh gosh, it's not that I don't like Sarah! I do! I was just like most mothers that over-love their sons; I secretly disliked any girl he brought home. But there comes a point when you can see that the son is smitten and you have two choices, either embrace that girl or lose your boy.'

'So you embraced her?' Kim leant forward, a hopeful tone to her question as she imagined Tait's mother holding her hand.

'No, not really. I lost my boy.'

Kim was stuck for a response.

Bea broke the tension. 'Would you like some carrot cake? I know it's cheating, but I picked some up from the new Plum Patisserie that's opened up in The Rocks – cakes to die for! And Flora and I were admiring their cupcakes on the forum – cupcakes from Mayfair, no less! They looked beautiful.'

Kim stared at the moist, walnut-laden crumbs topped with cream-cheese frosting. 'Mmmnn, please. Just a small piece. Wyatt and you are still close though, right? I mean, you're the first person he thought of when he needed help this week.' She gestured towards the lounge with her elbow as she bit into the chunk of carrot cake.

Bea sighed, thinking about how she had been excluded from their pre-Christmas plans. 'Not as close as we were. I think he resented being sent away to school, even though he loved it. And I think the boys he met at school made him realise how unconventional his mum was and he was embarrassed about that.'

'Christ, half his luck! Wish my mum and dad had tried to do what was right for me. If I'd gone to a place like Scotch College I'd have the prime minister's job or at the very least be with the Sydney Philharmonia by now!'

Bea laughed. 'Yes, I did try, but at Scotch there wasn't much room for anything that wasn't conventional or easily pigeonholed. The mums of his mates were all married to landowners or bankers. They spent their time keeping house and doing their bit for charity, so he was mortified when he worked out that his own mum, far from doing the rounds on the debutante circuit, had in fact been knocked up at eighteen and disowned by her Jesus-loving parents. It was difficult for him. I think he always felt that there was a chunk of him missing. He shared rooms with the sons of the Honourable This and That – or the 'Orrible This and That, as Peter used to call some of them! And it didn't really matter whether they were titled, extremely privileged or not, they all had something Wyatt didn't – a dad. He wanted his own dad more than anything else in the world.'

'But he had Peter.'

Bea smiled. 'Yes, he did.'

'I do miss him,' Kim said. 'He was a lovely man, Bea. The way he used to look at you. I would love someone to look at me like that, you know, like there's no one else in the room, no matter how crowded it is.'

Bea could only agree. 'Yes, yes, he did. I was very lucky.'

Her thoughts flew again to her son and his relationship with his stepfather. Neither of them had known how to behave with the other. She knew that Wyatt had never fully understood what his early years had been like for her, for them, how much of a battle it had been just to survive. Queuing for cut-price scraps at the market at the end of the day, living on broth. *We were both so lucky to find Peter.*

Bea gave an involuntary shudder. She remembered the day Peter had told her to close her eyes and had then laid in her palm a Chinese coin with a square hole cut from its middle. 'I found this on the kerbside. It's our good-luck charm! It's very appropriate: you're a round peg and I'm a square hole and yet we kind of fit together.'

'Peter, I… I can't feel how you want me to. I am fond of you, but…'

'I know. I know.' He'd placed his finger over her mouth and kissed her forehead before storing the coin in a small slit in his wallet, where it stayed until the day of his death. 'But I reckon I love you enough for both of us.' His kind eyes had crinkled into a smile as her chest filled with the bittersweet truth of his honest words.

Just before he'd passed away, she'd placed that coin in the special wishing fountain guarded by Il Porcellino, asking for forgiveness and sending him love.

'Anyway, Kim,' she said, bringing herself back to the present, 'lovely as it is to see you, darling, was there something particular you wanted – apart from to listen to me rambling?'

'You never ramble. Well, except when you do. I just wanted to say a couple of things.' Kim placed the empty plate on the counter. 'Firstly, Tait and I are perfectly capable of running the kitchen. If you have to take a day, or longer, I don't want you to worry. We would never let you down. And secondly, when Wyatt and Sarah are in Bali, you are more than welcome to come and hang out at mine. Only if you'd like to. I mean, you don't have to, but I know this time of year can be tricky and I don't want you to be alone, even though you're used to being alone.' Kim was getting more and more flustered. 'You know what I mean.'

Bea reached forward and hugged the girl she considered family. 'Thank you, darling girl. What would I do without you?'

'Well, you'd have one more chunk of carrot cake than

you currently do, that's for certain!' They both laughed.

Bea's phone beeped and she saw Wyatt's name flash onto the screen. 'Talk of the devil!'

'I'll let you crack on.' Kim gave Flora a small wave and left the apartment as Bea read her son's text.

Sorry about earlier. It's all a bit stressful. Shouldn't have taken it out on you. If Flora really doesn't want to come to Bali, can she stay with you?

She sighed and sauntered into the lounge. 'Just got a text from your dad, who says you can stay with me if you don't want to go to Bali, though I'm sure you'd much rather spend the lead-up to Christmas in a tropical paradise than washing dishes in the Reservoir Kitchen!'

'No!' Flora practically yelled. 'I would much rather stay with you. Can I?' Her eyes were wide with expectation.

'You can, but—'

Flora didn't wait to hear the 'but'. She leapt from the sofa and bounded around the room like Tigger, shouting 'Yes!' and 'Thank you!' alternately.

Bea shook her head. 'I never thought I'd be more attractive than Bali!'

'I really didn't want to go.' Flora flopped down onto the sofa again.

'I guessed that.'

'I would have wanted to go if you were going.'

'Ah, well, that's a whole other thing.' Bea sighed.

'Are you upset about not being invited to Bali?'

Bea nodded. 'Well, yes, if I'm being honest. A little. But

not angry so much as hurt. I guess I have more time to think here on my own, Flora, but I just can't imagine not including you all in my life and I've been dreading the build-up to Christmas, and I thought...' She looked towards the open French doors. 'I don't know what I thought, actually, but I would have liked to have been told of Mum and Dad's plans so I could make my own.'

The two were silent for a few seconds until Flora sat bolt upright and raised a finger. An idea had occurred to her. 'Why don't we go away somewhere together, just you and me, before Christmas! Just the two of us – we can have our own adventure!' She sat forward, eyes shining, eager for Bea's response.

'Oh, I don't know, it sounds like a lot of trouble at such short notice. You are of course welcome to stay here, darling, if that really is what you want to do. But I think a sedate affair is in order, a low-key December and then on the day itself a nice grilled lobster, some champagne and a trip to the beach to watch the sun set with Mum and Dad. Doesn't that sound good?' Bea tried to inject some enthusiasm into her voice.

'That does sound good, but I would love to go away with you, Gran!' Flora bounced up and down on the spot and clapped. 'Where could we go?' She tapped her fingers against her cheek thoughtfully.

Her excitement was infectious and Bea allowed herself to be swept along. 'Well, in theory, anywhere! As long as we aren't too extravagant. Pappy left me a little nest egg for a rainy day or an emergency, and I'd say that, despite the glorious sunshine, we *are* having a bit of a rainy day. He'd love nothing more than to treat me and his only grandchild to a trip somewhere together.' Bea smiled, warming slightly to the idea, or not wanting to quash her granddaughter's enthusiasm, she wasn't sure.

'We could go to Bali ourselves and stay in a better hotel than Mum and Dad and spy on them from behind bushes and walls!'

'Oh gosh, Flora, I don't know about that. As long as I don't have to shout anything rude at them from behind the wall.' She winked. 'I think I'd rather not. Bit too old to be sneaking around Bali hiding from your mum and dad.' She chuckled, picturing them doing just that.

'How about we go up to Mollymook? You know people there, we can sit on the beach, have a barbecue and you can drink wine, just like you used to with Pappy.'

Bea couldn't imagine going to Mollymook without Peter, but before she could counter that suggestion her laptop gave a loud ping as another email flew in. Immediately she pictured misty moors, a flash of tartan, long walks searching for white heather, and real fires blazing high to ward off the winter chill. 'How about Scotland?' she asked.

'Scotland! Isn't it going to be freezing cold? We'd have to get ski suits and snow boots. There's not even a warm beach to swim off!' Flora shivered at the thought.

Bea laughed. 'You're right, there's not much by way of beach holidays over there at this time of year, but we do have a ready-made guide in Alex and we might even see snow!'

Flora flung herself back against the cushions. 'Snow? Really? I'd love to see snow! Can we? Can we go?'

Bea looked at her granddaughter's face and couldn't remember the last time she'd seen her so excited about anything. She looked properly happy.

'Well, as long as Tait and Kim don't mind me slinking off, and Mario is free to work some shifts, and Wyatt and Sarah give us the go-ahead, then yes. Why not?'

'Really? Are you teasing me?'

'No, I'm not teasing you. Why not?' Bea grinned, feeling a jolt of excitement at the prospect. She looked at Flora, whose face had dissolved into tears.

'Oh, darling, why are you crying?'

'Because... because I'm happy.' She gulped. 'I want to go as far away from here as possible. I want to go to Scotland!'

'Then we shall. We can explore, go to the mountains and visit a loch, maybe go to St Andrews. And I bet the shopping is good. It'll be quite a hike, but as with any adventure, it's as much about the journey as the arriving!'

'Do you think Mum and Dad will let me go?' Flora gasped at the thought that they might say no.

'Well, there's only one way of finding out. I'll ask them.' Bea nodded, adjusting her bangles.

Flora slid off the sofa and jumped up and down on the spot, clapping. 'Whoop whoop! We're going on an adventure!'

Bea stood in the balcony window and dialled Sarah's

number. The two exchanged pleasantries and Sarah thanked her for looking after Flora.

'It was about Flora I was really ringing. We've had this bonkers idea of going away, to Scotland, no less, while you guys are in Bali...'

'I didn't know you were going to Scotland?' Sarah sounded surprised. *And I didn't know you were going to take my son to Bali right before Christmas...* Bea swallowed the words, knowing that Wyatt was a grown man and not a child held against his will. Sarah was his wife and not his jailer, no matter how it sometimes seemed to her. 'It's quite unplanned, but actually seems like a good idea. It's been lovely spending time with Flora. I told her that it's only okay if you both say so. Otherwise we're quite happy to stay in Surry Hills.'

'It sounds like a wonderful opportunity. I'd like her home before she goes, though. I think we need to lay a few foundations and talk things through...' Sarah sounded undecided.

'Of course,' Bea agreed. 'It might be just what she needs – a chance to get away and think about things in a neutral place.'

'It might, you're right. Rather than have her moping around the house longing for her horrible mates,' Sarah said. 'The more distance between her and that bloody crowd, the better.'

'Absolutely.' Bea nodded.

'Actually, I'm glad I've got you on the phone, Bea. I

wanted to ask, is there anything in particular I can get you for Christmas?'

'Good God, no! I've got far too much stuff as it is. Just a card would be lovely.' Bea wanted to spare her daughter-in-law the bother.

The call was ended cordially. She remembered her first Christmas in Sydney, alone, pregnant and pining. The pain in her heart had been so real, she'd thought she might die. Her ache for him was physical. Every couple she saw sent a stab of grief straight through her; every smiling girl reminded her of how happy she'd been. It seemed better to stay inside and figure out a way to let the sadness wash over her. She could only think about their last morning together, holding his head as he sobbed, begging him to stay and feeling like she couldn't carry on without him.

Flora skipped to the bathroom, from where Bea soon heard the sound of water splashing on the shower floor.

She looked at the photograph of Peter smiling from the wall and adjusted the silver bangles that he had collected for her over the years. 'Well, my love, looks like I'm going on a little trip.'

She swallowed the flash of guilt, shaking her head to rid her mind of the image of the man whose whereabouts she knew little of and who for all she knew might have died a long time ago.

She flipped open her laptop and perused hotels before continuing to read the rest of Alex's email.

Second Chance Cafe

The Christmas lights have been switched on along the Royal Mile and the whole city looks absolutely beautiful, bringing some much needed cheer and sparkle to these cold, dark nights.

Hoping tomorrow is less eventful for you.

Ax

From: BeaG

Subject: Re: Hello Again

I don't know about tomorrow, but my evening is proving quite eventful. I have big news. I AM COMING TO SCOTLAND! Can you believe it? Even writing that sounds crazy. Flora and I have decided quite last minute to take a trip and so that's where we're heading. We shall stay at The Balmoral, which looks lovely and will be such a treat. I know this is a busy time of year for you, Alex, so please don't worry about showing us round, but if you have time for a cup of coffee amid the merry mayhem, that would be good.

VBW! Bx

From: Christmas Café

Subject: Re: Hello Again

Well, that is quite a surprise, a great surprise! I can't believe it! I shall very much look forward to putting a face to the name and yes, a cup of coffee, hopefully a few cups of coffee, will be in order! That has warmed my spirit, more than I can say.

Ax

Bea smiled as she closed her laptop; she was filled with a sense of hope and excitement that she hadn't felt in quite some time. Maybe she should follow her own advice and feel happy about not knowing what was around the corner. As she'd said to Flora, it might just be great things. She picked up the green cushion and let her palm rest on its silky surface. It would be wonderful to see Scotland at Christmas time, to see the lights along the Royal Mile and to meet the lovely lady with the cat who was her e-penfriend.

She was returning to the UK after all this time, returning to the strange land that she had once called home.

Ten

A fortnight later and Bea was pottering in the Kitchen, reluctant to leave and feeling more and more anxious as the time to go approached. 'I've told you about paying the fish man, and the Wednesday delivery, haven't I?'

'Yes, boss.' Tait smiled. 'Twice.'

'Sorry! I'm a bit nervous.' Bea twisted her bangles.

'You don't say?' Tait laughed as she paced in front of the sink.

'You're going to have the best time!' Kim interjected from inside the fridge.

'I know.' Bea nodded. 'I got a lovely email from Alex, saying how it will be nice to put a face to the name. Must admit, we have really clicked! Despite her love of cats.'

'Well, we don't have to wait till you get there, we can google her if you like,' Kim offered, opening the laptop on the sideboard. 'Miss Alex McKay, Christmas Café.' She sounded out the words as she typed.

Bea smiled at her in the seconds they waited for the results.

Kim leant forward, twisting her body slightly and manoeuvring the screen, making it hard for Bea to see.

'Oh. My. God.' Kim slammed the lid shut and turned to her boss. 'On second thoughts, I think you should just turn up and be surprised!' She gave an awkward smile.

'Don't be daft, Kim! Show me! What's wrong? You know me, I don't judge people, and neither should you.' She gave her a knowing look. 'Let me see her!' Bea made a grab for the laptop.

Kim shook her head. 'I'm afraid you can't.'

'Kim, you're starting to bug me. Come on, just show me her picture!' Bea raised her voice, alerting Tait, who came over to investigate.

'What's all the racket?' he asked.

'I want to see a picture of Alex, my e-penfriend who's in Scotland, and Kim, for some bizarre reason, won't let me see her!'

Kim sat tight. 'I told you. I c-c-can't!' The close proximity of Tait had thrown her a little.

Bea folded her arms. 'Kim! Wyatt will be here any second and I insist you show me her picture, right now!' The joke was wearing thin.

Kim opened the laptop and pressed a button that made the picture spring back up. 'I can't show you a picture of her because she isn't a she. Alex McKay, proprietor of the Christmas Café, is in fact...' She turned the laptop so Bea had the best view. 'A man!'

Bea stared open-mouthed at the image on the screen. It showed a youthful grey-haired man with quite a large nose and a smiling mouth that revealed even teeth. He was wearing a denim shirt and what looked suspiciously like a silver bangle. 'Well, there must be a mistake!' Bea bent close to the screen. 'It must be a different Alex McKay!'

'Nope.' Kim scrolled through some other documents. 'It's definitely him. Does it matter?'

Bea placed her hand on her chest. 'Oh shit! Oh no!' She put her head in her palms and cringed as she bent double.

'I don't see what the problem is. Your e-penfriend is a bloke, big deal!' Tait shrugged. 'It's 2014, men and women can be mates without it meaning anything – isn't that right, Kim?'

'Yup. Uh-huh.' Kim swallowed her desire to scream.

'You don't understand.' Bea's breath came in shallow pants. 'The way I wrote to him… I would never have been so open had I known he was a bloke. I told him about how I was feeling in quite an intimate way.' She screwed up her face as if in physical pain. 'I admitted to him that I have a pouchy stomach!' *And a lot worse besides*, she thought. All that confessing about how lonely she was without a man by her side. 'Oh no!' She cringed again.

Kim threw her head back and let out a loud, resonating laugh. 'That's hilarious!'

Bea shook her head. 'No. No, it isn't! It's terrible. What must he think of me? Telling him my most personal thoughts. The sort of stuff I only share with my girlfriends. I had no idea!'

Kim laughed into her palm. 'It's too funny! Mousy Miss McKay with her cat friends is actually this hunk!' She clicked on another picture and turned it to face Bea. This time he was in a dinner jacket, raising a glass towards the camera.

'Oh, stop!' Bea sighed. 'We've even been putting kisses at the bottom of our emails, which I thought nothing of because she's a woman! But she's a man! He's a man! Oh God! Oh no!'

'Bea, look on the bright side, if this is a budding relationship, at least you haven't got to worry about the slow burn of getting to know each other. He already knows so much about you!' Kim chuckled.

'Oh, please don't, Kim. You're not helping.'

Kim beamed. 'I'm sorry, but it's just too funny!'

'Think of it as speed dating!' Tait added.

'Oh, for goodness sake, you two, we are not dating!' Bea shouted a little louder than she'd intended. 'I just thought I had made a lovely new friend.' She ran her hand over her face, wincing with embarrassment. 'Maybe we won't see him after all. Maybe it's best we just don't make any contact and he will forget we are arriving and that'll be that.'

'Good luck with that!' Tait snorted.

Bea glanced at her watch, willing Wyatt to appear sooner rather than later. 'God, the waiting is killing me! I just want to get under way.'

Tait swung through the doors into the café, leaving her and Kim alone.

'I was thinking, this might be very exciting. Are you

sure you didn't know Alex was a bloke? Maybe at some level you were looking for a nice little dalliance?'

Bea stared at her employee in confusion. 'Kimberley, I think you think too much!'

'You're still blushing!' Kim teased. 'I was just wondering if maybe you had hooked up on Tinder and the sausage club is just a ruse and you are in fact planning on liaising with your beau in the Highlands!' She threw her head back and laughed.

'Goodness me, do people actually do that? Hook up on Tinder, whatever that is? No, in fact, don't answer me, I don't want to know.' Bea raised her palm. 'And as if I *would* go all the way to Edinburgh for some sex! The very idea.'

'Even the way you say "some sex" makes me laugh. It's like, "Would you like some chips, some advice, some sex?"' Kim snorted the laughter through her nose.

'Well, I'm glad you find it funny, although the very thought of heading off anywhere for a Tinder, or whatever it is, I find quite disturbing. If I was looking for a man, that wouldn't be how I'd do it. I'd rather be introduced by someone that knows me. Not that I'm looking!' she emphasised.

'I thought it seemed logical. Wanting to make an illicit trip but not wanting to go alone. Taking Flora as your decoy.'

'Logical to you, maybe, but I can think of places a darn sight closer to Surry Hills to go for sex!'

'Really? Where? Do tell!'

Bea tutted and adjusted her bangles. 'I was speaking figuratively.'

'Oh, how disappointing. Although, as you've hinted, maybe your days of illicit sex are behind you...'

'Is that right? What do you think happens, Kim? It's not that my body and mind aren't willing; of course they are! What holds me back is more an acute sense of embarrassment at the thought of stripping off in front of someone. That, and I think I've actually forgotten what to do!' She leant on Kim, laughing, trying to imagine conducting a similar conversation with her boss, however many moons ago. 'But that's the point, darling. No matter how past it my age might seem to you now, it really isn't. And you will one day discover that there isn't a switch that gets flicked at forty-seven that stops you thinking about, indulging in or desiring sex! It's not as though we all stop fancying each other and turn our attention to doing crosswords and growing tomatoes!'

'Well, no, not at forty-seven, obviously. But at forty-eight, surely!' Kim smirked.

Bea pushed her hair behind her eyes. 'I live in the same world as you, where sex sells products, where every advertisement and every magazine article is illustrated with the perfect body of some unfeasibly gorgeous twenty-year-old. The world sells its objects and services using sex and I am part of that world, no matter how removed I might feel from it or how unpalatable that might be to you and your peers. Just because I have the slightly crumpled body of a woman in her fifties does not mean I don't still have the mind and desires of a woman much, much younger. Sadly.'

'I guess.' Kim looked a bit nonplussed. 'But it can't be like it is for me and my friends, can it? On a quest for sex half the time. It must all calm down, surely?'

Bea smiled at Kim's expression, could see that she was desperately hoping the answer would be no.

'No. It's not like that. Granted.'

Kim exhaled, looking relieved.

'But that doesn't mean I don't find people attractive or that I don't want companionship or comfort from another human, a man. I still want that, but as you hit middle age, it's difficult, different.'

'Why, because there aren't nightclubs and bars that you can drop into and pull?'

Bea rolled her eyes. 'No, because everyone my age is slightly bruised by experience and many of us either can't be bothered or life has put us off trying. It can feel like too much effort, too disrupting.'

'That sounds depressing! And I thought it was tough being my age.'

'I guess it *is* slightly depressing. We certainly can't be taken in by the sort of rhetoric that used to work when we were young. We're far too cynical. Plus we all carry a large amount of guilt.'

'Ooh, what, like skeletons in the cupboard and dodgy dealings that you don't want discovered?' Kim raised her eyebrows but kept her eyes fixed on the counter in front of her.

'No, not that!' Bea chuckled. 'But old age does leave you feeling a little exposed; it's difficult to hide anything. We tend to carry the guilt of things we should or shouldn't have done. Our successes and failures aren't hypothetical any more – they're visible right there on our faces, in our histories. We can't invent a future or hook people in with our marvellous potential.'

'I thought you might have less to worry about as you get older, making you a bit more jolly about life, more optimistic.'

Bea liked her rationale. 'It's not that you worry less but that your worries evolve. Like when you have babies, you worry are they too hot, too cold, are they going to die in their sleep? And then when they start school, will they run out in front of a car? Then suddenly they are *driving* a car and you worry that they might crash! And then we worry that they'll get their hearts broken or take drugs... On and on it goes. You never stop worrying, it's just that the worries change.'

'God, I never realised that kids were such a pain in the arse! Not sure if that's a road I will travel anyway. I don't think Tait wants kids, not for a long while. In fact I know he doesn't.' She gave a wry smile.

'They *are* a pain in the arse, as you put it. But they are also the greatest joy.' She shot Kim a steely look. 'And you certainly can't decide now whether it's a road you will travel or not. Trust me, despite what the media would have you believe, it's usually a road that chooses you. The world's moving fast and who knows how you will feel or who you might meet – next month, next year. Maybe your future is with Tait, maybe it isn't! And that's the point, really; the longer you're on the planet, the more balanced your view.'

'Because you've been around long enough to see everything...'

Bea smiled and thought of the things she still hoped she would see and achieve. 'Yes, something like that. I guess the older you get, the harder it is to be surprised.'

'Oh, a life without surprises would be brilliant!'

Bea gazed at Kim's profile. Her own philosophy was the exact opposite. 'Older people are like a book that's two thirds written, so the scope to change the ending is reduced. Much more importantly, however, we also share a secret that we almost never divulge. But I shall let you in on it – okay?'

Kim nodded. 'I shan't tell a soul!'

'Life is for the brave, Kim. You have to chase the life you want and grab it. So if you really want Tait, and I believe you do, then make it happen! Don't be defined by anyone else; don't worry about Janine, or whoever. Just be yourself, because one day you'll blink and it will be too late to tread your own path. You might find you're walking the route that someone else has ploughed for you.'

'Jesus Christ, Bea, you are on a downer!'

'I don't mean to be. You just have to make sure that you, like me, have an amazing and rich life, a real roller-coaster that takes you as high as you can possibly go. Getting older is nothing to be sad about; it's to be celebrated!'

Kim sighed. 'I know you're right, I do need to dive in, I can just never find the right time. And I know that time is ticking by and nothing changes for me.' She looked towards the swing doors. 'No matter how much I want it to.'

'You need to make the change, Kim; you can't wait for it to come to you. I'm double your age and I am raring to go!'

'Ooh, lucky Alex!' Kim laughed.

'Oh, for goodness sake, Kim, do stop!' she snapped.

'I'm sorry. I was only mucking about, I didn't mean to tease you.'

'I think we both know that's a lie.'

Kim laughed. 'Are you sure you're not the teeniest bit interested in Mr McKay, the silver-fox charmer?'

'No! Absolutely not. I'm just mortified.' Bea shook her head, rather embarrassed by the suggestion.

A horn honked in the road.

'Oh, that'll be Wyatt.' Bea gathered her bag and for the umpteenth time checked that her passport, wallet and phone were all in their little compartments, before making her way out to the front of the cafe.

She kissed Kim on the cheek. 'Thank you, darling, for everything.'

'Go! Enjoy yourself! And don't worry, we can handle things here,' Kim assured her.

Second Chance Cafe

Bea hugged Tait. 'Right, you two, you have all my numbers if you need anything. Mario will be here tomorrow and I shall see you in a couple of weeks!'

'Have a great time, Bea, we shall miss you both!' Kim pushed out her bottom lip.

'We'll be right though, Kimmy?' Tait winked.

Kim nodded briskly; her blush was fuchsia, she didn't trust herself to respond.

'And if you bump into my aunty or my cousin Gideon, give them my love.' Tait beamed.

'Oh yes, of course. Where do Gideon and his mum live?' Bea asked.

'Weston-Super-Mare.' Tait smiled.

Bea laughed. 'Tait, if we are anywhere near Weston-Super-Mare, our travel plans will have gone drastically awry. It's about as far from Edinburgh as you can get!'

'How should I know?' Tait shrugged.

'I've left a little something for you both in the larder. Not your actual Christmas pressies, but a pre-Christmas thank you.'

'Aww, Bea! Thank you!' they chorused.

She had left them both beautiful wicker hampers full of tempting festive treats, including a bottle of bubbly and a dainty, beribboned box of fancy handmade chocolates from Haigh's in the Queen Victoria Building.

Bea blew kisses as she wheeled her suitcase ahead of her and made her exit. She climbed into the passenger seat of Wyatt's Holden and immediately sensed that she'd entered the scene of an argument. Flora looked tense, her scowl giving way to a weak smile as she greeted her gran.

'Excited?' Bea asked.

Flora nodded and popped her earphones into her ears.

'Talk some sense into her while you're out there, won't you?' Wyatt said as he navigated Elizabeth Street, passing the train station. He addressed his comment to the windscreen from behind his mirrored sunnies, speaking as if Flora wasn't there.

'Gosh, Flora is far more sensible than me, I should think it'll be her giving me advice!'

Wyatt gave an almost imperceptible shake of his head.

As the car turned into Botany Road, Bea spotted Mr Giraldi hovering by the kerb. His straw trilby was keeping the sun from his head and he was dabbing at his face and neck with a blue spotted handkerchief. He had obviously just been shopping as his Harris Farm bag was straining at the handles, no doubt full of the large oranges that he loved. Bea waved furiously. Mr Giraldi caught her eye and, quite forgetting his cantankerous reputation, waved back as his face broke into a beautiful smile, his eyes following her face until she was out of sight.

Wyatt's hands tightened on the steering wheel, letting her know that even this interaction had somehow irritated him. But as she had said to Flora only recently, that was just tough luck.

Wyatt dropped them at Terminal One, awkwardly hugging his daughter and grazing his mother's cheek with a misplaced kiss. They would reunite just before Christmas, after he and Sarah had returned from Bali. Both Bea and Flora were excited at the prospect of flying from the international terminal, even though the flight would take them a whole day; it was nearly ten hours to Hong Kong, then another sixteen via Amsterdam to Edinburgh.

'Are we going to visit Miss Alex and her many cats when we arrive?' Flora asked suddenly as they were boarding their plane. She dissolved into giggles, which made Bea smile. 'Kim sent me a text and told me to ask you that! I don't even know why it's funny!'

'Ha.' Bea tutted. 'Tell Miss Kim that maybe we will.'

Despite the seemingly interminable flight, there was something about being cocooned in a warm plane with a blanket wrapped around them and having nowhere to go and nothing to do that lulled them to sleep. Having watched the couple of movies that jumped out at them, they both slept soundly for the best part of eight hours.

After she woke, Bea lay in the dark with her little green silk pillow under her cheek and remembered the last time she'd made that journey, in the opposite direction, all set to start a new life on the other side of the world, surrounded by her family. Her gran had wished them a tearful farewell at the airport and her mum had cried; Bea remembered her dad telling her mum that tears were infectious and that she should try to buck up for her girls' sake.

At fourteen years old, just a few months older than Flora was now, Bea had imagined her new home in

Australia would be very much like the British seaside that she loved: all sunshine, beaches and ice creams, with nothing much to worry about except whether she'd packed enough pairs of flip-flops and if they had an equivalent of the Top Forty. The reality of Byron Bay was a shock. Apart from the church and a few solid structures along the high street, everywhere seemed quite flimsy and temporary – a world away from the solid Surrey suburb where she'd grown up. Her overwhelming memory of her arrival in Byron Bay was the truly nauseating smell, a product of the abattoir and a large dairy factory whose odours were pumped out into the locality. The intense heat was a torment. Midges buzzed relentlessly in the blistering sunshine, flies continually settled on her lips and tongue, and she tried not to think about the crocodiles and sharks as she took refuge in the ocean or under the shade of the eucalypt trees on the beach. The place was nothing like she had imagined – about as far as she could get from the tender embrace of a warm summer's day at home. And she longed for her favourite foods, wished they'd packed a lifetime's supply of Bird's Instant Whip and Ovaltine.

Bea's thoughts turned to Diane, her sister and friend. It was now more than thirty years since they'd last seen each other and she missed her dearly. Of all the losses, it was Di's that she still felt most keenly. But she had done as her parents had instructed, had remained true to her word and stayed away without contact. *I miss you, Di...* She'd never been back to Byron Bay, afraid perhaps of what she might find there. Though by all accounts the town was now unrecognisable: the unappealing outpost had been transformed into a fashionable centre of alternative lifestyles and eco retreats. She wondered if Di was still there, whether she'd turned into a Byron Bay hippy, whether she thought of Bea still. She hoped so.

Flora stepped from the plane first. The ground was covered with a light dusting of frost. She turned to her gran from the top step as she wrapped her arms around her trunk. 'Oh, Bea! It's absolutely freezing!' she shouted against the cold wind that whipped her hair back and froze her nose. It was the coldest she had ever been.

Bea laughed, having quite forgotten just how cold cold could be. This was not a case of reaching for an extra jersey at the end of a day on the beach as the big sun sank into the sea, or popping on a pair of socks to ward off the early-morning chill; this was the kind of cold that shrank your goosepimpled skin against your limbs and chilled your bones until they felt brittle. The kind of cold that hurt your ears and made you want to crawl beneath a big fat duvet and not emerge until the summer showed its face. She had a sudden flashback of walking home from primary school with Diane in the dead of winter and it being already almost dark at three o'clock. She recalled the way her face would feel raw to the touch, how they would race home in their wellies to sit in front of the fire, their fingers and toes numb, and then the unpleasant smell of damp wool as their mum laid their mittens and scarves on the unwieldy metal fire cage to dry out. 'Is it too late to choose Bali?' she quipped, laughing at her granddaughter through chattering teeth.

As soon as they'd reclaimed their luggage, Flora pulled her ski jacket from her backpack, along with her woolly beanie and thick angora scarf. Bea wrapped her pashmina twice around her neck and fumbled in her case for her long navy wool coat. As they headed for the car-rental office, her teeth seemed to knock in her gums and the icy air sent a chill right through her body. 'God, it's so cold!' she repeated every few minutes, rubbing her hands together. Flora merely nodded, as though the shock of the temperature had rendered her unable to speak.

Airport hoardings carried posters of the festive food and beribboned gifts that awaited them in the stores and restaurants of Edinburgh. Bea felt a jolt of excitement. It might be cold, but it was proper Christmas weather.

'Are you feeling okay to drive, Gra— Bea?' Flora asked.

'Perfectly! I'm wide awake and raring to go!' Bea beamed, her shoulder-length grey hair sitting neatly on her shoulders beneath her hat.

The two took possession of their little red Fiat 500, laughing at the novelty of it. They thanked the smiling Andrew from the car-rental company, who spoke so quickly and with such a strong Scottish accent that Bea only caught about every third word. Flora threw one bag on the back seat; the other fitted easily into the surprisingly roomy boot. Bea slammed the lid before jumping into the driver's seat and punching the coordinates into the satnav, which beeped.

'I love this car! It's like driving in a little cherry tomato!' Flora chuckled as Bea turned the key in the ignition, cranked the heating up to full blast and held up her hands in front of the vent.

'No, it's like a Christmas bauble!' Bea laughed.

'Whatever it is, I wish it was warmer. I can't feel my feet!' Flora stamped her trainers against the rubber mat on the floor.

'It'll soon heat up.' Bea hoped she was right as her hand shook against the steering wheel, rattling her bangles beneath her coat.

They were apparently eight miles from The Balmoral Hotel, their home for the next couple of weeks. Neither had been to Scotland before and, other than what they'd gleaned from pictures on the internet – all high mountains and dense forests – and from watching *Highlander* and *Taggart*, they had no idea what to expect.

Bea fastened the seatbelt and pulled at her cream chinos to ensure minimum creasing in transit. She gathered the folds of her coat over her lap to act as a blanket and adjusted her silver bracelets, as was her habit.

'You haven't driven me in a long time.' Flora yawned and tossed her head, shrugging off the tiredness that threatened.

Bea nodded. 'Nope, but don't worry, I think I just about remember how.' She winked. 'At least they drive on the correct side of the road!'

Flora laughed.

'Are you excited?' Bea asked as she revved the engine.

'I really am!' Flora squealed.

Bea felt a flicker of unease at the responsibility of driving her granddaughter. It felt like the biggest privilege that Wyatt and Sarah were entrusting their only child into her care on the open road in a foreign country.

'The sky is quite grey here, isn't it?' She bent low in her seat and peered up through the windscreen at the low, thick cloud, which made everything seem very wintry. 'It adds an air of mystery to the place, don't you think?'

'Yes. It reminds me of *Harry Potter*.' Flora chuckled.

Bea switched the indicators left then right and practised turning the lights on, off and to full beam, trying to familiarise herself with the controls of the Fiat. Sitting bolt upright in her seat and concentrating with every fibre of her being, she released the handbrake and pulled into the flow of traffic that was emerging slowly from the car park. She navigated three roundabouts, following signs for Edinburgh city centre. The roads were neat grey asphalt and the mini roundabouts with their high, pale kerbstones were turfed with well-kept grass and dotted with the occasional advertising board staked into the soil.

Two coaches swamped the little Fiat as it continued sedately down the middle lane. 'Crikey, I feel like a minnow!'

'A shiny red minnow!' Flora corrected.

The heavy traffic continued as they tootled along the A8. 'I think the satnav's half-hour estimate might be a bit optimistic,' Bea said. 'I can't believe there's this much traffic! I remember there being hardly any cars when I was growing up, especially round us. Diane and I used to play games on the little roads near our house, if you can believe that – tennis and football, right there in the road. If a car did come along, it would simply beep and we'd get out of the way. But look at this! It's crazy!'

As they crawled along, slow enough to peek into the cars on either side of them, Bea and Flora smiled inanely at their occupants, ridiculously excited at being in a traffic jam – a Scottish traffic jam, no less! Bea peered at the houses as they passed through Corstorphine, studying the sturdy detached granite homes. Elaborate castellations sat above the top windows, giving the properties an air of grandeur quite unlike the more modern buildings they were used to in Sydney.

'I am actually here...' Bea shared her thoughts out loud. 'I am back in the UK, but I am a grown-up. How did that happen?'

'I don't know.' Flora shrugged. 'I wish Mum and Dad could see us, driving along in the bauble while it's so cold outside. Dad would love it here, exploring. He likes adventure, doesn't he?'

'He sure does.' Bea smiled, happy that Flora spoke about her dad with fondness and none of the aggression she had witnessed of late.

'Do you think they'll miss me?' Flora's voice was small.

'Miss you? Of course they will! But they'll be happy that we're having a good time.'

'I'll call them later.' She stared out of the window.

'Good idea.'

Flora shook her head. 'It will be nice for them to have some time on holiday on their own. Without work or anything.'

Bea thought she sounded remarkably grown-up. 'Are you missing them?'

Flora nodded. 'A little bit.'

'Well, that's a good thing. Just think how lovely it will be when you see them again.'

'I'm going to buy them presents and maybe something for Marcus.' Flora continued to gaze fixedly out of the window.

'Marcus who you hate? Who you punched in the mouth?'

'Yes.' Flora sighed. 'I don't really hate him. I like him. I might love him.'

'Oh, darling girl! Well, a little tip for you: if you do like someone or maybe even love them, punching them in the mouth is not necessarily the best way to start a relationship.'

'I know that.' Flora looked at her gran. 'I didn't like him immediately. Lori said she wanted to go out with him, so I didn't say anything to anyone. But then about three weeks into term, we were on the bus back from the beach and I saw him walking on Darley Road. He was on his own and my heart kind of fluttered. I knew I wanted to speak to him and get to know him, but I knew that Lori liked him, so I didn't say anything. I thought about him the whole way home and when I saw him at school I felt the same. But then the whole period thing happened, and then I punched him.'

Bea remembered what it was like to have a teenage heart bursting with love. Undistracted by work or other responsibilities, her young mind had been free to ponder the object of her affection morning, noon and night. 'Have you spoken to him? Told him how you feel?'

Flora shook her head. 'No. I was way too shy and Lori would kill me. But I remember what he was wearing when he walked along Darley Road and every time I think about it my tummy gets real flippy.'

Bea focused on the grey sky, a blue button-down shirt, a dark green silk scarf, grey twill slacks, a lick of fringe that dangled in his eyes, the size of his hand, into which hers fitted as if made to measure...

'Do you know what I mean?'

'Yes,' Bea mouthed, quietly. 'I do.'

Flora straightened her shoulders, sitting upright in the seat. 'Not that there would be any point in telling him. He hates me.'

'I bet he doesn't.' Bea spoke from the side of her mouth as the line of cars moved forward.

'Well, it doesn't matter anyway. Lori says he's going to go out with her and that's that.'

'Doesn't he have a choice? Poor bloke! Don't you think you should tell him how you feel, give him the chance to decide?' Bea gave her granddaughter the same advice she'd only recently dished out to Kim.

'Suppose. How do you know when you've met the love of your life?'

'That's a good question.' Bea smiled. 'I suppose the answer is that you just have to trust your little voice of instinct.'

'I think I love him, but I might have blown it...'

'What, with the whole punching him thing?'

Flora nodded defeatedly. 'The zoo!' she suddenly shouted, changing the topic and the atmosphere as she pointed to a sign on the left-hand side of the road. 'And they've got pandas! Actual pandas! We've just got fat dugongs. I hate to think how cold they must be! Can we go see them?'

'People from Edinburgh would probably love to see the fat dugongs! And yes, we can do whatever you want, but not today – I need a hair wash and a soak in a bubbly bath.'

'I am so excited!' Flora yelled.

The car picked up a little speed as the traffic flowed more freely and it was Bea's turn to shout. 'Look! Murrayfield! That's incredible! I saw it on TV when the Wallabies played Scotland last year. We watched it in the café, Tait was going crazy for Lealiifano, who played a blinder! And here I am! That's just crazy. I have to get photos and send them back.'

Flora laughed, buoyed up by her gran's excitement and tickled to see her dad's mum sharing his passion for a sport she herself had only the vaguest interest in.

The two marvelled at the Christmas decorations on the

houses that lined the streets. Neon Santas dangled from ladders and hung from window ledges; trees and shrubs glowed and twinkled with fairy lights; and one driveway even sported an illuminated sleigh with four reindeer pulling it. Inflatable snowmen and a variety of green, red and gold displays shone against the grey afternoon sky, lighting up the solid flint walls and drab rendering. Children wearing thick coats, woolly hats and scarves gripped their parents' hands as they scurried along the damp pavements, clutching carrier bags decorated with Christmas trees and cheerful slogans.

Bea stared at the parades of shops, having quite forgotten that in the UK they didn't have the heavy canopy roofs they needed in Australia to keep the sun off their rows of shops and cafés. The facades here looked a little flat by comparison, exposed, but also lighter and more accessible. A memory flashed into her head of her six-year-old self clutching a silver sixpence. She was standing with her nose inches from a glass-fronted domed cabinet as she chose sweets from a mouthwatering display to be put into a small paper bag. Having to make the choice between Foaming Yellow Bananas, Pink Shrimps, Rhubarb and Custards, Black Jacks, Liquorice Pipes, Jelly Worms and packets of Parma Violets was excruciating! She would then suffer from post-choice regret when she saw that Diane had gone for Strawberry Laces or another goody that had escaped her own eagle eye. She had forgotten all about those Saturday morning trips to the sweet shop.

Eventually they turned into Princes Street. Bea gasped and her heart jumped; there it was, just as she had imagined it for all those years. Alex was right: the city did look absolutely beautiful. It was only early afternoon, but the sky already had a tinge of purple to it. Lights had been strung between the Victorian lamp-posts and under them a throng of shoppers and tourists ambled. To the left, the tall flint and granite buildings were crammed together like sentinels overlooking majestic Edinburgh Castle, and beneath the castle walls Princes Street Gardens swept up to meet the bustle of Princes Street.

Bea felt her pulse race, hearing the words he'd whispered into her ear as they waltzed under a hunter's moon. *'She stands like something from a grand painting, framing your view. There is nowhere else in the world you could be but Princes Street. On a rainy day or with the sun glinting off the old red sandstone, the castle is equally beautiful. For me it means home and I guess it always will.'*

'Oh, look, a funfair!' Flora pointed up ahead.

Bea pulled her gaze from the Christmassy shop windows, her eyes lingering on the frontage of the kiltmaker's Hector Russell, whose three floor-to-ceiling windows each showed a fantastic array of tartan, complete with mannequins decked out in Santa hats sitting askew on their heads. She wanted to run up the sweeping staircase and explore inside.

'A big wheel! The view from there will be awesome. We have to go!' Flora's excitement spilled from her and Bea was happy to hear it, mindful that, despite all the upset at school, Flora was still just an exuberant young girl. She hoped she would remain that way for a long time yet.

'We can do whatever you want. Put it on the list.' Bea smiled.

'Eat is what I want to do. I'm starving.' Flora patted her stomach. 'What's the time at home?'

With one hand still on the wheel, Bea delved blindly into her rucksack pocket for her phone and switched it on for the first time. It took a minute to find the network before her phone issued all manner of beeps. 'Ooh, look, I'm on O2!' She faced the phone screen towards her granddaughter and laughed, as if proof were needed that they were indeed in a foreign country. 'The time in Sydney is... Gosh!' Bea squinted at the screen. 'It's two in the morning! No wonder we're a bit out of sorts.'

'That is way past my bedtime!' Flora yawned.

'And mine.' Bea laughed.

The satnav spoke and Bea indicated. 'We have to go around. I think it's one-way ahead!'

Flora pointed at the satnav. 'Ooh, look, we're going over the Royal Mile! Hello, Alex!' She waved through the window.

Bea tutted, feeling an unexpected sense of embarrassment and a frisson of excitement about meeting the mousy, cat-loving woman who was in fact a man. She quickly changed the subject. 'Wow! Look! Here's The Balmoral. Doesn't it look old! And very fancy-pants.'

As the two weary travellers wheeled their suitcases into the hotel, they gawped admiringly at the cool grandeur of their surroundings. High ceilings, ornate cornices and colonnades drew the eye upwards. The plushly carpeted floor was dotted with potted palms, a real fire was burning in the hearth and nearby stood an elaborate Christmas tree. It was breathtaking. As they waited to check in at the darkwood reception desk, Bea and Flora looked at each other and giggled. They were actually in Scotland, and this very grand hotel was to be their home for the next two weeks!

Eleven

'Oh, cool! Look at this! I can see the castle and the gardens! It's all so old!' Flora stared through the bay window of their room at the dazzling array of ancient buildings, Christmas lights and shoppers enjoying the spectacle.

It was a good-sized room, with two double beds whose crisp white linen looked more than a little inviting. The light came from a multitude of elegant lamps that had been artfully placed on the dark-wood dressing table and bedside cabinets. The luxurious carpet was a pale tartan. Someone had arranged a stunning bouquet of lilac-coloured thistles and white roses as a centrepiece. They smiled at each other; their room and the view were just perfect.

'Come on, Bea, let's go exploring before I crash out on that bed and fall asleep for a hundred years.'

'Okay, my little would-be Sleeping Beauty, if you're sure you're up to it. I feel a bit scruffy, have I got time to shower and change?' Bea released her thick hair from its barrette and ran her fingers through her tangles before refastening the clip, making sure she caught all the stray tendrils.

'You always look très chic, Bea. Mum tells her friends

the story of when she first met you and you had an outfit on like Coco Chanel, with a silk shirt, strings of pearls and wide-legged pants. She says you looked beautiful, elegant and very fashionable and that it made her feel nervous.'

'Ah, well, thank you, Sarah!' Bea was genuinely happy and rather surprised to learn that this was how her daughter-in-law referred to her. 'I do love clothes, it's true. I think it's because I didn't really have any when I was growing up – just a couple of drab outfits my mum made. Me, my sister and my mum always had the same clothes. Once or twice a year, my dad would buy a cheap bolt of quite plain fabric and my mum would lay it out on the floor and pin three different-sized paper patterns to it, one for each of us – enough for three skirts, blouses or whatever. She was a very clever seamstress and the electric sewing machine was forever whirring away in the house. But I secretly longed for shop-bought clothes that were different from my sister's. It wasn't until I met Peter that there was spare money for good clothes. Ever since then I've always bought well and kept them for years. Still do.'

'And you have a lovely figure.'

'Oh, well, bless you, Flora! What a nice thing to say.'

'Have you ever been fat?' Flora asked, with typical teenaged bluntness.

Bea pictured herself on a bed, looking like she had swallowed a barrel. Her skin had stretched to accommodate the new life within her. She remembered standing in the bathroom and looking down, unable to see her toes. She had been huge and had rather loved it, despite the gnawing embarrassment at the fact that she was pregnant and alone.

'Not really, no. What do you fancy for supper?'

Neither commented on the change of topic. Flora shrugged. 'Shall we wander? I don't really mind, but I would like chips, but then I always want chips! I got this leaflet from the foyer.' She waved a piece of paper in front of Bea. It showed a pub sign that was in fact a large lobster. 'It looks nice.'

'Yes, it looks great! Good idea.' Bea grabbed her rucksack and threw it over her shoulder. Her phone buzzed. 'Oh, it's an email from Alex.' She placed her finger on the screen and moved the icon as she'd been taught. 'He hopes we had a good flight and has invited us for a coffee tomorrow, and he's given us directions. It feels weird saying "he"!'

'It will be great to see him, meet him finally!' Flora clapped.

'Hmm, maybe.' Bea wasn't so sure. She reached for the room key card and busied herself with her pashmina to try and hide her blushes. 'I'm a bit nervous in case I've given him the wrong impression. I'm not really interested in those kinds of shenanigans, not with someone on the other side of the world. And certainly not with someone who knows so much about my innermost thoughts!' She cringed again at the memory.

'Well, you're not on the other side of the world – not any more. You're here! And what do you mean, "shenanigans"?' Flora stared at her gran.

Bea rubbed her aching back. After twenty-four hours on a plane she could feel her joints seizing up, not helped by the fact that she hadn't done her morning exercise routine nor put herself through the physical workout of a day in the Reservoir Street Kitchen. 'I'm not exactly sure, but trust me, it's nothing I have to worry about right now.' She laughed. 'And "shenanigans" is not a swearword so there's no point putting it on your list!'

Flora blushed at the mention of her list.

The two strolled out of the hotel, smiling at the suited and booted men who stood in the reception area.

'God, it's so cold!' they both chorused as the icy air hit them full in the face.

Flora linked arms with her gran. 'We could have gone anywhere in the world and we chose here! Where I can't feel my feet or my face. It's freezing!'

Bea looked down the length of Princes Street. A young busker wearing a kilt and sporran stood on the bridge pulling a soulful tune from a set of bagpipes. It was hauntingly beautiful; it sounded almost like crying. A lump grew in her throat; she swallowed and coughed to clear it. She remembered him telling her about its sorrowful sound, how it had the power to move to tears any Celt who was away from home. In that moment she understood precisely what he meant.

'You're right, Flora, we could have gone anywhere in the world, but I'm glad we're here because it's a beautiful city with some amazing architecture. And it feels like Christmas, doesn't it?'

'It does.' Flora tightened her grip on Bea's arm. 'Thank you for bringing me here.' She stopped in her tracks, shivering on the spot, and stared at her gran. 'I was thinking that maybe Kim is right: Alex could be your boyfriend. Pappy loved you so much he would just be happy that you were happy.'

'Oh, love! That is a sweet thing to say and, yes, Pappy would be happy that I'm happy.' Bea recalled the wonderful note Peter had left hidden in his book. *So go find happiness and let yourself love!* 'But Alex is not going to be my boyfriend.'

'He might be! You haven't actually met him yet.' Flora grinned impishly as they resumed their walk down Princes Street.

The pavement was crowded; there was a constant burble of laughter and conversation, punctuated by squeals from the funfair. It had the atmosphere of a party, which lifted the two weary travellers from their fatigue. Women walked arm in arm in groups, wearing high heels, sparkly tops and no coats. Bea shivered at the sight of the bare flesh exposed to the cold evening air. She chuckled as three men, arms linked, staggered towards them, all wearing Santa hats, clearly drunk and singing fit to burst.

'Happy Christmas, hen!' One of them pulled away from his buddies and lunged towards Bea, who ducked away from his puckered lips.

'Thanks! You too!'

'Hey, are you from New Zealand?' One of the revellers leant towards Bea.

'Close enough.' She laughed, knowing it was pretty pointless to discuss geography and accents with someone that many sheets to the wind.

'Do you know my cousin Bradley? He lives in New Zealand!'

'Oh, right, what bit?'

'Fuck knows. Ooh, sorry!' He clamped his hand over his mouth when he noted Flora's age.

'That's okay,' Flora replied, quick as a flash. 'It was already on my list. And anyway I said it three times the other day, didn't I, Bea?'

Bea gave a brief nod, not wanting to encourage her.

'So... Bradley.' The man drew them back to the point. 'I don't know exactly where he stays, but it's near a mountain and they've got a bungalow with an extension.' His words were slurred. 'He's quite tall.' He raised his hand above his own head to show cousin Bradley's comparative height.

'Oh, sure, quite tall Bradley near the mountain in the bungalow with the extension! Yeah, I'm not far from him.'

'Give him ma best! And tell him, sorry about the dog.' He saluted, wobbling on the spot, happy as he joined his pals and they all continued on, staggering in and out of the kerb.

Flora laughed loudly and leant on her gran. 'I think he's had too much wine!'

'I think you might be right. And too much beer and too much whisky!' Bea chortled. 'I was tempted to ask if he knew Tait's cousin Gideon from Weston-Super-Mare!'

Second Chance Cafe

She knew the Café Royal was a good choice as soon as they stepped through the revolving door. The air was heavy with deliciously rich cooking scents that made her mouth water. Her cook's nose twitched as she inhaled the aroma of a heady red-wine reduction, roasted garlic and shallots. She and Flora exchanged glances, relieved that the place looked just as good as the leaflet had promised. They shed their hats and coats, taking in the grand 1920s interior, their eyes lingering on the unique murals. It was part ornate parlour and part speakeasy. The Christmas decorations were subtle; fairy lights were intertwined with sprigs of spruce and were looped around the bar.

The rather suave maître d' treated Bea like a film star. He showed them to a table near the carved walnut screen that separated the oyster bar from the pub next door, then swiftly reappeared with a glass of chilled champagne.

'May I ask if you are old enough to drink?'

Flora stared at him anxiously. 'I don't know – I'm nearly fourteen!'

Straight-backed, he looked down at her through his pencil-thin moustache. 'I was talking to this lady.' He gestured towards Bea. It made her night.

The decor could have come straight from the *Titanic*: low-hanging crystal chandeliers, gold-leaf detail, etched glass and shining marble. It was beautiful. They ordered lobster and chips and sat back, Bea sipping her champagne and Flora her water.

'This is so posh. How lucky are we?' Flora said.

'Very, my darling.' Bea raised her glass. 'To us, Flora, and thank you for accompanying me on this marvellous if unexpected adventure!'

Flora clinked her glass of water against her grandma's. 'Can I ask you something, Bea?'

'Of course. Fire away.' She sipped at her chilled fizz, which sparkled on her tongue. Loud laughter, conversation and the odd snatch of a Christmas carol floated from the bar next door, providing just the right level of Christmas cheer.

'I was thinking about what you told me and I was wondering, why do you think my dad is so angry about something that happened so long ago, when he was little? Why is he angry and upset if it was just the way things were? So he didn't have a dad, so what? Lots of my friends don't have dads, it's no biggy.' Flora looked at her lap, avoiding eye contact and hoping this wasn't too intrusive.

Bea steadied her glass and placed her forearms on the white linen tablecloth, flat-palmed, before arranging her bangles just so and settling her pose again. 'You have to understand, Flora, that things were so very different when I was your age. Goodness, what an awful phrase – "when I was your age"! It makes me sound absolutely ancient. But there it is, the truth; things *were* so much harder. Things that don't matter a jot now were indeed "a biggy", to steal your phrase. Your generation has so much freedom now, you really are very fortunate.'

'I don't feel very fortunate,' Flora whispered.

'Well, you should. I know you feel you're having a difficult time right now, but it's just a bump in the road. Thirty, forty years ago, young women were judged rather negatively and I was only eighteen when I went through a terrible time, a terrible and wonderful time, if you can imagine such a thing. I blamed myself for years, but I wasn't really guilty of anything, just being young. I wasn't trying to cause anyone harm and I certainly acted with more discretion and judgement than some of the girls you see in the newspapers these days. It's so much better now that you can build your own life and not be defined by your husband's career, or judged for simply following your heart.'

Flora knitted her eyebrows together, trying to figure out exactly what her gran was talking about.

Bea continued. 'You can be who you want to be. You have an infinite number of choices, Flora, that simply weren't open to me.' She took a deep breath. 'I wasn't married when I had Wyatt and it was a huge stain on my character.'

'"*Stain on your character*"!' Flora chortled. 'I don't really know what that means, but it doesn't sound very nice.'

'It isn't very nice.' Bea smiled at Flora's simple assessment. 'It means that you've done something or had something done to you that taints the way people view you – a scar, if you like, and you can never remove it.' Flora grimaced. 'I know, it's horrible, isn't it? A really terrifying thought. But it was a reality nonetheless. In my community it was considered a terrible thing.'

'What happened?'

'When?'

'When you had my dad. He never talks about it. Did he know his daddy? Did you love him?'

'Gosh, Flora, those are two big questions right there.' Bea sighed. 'No, Wyatt never knew his daddy and his daddy didn't know about him.'

'How did you hide him?' Flora looked puzzled.

'Oh, I didn't hide him, not exactly. His daddy didn't know I was having a baby. I didn't even know myself for a long while. I was only young, and, looking back, I didn't know a lot of things, things that you are probably much more worldly about than me. We didn't have the lessons you have in school. Everything was more secretive. I couldn't even say to my family that I'd started my periods, that would have been too personal!'

'I wish I'd started mine.' Flora scratched at the tablecloth.

'Oh, darling, don't wish your life away. Periods are not that great, trust me!'

'Do you still have them?'

'Yes, not as regularly as I did, but yes I do. And, funnily enough, as eager as you are for them to start, I can't wait until mine finish for good!' Bea laughed.

'So, did you love him, my dad's dad?'

Bea gulped the last of her fizz and welcomed the refill that the waiter hurried over to her. 'Gosh, it feels strange mentioning him, especially to you. I don't talk about him much...' *But I think about him nearly every day.*

Second Chance Cafe

'Why not?'

'Because it's too hard. It hurts, even now.' She pictured her young self, waiting to give birth, feeling the excruciating shame of her parents' words every time she looked in the mirror at her swollen reflection. 'My father, as you know, was a minister, came over from the UK to look after a church in Byron Bay. Well... every year they used to organise a summer cruise.' She smiled at the memory. 'It was a big deal in our rather empty social calendar. My sister Diane and I used to plan and plot, thinking about what we might wear and trying to get hold of rouge and other things we weren't really allowed. One of my dad's congregation skippered a tall ship that used to take us from the beach up around to Cape Byron lighthouse and back again. It was so beautiful, always a wonderful evening. All the women would bake for a fancy picnic on board and the men would decorate the ship with Chinese lanterns strung from the rigging and flaming torches dotted around the deck. I've never seen anything as beautiful before or since.' She gave Flora a small smile. 'The atmosphere was electric. There'd be dozens of people and we'd all sing and dance to an Irish band who came aboard with their fiddle, whistle and flute, concertina and of course their bodhrán.'

'What's a brodan?'

'A bodhrán. It's a large Celtic drum. It has a wooden frame.' Bea drew a circle in the air. 'And used to be made of goatskin.'

Flora nodded, happy at the picture her gran had painted.

Bea continued, sipping as she spoke. 'They always played until the early hours. The music was like energy that kept us going. As long as they played, we danced. Our feet would thump against the ship's deck as we wheeled round and round, and that sound became part of the music.' Bea bounced her flattened palm on the table, her eyes closed, reliving the jolt of the wooden deck against the thin soles of her shoes as she beat out the rhythm of the dance.

Flora sat forward. 'It sounds brilliant, like a festival.'

'It was.' Bea sniffed, opening her eyes. 'It was an event like no other; the music brought everyone together, the food gave happiness and the atmosphere affected everyone. The last time I attended, I was eighteen. We set sail at dusk and everyone was mingling, the girls all keen to see what the other girls were wearing and of course to catch the eye of any boy they might like to dance with later on when the sun disappeared. My dad was in high spirits, I remember, laughing and dancing with my mum, his arm around her waist. She looked so happy, it made her seem very young. I didn't often see her like that. I walked to the side of the boat to watch the shoreline get further and further away and I became aware of someone standing next to me.' Bea swallowed, as if lost in the memory. 'It was a young man. We stood side by side, watching the beach getting smaller and smaller, and then he spoke. He said, "I don't think there is anywhere else on the whole of God's earth that I would rather be." I looked up and he was smiling at me. He had a shock of dark red hair and green eyes the same colour as his scarf.'

'Like mine?' Flora smiled and touched the tip of her eyelashes with her finger.

Bea nodded. 'Yes, like yours. He was smiling at me as if he knew me and all of a sudden it was like being punched in the gut – in a good way, of course! I stared at him and I desperately wanted to get to know him. Even in those first few moments, I would have gone anywhere he asked and done anything he wanted.'

Flora was transfixed, staring at her gran as if she was watching a movie, taking in the detail with a mixture of fascination and shock. She was delighted that her gran was sharing this with her, treating her like the grown-up she craved to be.

'One of the churchwardens came up behind me and broke the spell; she was a sweet lady, rushing to introduce us. As the minister's daughter I had a little bit of status – things like that mattered back then. "Miss Gerraty, this is Dr John W. Brodie," she said, emphasising the word "doctor", giving him his full name, a bit impressed. Then she rushed off again. But his name was a small detail to me. I was already under his spell and he under mine.'

'Did you fall in love?' Flora whispered, totally enthralled.

Bea nodded. 'Yes, we did. Well, I was only eighteen. I say "only" now, but at the time I thought I was a woman of the world. Of course I wasn't. I thought it was enough that I had been on a plane, travelled to Australia from

England and attended a few socials. But I wasn't worldly at all. Nothing like the eighteen-year-olds of today. I couldn't be, I hadn't done anything or seen anything and I had no idea what was in store for me – which, with hindsight, was a good thing.' She gave a wry smile. 'My family was very traditional, strict. Even at eighteen I wasn't allowed out with boys by myself – goodness, perish the thought! And we were miles from all the excitement of big-city life. We lived on the coast next to the church. My mother was terribly house-proud and worried constantly about what my dad would think. I always thought her life was rather boring and with the glorious gift of hindsight, I can say that I might have been right!'

Bea straightened. 'I don't want to go into the details, but suffice to say, I had a lot of fun with... John.' Bea paused. It still felt strange saying his name out loud. 'He was a visiting physician, just graduated from medical school, and we had three months together – three months that I can only describe as absolutely magical.' She beamed at the memory.

'My granddad's name was John,' Flora practised, before blinking up at Bea. Both of them felt a stab of disloyalty about her pappy.

'Yes. Yes, it was.'

'Why didn't you stay together if you loved each other?' Flora buttered a piece of bread and popped it into her mouth.

'John's time at Byron Bay came to an end. We spent our last night together on the beach, in secret, of course. Before

I knew it, dawn was breaking and that was when...' She paused.

'When what?' Flora was rapt; she swallowed the lump of bread.

'When he told me that... that he was married and had two small children.' She lowered her eyes.

'He was married to someone else! No way!' Flora shrieked, shocked. This was not quite the fairy-tale twist she was expecting

Bea raised her palms and nodded. 'He was five years older than me, still young, but old enough to have had a bit of a life. Even if it was a life he didn't choose. He'd had a fling with another student while he was at med school, she fell pregnant, and that's how he ended up with twin babies. He'd done the honourable thing, got married and all that, even though it didn't sound like a match made in heaven. It was what you did back then, there was a sense of duty and happiness or anything as frivolous as true love was kind of secondary.'

'I'm glad I wasn't born then, it doesn't sound very good.' Flora imagined being paired off with someone who wasn't her first choice. 'He sounds sneaky, making you fall in love with him and all the time his wife was at home, waiting for him.'

'No, it wasn't like that at all, Flora. I know it's hard for you to understand – it was hard for me to understand!' She wrapped her arms around her trunk, soothing away the quake that was still almost as raw as on the day he'd told her.

'He wasn't looking to fall in love with someone – he hadn't planned it, quite the opposite. He was determined to make the best of it with his wife. But when he and I met that night on the boat it was like we were meant to be together. We both felt it, right from the first moment. He was as surprised by the whole thing as I was. And he was quite broken; ashamed and torn. A good, good man who suffered because of a rotten twist of fate when he was still quite young. He felt the weight of his mistakes. He was so upset that night on the beach and he cried and cried.' *He cried because I begged him to leave his family, asked him to leave his children. I told him they were too little to remember him. I begged...*

'Oh, poor John!' Flora said.

Bea smiled at her rapid change of heart. It was also quite wonderful to hear her granddaughter use the name that was always there on the tip of her own tongue but never spoken. 'Yes, poor John. I knew then and I know now that if he hadn't been such an honourable man he would have stayed with me. He loved me, I've never doubted that, but he had a strong sense of duty towards his wife and kids. He said that going home was like settling for second best now that he knew it was possible to find true love. So he left. I was distraught. Oh, Flora, I grieved, ached for him...' She rubbed her arms as if to rid her body of a chill that was spreading through her.

'And then you found out you were having my dad?'

'Yes,' Bea whispered. 'My parents went crazy when they found out. Beyond crazy.'

'I know how that feels!' Flora sighed.

'Oh, trust me, Flora, my parents' crazy makes Wyatt and Sarah's outburst seem like praise! It was terrible, a truly horrible time. I never told them it was John's. But being unmarried and "with child", as they called it, was a source of great shame in those days, especially for a minister's daughter. I can only imagine how bizarre that sounds, but it was. It ruined people's lives. My mother wasn't really interested in how it was affecting me or how it might affect my future, it was all about keeping it a secret, that was the main effort.'

'But you were having a baby! You'd think she'd have been so happy to be becoming a granny! My mum says she can't wait for that day, she says it will be the best time in her life and she's going to decorate a room for it and all sorts.'

Bea smiled up at the ornate ceiling, glad that Sarah felt that way. 'No, it wasn't quite like that. In her eyes I had done something unforgivable, committed a sin. She was emotionally constipated at the best of times and was very cold about my pregnancy, made it all feel dirty, shameful. There was no room for tears or hysterics; it was simply something that had to be dealt with. I was lucky; I was stronger than most, quite resilient, and actually my misguided belief that I was a worldly girl-about-town gave me the mettle to plough on, even though I didn't always feel like it.'

'So that was when you came to Sydney? I mean went to Sydney?' It was easy to temporarily forget that they had travelled to the other side of the world.

'Yes. I took rooms in a horrible place in Kings Cross and struggled to make ends meet. Oh, Flora, it was awful. I don't know how I got through it really. I was often hungry. Afraid to sleep in case the rats got into the cot or the cockroaches that dropped from the ceiling landed on him. It was a dark time.' She shivered. 'And that was how we lived until I met Pappy!' Her face brightened.

'Why have you never spoken to my dad about it?'

Bea considered how to respond to her granddaughter. 'I guess because it never really crops up and the longer we go without speaking about it, the harder it is to start.'

Flora drew a sharp breath and her lower lip wobbled.

Bea ran her hand over her brow as she opened her rucksack and fished for a tissue.

'That's just so sad!' Flora sniffed. 'And I never realised. I hate to think of you and my dad living like that. I love you both so much and I can't imagine being kept from someone you love.' She scrunched the tissue. 'Sorry, I didn't mean to cry.'

'Don't be sorry for your tears, darling. It is sad. There's no way that you can imagine it because the world is a very different place now, thank goodness. And, you know, I wasn't so unlucky compared to some. Other girls in my situation often used to have to give away their babies, so all that heartache was for nothing.'

'At least you got to keep Dad,' Flora almost whispered.

Bea nodded and dabbed at her eye with the corner of a Kleenex. 'Yes. Yes, I did. And I am thankful for that every day. And for you.' She reached out and took her granddaughter's young hand inside her own.

Replete but weary, Flora linked her arm with Bea's as they stepped out of the Café Royal and into the dark evening.
'Oh, wow! It's so—'
'Don't say it!' Bea waved a hand in front of Flora's face. 'We can't keep complaining about the weather. It is what it is and us moaning about it will not make it any warmer. As my grandma used to say, there's no such thing as bad weather, only the wrong clothes. A few more layers and some sturdy boots and we'll be right.'

Flora nodded, trying not to let her chattering teeth give her away. Bea kissed her granddaughter on the back of the hand and squeezed her arm even tighter as she fell into step beside her. She loved the new closeness that she now shared with her.

'I'm having a lovely time, Bea.'
'Me too, darling.'
Their hotel room was warm and welcoming. The lamps had been turned on and the pristine white Egyptian cotton sheets and gold silk counterpane had been turned down to reveal the plumped, inviting feather pillows.

'I could get used to this.' Bea laughed. The elaborate decor, tartan carpet, patterned wallpaper and ornate lamps would have seemed way too fussy in her own home, but there, in that unique setting, it was quite charming.

While Bea sat at the little dressing table between the

windows and removed all traces of make-up, Flora cleaned her teeth in the bathroom. She spat into the sink and ran the tap, then wound her hair into a fat plait. 'Where did he live, this Dr John W. Brodie?' she shouted into the mirror, as though that would somehow help her words bounce out to her grandma in the bedroom.

Bea turned on the stool and faced her granddaughter. 'Where did he live?'

'Yes, when he left you, where was he heading back to? Where were his wife and kids?'

There was the faintest pause. Then Bea spoke with only a slight quaver to her voice. 'Edinburgh. He lived in Edinburgh.'

Twelve

Bea and Flora sat at their beautifully set breakfast table in the brasserie of The Balmoral. Their tea was served in an elegant silver pot and the cutlery sparkled under the impressive chandeliers.

'This is nice.' Bea winked at her granddaughter. 'Don't think it'd go down too well with the Reservoir Street Kitchen customers, though. They prefer the more rustic decor. Or my "bits of junk", as Mr Giraldi calls them. I can just see him in here, bashing his cane to get the best table. Don't think it'd cut much ice.' The two chuckled.

'Do think they've got Choco Pillows?' Flora wondered as she surveyed the pristine menu card.

'Doubt it, but you've made a sensible choice with eggs and croissants. It's good to start the day with something warm, keep that chill at bay.' Her mind turned to breakfast service at the Reservoir Street Kitchen. 'I wonder how Kim and Tait are getting on.' She voiced her thoughts out loud. 'She is totally in love with him, you know.'

'What?' Flora squealed. 'Kim and Tait? No way! That's so exciting! Do you think they'll get married? Oh, I hope they do. He's so lucky, she is so out of his league, and she plays an instrument in an orchestra, doesn't she?'

'Yes, the cello.' Bea spoke with pride, as though talking about her own daughter. In a sense they were like her children; she certainly loved them like her own.

'That's awesome. I love Kim. I want to be like her when I'm older. She's got a nice apartment and everything.' Flora sipped her fresh orange juice and looked across the dining room towards the kitchen: the scrambled eggs she had decided on couldn't come fast enough.

Bea smiled. If only Kim could hear them. 'She has, but no hot tub in her bedroom and as far as I know, no 5 Seconds of Summer posters over all the walls instead of wallpaper! Oh, and no dog.'

Flora laughed, happy that her gran had remembered. 'I've been thinking about what you told me last night.'

Bea nodded, sipping her coffee.

'And I was wondering, what are we going to do about Dr Brodie?'

'Sorry to interrupt, but are you wanting a doctor?' Neither had noticed the waitress clearing the table behind them.

Bea pivoted round, feeling her neck turn crimson. 'Oh, no! But thank you.' She smiled, turning back to Flora. 'We are not going to do *anything*,' she said firmly.

'Sorry!' Flora mouthed before leaning in conspiratorially and saying, in no more than a whisper, 'I wonder if he's still alive. I've been thinking about him all night.'

Me too... Bea nodded and swallowed; she had of course considered this over the years. 'Who knows? He'd only be fifty-eight, but anything could have happened. He might not even live here any more. People do move. As I said, we shan't do anything. It was a long, long time ago.'

'Have you not spoken to him since the morning you waved him off from the beach?' Flora shook her head as if the image was too sad to contemplate.

'No,' Bea admitted.

'God, that's awful.'

'Although I did keep his scarf. It was dark green silk and I had it made into a little pillow.'

'Your little pillow? I know the one!'

'I like to have it close. I place it under my cheek at night. Ridiculous really.' She coloured at the admission, which she'd never shared before.

Flora jutted her chin out. 'It's not ridiculous. I have one of Marcus' T-shirts. It smells of him and I put it on when I feel like it. I haven't told Lori or Katie that I've got it. I found it by the goal after he'd been playing soccer and I put it in my bag to give him, but then just kind of didn't. It's not stealing, not really.'

Both considered the bag full of make-up that had found its way under her bed. Flora felt her cheeks blush and her heart thump.

Bea shrugged. 'I know very little about him, actually. Apart from that he was a physician, was married to Margaret and had a girl and a boy, Moira and Xander.

Thing is, as I say, even if he is still alive, he might not still live in Edinburgh; he could have gone anywhere in the world. I just wanted to see where he came from. I've always wanted to. I'm happy to be here – that's enough for me. He told me such beautiful stories about life in Auld Reekie!'

'Old what?' Flora wrinkled her nose.

'Auld Reekie. It's the Scots name for Edinburgh,' the waitress explained as she placed the plate of scrambled eggs and smoked salmon in front of Flora. 'It means Old Smoky. We used to have a lot of chimneys, so the old town was always full of smoke.' She set the bowl of porridge with honey and blueberries before Bea.

'That looks lovely. Thank you.' Bea smiled and picked up the silver spoon, her appetite suddenly raging at the sight and scent of their breakfast.

Flora tapped her fork on the side of the plate, hesitating despite her hunger.

'What's wrong, darling? That looks lovely.'

'I did something,' she whispered.

'Oh no, what now?' Bea pictured more scrapping, fibbing, harbouring bags of swag...

'I googled him.' Flora spoke with her eyes on the plate.

'You googled who?'

'Dr John W. Brodie.' Flora concentrated on balancing her egg on her fork. 'This morning, when you were in the shower.'

'You did?' Bea was intrigued and annoyed in equal measure.

Flora swallowed her food without really chewing. 'I was just curious.'

Bea felt her pulse race. 'What did you discover?'

'There were two of them. But your John was listed as retired. It says a Dr J. W. Brodie, retired, lives in an area called Davidson's Mains, Edinburgh, wherever that is. It sounds like an odd address.'

Bea held the spoon by her mouth and watched the blueberries shiver as her hand shook. She felt a rush of nausea as she sat back in the high back chair. *Your John, he's here, in Edinburgh, minutes from you at this very moment.*

'You okay, Gran?' Flora reached out and touched her arm. 'You don't look too good.'

Bea placed the spoon in the bowl and folded her hands in her lap, taking a deep breath as she arranged her bangles on her wrist. 'Goodness me, Flora. I've waited for over thirty years and you're saying, after one little tap on a screen, that I could be in the same city as him? Right now?'

Flora nodded, still unsure if she had done the right thing.

'Oh, God help me!' Bea lifted the linen napkin and held it over her face, reminding herself to breathe. *What am I doing? I should leave things well alone! What's the point, Bea? What's the point of disturbing his life after all this time? What would he say to his wife? You could ruin his life! He must never know you are here. Never.*

Standing on the steps of the hotel, kitted out in fleecy layers, a windcheater, gloves and trainers, Flora turned to

Bea, pulling her hat over her ears and exhaling a long smoky breath into the morning mist. 'I know I'm not allowed to say it, but—'

'You're right!' Bea interrupted, raising her palm. 'You're not allowed to say it!'

'Okay! But can I just say instead that Mum and Dad are on a beach in Bali right now, probably dipping into their private pool to keep cool?'

'No, you can't!' Bea fired back, hopping on the spot to keep the chill from her toes. 'Have you spoken to them?'

'I emailed them, because I wasn't sure about the time and stuff. I told them we'd arrived safely and that we're having a really cool time. Mum replied to say they had a great view of the ocean, blah, blah, and ended on a cute nagging note that I need to use this time to think everything through!' Flora rolled her eyes.

'She's your mum and she's worried about you because she loves you.' Bea had been pleased to note the affectionate tone to Flora's words. 'Come on, we're going hiking.' She practically ran down the steps.

'Where is it we're going again?' Flora shouted as she raced after her.

Bea pointed towards the Royal Mile. 'To Arthur's Seat!'

'I haven't come all this way to look at some bloke's chair!' Flora moaned, her words evaporating in the gusting wind.

They took the bus to Holyrood Palace, at the far end of the Royal Mile, then walked past the entrance to the

Scottish Parliament and on into Holyrood Park. Flora stared up at Arthur's Seat. The hill looked massive so close up, dominating the park and looming large over the edge of Edinburgh's city centre. 'Are we going all the way to the top?' she asked.

Bea nodded, striding forward, her nose and cheeks quite pink. With her head down, she trod the path, zigzagging up the steep slope. The grass was springy underfoot and, just as John had described it all those years ago, she had a real sense that where she was heading was somewhere special. Her stomach fluttered with anticipation. Flora raced ahead, unfazed by the gradient.

At the top of the rocky summit, Bea bent over to catch her breath, resting her palms on her thighs, enjoying the feeling of her heart beating fast in her chest and the warm slick of sweat that covered her skin. As her pulse slowed, she straightened up and took in the view.

'Oh wow!' she gasped, looking left to right and back again, then spinning in a slow circle, trying to take in the full panorama of city spires and the coast and rolling green mountains beyond.

'I can see why old Arthur wanted his chair up here,' Flora said. 'It's awesome.'

'The same reason Mrs Macquarie wanted hers where it is, I should imagine: the best viewpoint in the city to watch the comings and goings! And it is awesome, isn't it?'

John had loved it, she remembered, had mentioned it often. *'You can see as far as your eye will let you. Every way you turn reveals something new.*' She squinted to focus on the sooty spire of the Scott Monument, then took in the sweep of Princes Street beyond it. 'Could it be that you are below me, somewhere in that sprawl?' she whispered into the scarf wrapped around her nose and mouth. 'I wonder, are you there, John, close to me now?'

As if in tune with her gran's musings, Flora turned to face her. 'Barnton Avenue West.'

'Sorry?' Bea turned towards her granddaughter.

'That's where he lives. Barnton Avenue West. He's been there for the last thirty years, according to the records.'

'Oh, Flora!' Bea exhaled slowly, trying to decide what to do with the information.

'Phew! That's some view, eh?' Neither of them had heard the man approach from behind. He stood huffing and puffing next to them on the rocky outcrop.

'It sure is,' Bea replied.

'Oh, you're Australian! No way! It's a small world.'

Bea wondered if he was going to ask if she knew tall Bradley with the extended bungalow by the mountain...

'My boy's over there just now, been working on a dive boat off the coast of Cairns. Says he's homesick but loves the weather. He's a fisherman here, sounds like a bit of a busman's holiday! I says to my wife, boats are boats and weather's weather, how much different can it be?'

Bea wriggled her fingers inside her gloves and tried to halt the shiver along her spine. She laughed loudly. 'You'd be surprised!'

Down at the bottom of the hill again, they waited for the bus.

'I don't know what to do, Flora. I wanted to see his city, but I didn't consider seeing him.'

'I've been thinking that you might actually bump into him – literally, in the street!' Flora said, pulling her hat down over her ears. 'I keep looking at all the old men to see if they look like my dad!'

'Oh, goodness, don't say that!' Bea felt both horrified and thrilled by the idea. 'And he's not an old man, he's only fifty-eight!' She stared into the distance. 'I used to imagine all sorts – him coming to find me and what it would be like when we first saw each other again, how that would either confirm or shatter what I thought I knew. And then I used to worry about him coming to find me when Peter was alive. But it's been so long, I gave up on that years ago.' *I would be content to know that he is happy and that he has been happy. That's what I want for him, what I've always wished for him.*

'Who would you have picked?' Flora asked, straight out, as though they were discussing something far less emotional.

'Hmmm?' Bea had heard but wanted a second to consider how best to answer, if at all.

'I was wondering who you would have chosen if John had turned up at your house where you lived with Pappy and you'd had to choose?'

Bea looked up at the green hill in front of them and breathed in the crisp, sweet Scottish air. 'I'd have picked

Pappy every single time. I loved him, Flora, and he made me happy for twenty-seven years.' This was the truth and it felt good to say it aloud, especially there.

Flora considered this. 'But you loved them both?'

'Yes.' Bea nodded. 'I loved them both and I loved them differently. John was my first love, a desperate, passionate love that was all-consuming, like a storm; it took me by surprise and left me broken. The love Peter and I had was like the summer, gentle and lingering, and it felt good to be living in it. It warmed my bones and my soul.'

'Kind of like Scotland and Australia,' Flora whispered.

'Yes, I suppose so.' It was the first time Bea had seen it that way.

'Do you think you can love more than one person?' Flora kicked her toe against the pavement.

'I know you can. And each love is different, you'll see.'

'I don't think Marcus is even talking to me, let alone loving me.' She flicked her hair over her shoulder.

'You are so young, Flora. Who knows – maybe Marcus is for you, maybe he isn't. Don't forget, it's the journey that's the exciting bit.'

'I guess. Do you think we should go and see his house?' Flora let the idea hang.

Bea shook her head. 'No, Flora. I'm not sure that's a good idea.'

'We won't go in or anything like that. We could just sit outside and you can have a quick look. We can hide a bit or wear disguises and then we'll leave!'

'You've obviously given it a lot of thought! But it's not a good idea, love. I think we need to change the subject,' Bea said, relieved to see the red double-decker bus pulling into their stop.

Alighting further up the Royal Mile, they navigated their way along the cobbles. They peered into the festive window displays and resisted the temptation to stop for the tea and Dundee cake that one coffee shop was offering. Instead, they ploughed on towards their date with Alex. But they'd only gone a few yards before Bea was diverted by the sight of an antiques shop set back from the street. She pointed excitedly at the grimy double frontage.

Flora rolled her eyes.

'What? Don't look at me like that. I'm only going in for a peek!' Bea smiled, the prospect of a potential discovery bringing a twinkle to her eyes.

The shop wasn't much warmer than the street. A single Calor gas fire pumped heat towards the legs of the owner, who sat behind a counter watching a tiny TV tuned to a gameshow; canned laughter filled the dusty air. He raised his hand in welcome without taking his eyes off the programme.

Bea strolled around the cluttered shop, her eyes roving over the walls. She pointed at the giant stuffed stag's head, which was mounted on a wooden shield. 'How much room do you have in your suitcase?' she asked.

Flora smacked her forehead with her cupped palm. 'I knew it was a mistake to let you come in here! Kim said I had to keep an eye on you.'

Bea laughed. 'I'm only teasing.'

They left, waving at the man behind the counter, who ignored them, pushed his glasses further up his nose and concentrated on his flickering TV.

They eventually found the Christmas Café up an alleyway past the Scotch Whisky Experience and the Tartan Weaving Mill. Bea would have recognised it anywhere; she smiled at the sight of the window with its tartan swags and pine-cone decorations. It looked even prettier in real life. The window was steamed up and had fairy lights around it. A potted Christmas tree stood by the door, speckled with warm, white lights and topped with a red and gold tartan bow. The front door was peppered with stickers and flyers for local Zumba classes, a Kiss Goodbye to Sepsis fundraiser at Dobbies Garden Centre, a Christmas fair and much else besides.

It looked like a fabulous tearoom: homey, cosy and inviting. Christmas all year round, how wonderful. Bea took a deep breath. She was more nervous than ever at the prospect of meeting this man she had shared so much with. She smoothed her hair and pushed the door.

Thirteen

Bea stooped to enter the low doorway and found herself in a long, higgledy-piggledy room with a step bisecting it and small round tables and chairs in clusters on both levels. Couples occupied several seats. They had removed their hats and scarves and slackened their coats; some were nursing mugs of hot, strong tea to go with the slabs of homemade cake crammed full of plump, glistening cherries; others were biting into deep bacon sandwiches that oozed brown sauce. A large fire roared in the grate, its white-hot embers crackling as the scent of fresh pine wafted from the beautifully decorated mantel. It was a most elaborate display: nests of pine cones sat among a lattice of woven branches, and tartan and gold ribbons had been tied into bows at regular intervals. The walls were crowded with pictures and photographs of different festive scenes from times past. There were Victorian urchins selling roasted chestnuts from a brazier; a family circa 1970, gathered around their vast Christmas tree and all wearing matching Christmas jerseys and heavy-framed glasses; and a black-and-white photo of the tree outside the Rockefeller Center in New York.

A man made his way from the back of the shop, presumably where the kitchen was. He drew closer, waving with both hands, smiling widely to reveal impossibly white teeth beneath his clipped moustache; his denim shirt was unbuttoned low enough to show his tanned, hairless chest. He looked much younger than in the photos – under forty, for sure, thought Bea.

'There she is! Welcome! Welcome to Scotland!' Alex McKay bent low and threw his arms around Bea's shoulders, enveloping her in a cloud of delicious aftershave. 'My favourite e-penfriend, all the way from Australia!' He clapped. 'We are going to be the best of friends, I just know it! And the first thing I am going to do is cut that hair – you know the rule about over fifty and below the shoulders, right? You're breaking it by about two inches, but no matter.' He batted his words away.

Bea chortled, enjoying the warmth of his Scottish burr, which poured over her like soft caramel. Alex pulled out a chair and sat her down, beckoning for Flora to do the same as she slipped out of her coat. He joined them, crossing his legs. Bea grinned. She didn't know the hair rule, but she did know that she no longer had to worry about giving Alex the wrong idea; shenanigans would be the furthest thing from his mind.

'It's good to meet you face to face, Alex!' Bea felt her face break into a smile.

'You too, sweets. And don't worry, we have a gym in the spare room if you need to work on that saggy tum.' He pointed a manicured finger towards the ceiling.

Flora chuckled loudly and even Bea, who had covered her eyes in embarrassment, felt her shoulders relax. 'Oh, don't!' Her new best friend was quite wonderful.

'And you must be Flora?' Alex turned to face her, giving her sparkly eyes and open smile an admiring appraisal. 'Well, you are as pretty as a picture.'

Flora beamed, feeling pretty for the first time in a long time.

For a few minutes the three chatted and laughed about nothing in particular, exchanging small talk, happy to be in each other's company.

'It's so lovely to finally meet my new best friend!' Alex leant forward and crushed Bea to him in another hug.

She was once again engulfed in a delicious fog of aftershave. 'This is lovely, Alex, so cosy! And the fireplace looks stunning.'

'Aww, thank you!' He was clearly delighted by the compliment. 'Now, what'll we go for? The turkey with all the trimmings or do you want to jump straight to Christmas pud?'

'Very funny!' Bea smiled.

Alex clapped his hands. 'I think warm soup and homemade soda bread might be in order. How does that sound?'

'Sounds lovely!' Bea finally pulled off her coat, resting it on the back of the chair.

'And for you, doll?' He looked at Flora.

'Soup sounds good!'

Alex issued instructions to the kitchen and appeared minutes later to take up a chair at their table. 'What made you decide to come over to Scotland? I mean, it's wonderful, but a bit sudden!'

Flora sat up straight. 'My parents have gone to Bali and I was supposed to be going, but that kind of fell through.' She pulled a face. 'They're not too happy with me at the moment.'

'That's parents for you.' He winked at her. 'Why are your parents not too happy with you, young Flora?' He leant forward, interested. 'What did you do? Messy room? Ignore your homework?'

'No, I had a fight with a boy and got suspended from school and then they found some stolen things, which I didn't actually steal, but they were in my room.'

Bea pulled a face at Alex and reminded herself to brief Flora on what was and wasn't appropriate to share with relative strangers.

'Well, I'm sure they'll come round.' He patted her arm.

Flora shrugged. 'So Bea and I got to thinking about all the places we might like to visit in the whole wide world and we ended up here.'

'I think I was influenced by your vivid descriptions of your walks. It sounded so peaceful,' Bea explained.

'My walks?' Alex looked confused.

'The misty moors, the tranquil lochs, the smoke hovering above the water.' She sighed wistfully.

'Oh, *those* walks. Yes, very lovely.' He smiled. 'And so

you just jumped on a plane – how very jet-set!' Alex laughed. 'Not sure it would have been my first choice if the whole wide world was on offer. I think the Maldives would rate pretty highly, or maybe New York for New Year, that would be fun. Mind you, I've always wanted to go to Sydney.'

'You'd be welcome any time,' Bea assured him.

'Yes, great and I could hire Flora as my very own security! Which is handy.'

Bea laughed. She liked Alex, a lot. 'Tait, who I work with, calls her Little Klitschko.' She tutted.

'I like that.' Alex grinned.

A middle-aged woman in a long red cardigan with a striped apron over the top approached their table with a tray on which sat two deep bowls of steaming soup, a wooden breadboard with a dense loaf cut into chunks, and an ample supply of butter.

'You'll love this, especially after a chilly walk up at Holyrood; it'll warm your bones. My mother's recipe. Thank you, Elsie.'

The woman gave the slightest nod of her head as she deposited the bowls in front of Bea and Flora. 'I used to take ma bairns up t'Arthur's seat. They'd sit atop and eat a jeely piece and if it was real cold they'd get a poke a cheps on way home. Long time ago, eh?' She sighed.

Flora and Bea stared at Elsie; it wasn't just that they couldn't understand half the words she'd used, it was the speed at which she'd delivered them. Bea nodded, to be polite. Flora took the bull by the horns. 'What part of Poland are you from?' she said slowly, courteously.

'Glasgow,' Elsie replied as she sloped back to the kitchen, shaking her head.

Bea ladled a spoonful of soup into her mouth. 'Ooh, this is good. What is it?'

'Cock-a-leekie.' Alex nodded matter-of-factly.

Bea bit the inside of her cheeks; this was no time for childish giggles.

'So, do you have a boyfriend, Flora?'

Flora shook her head. 'Not really. I do like this one boy though. Marcus. In fact he's the one I punched.'

'You punched him?' He placed his hand on his breastbone and looked at Bea. She raised her eyebrows in confirmation. 'Is this some Australian courting ritual that I don't know about? Do you all go about punching people you like? Goodness me, child. Should I punch *you*, Bea? I mean, I do like you.'

'I'd really rather you didn't.' Bea drank spoonfuls of her soup in quick succession.

Flora pulled off a lump of bread and slathered it with butter. 'I'm not a child. I'm fourteen in a couple of weeks.'

'Flora! I have underwear older than you,' Alex replied.

Flora was unsure of the relevance. 'I don't know if I love him, but I really like him. I want to be with him all the time.'

'I guess the question is, does he love you back?'

'I... don't know. I sometimes think he might, but I don't know.' Flora stared at the table.

'You sometimes *think* he might? Well, that's what you need to find out! No point going through all this upset if you don't even know if it's got legs! You need to make sure, honey. Don't be living in sadness, otherwise you might end up like Bea and me, sitting on our own, tip-tapping into our laptops at all hours of the day and night!' He chortled and banged the table.

Bea laughed. It was fun to be with this loud, exuberant, jokey man. He was quite different from how he'd come across in his emails, which had been considered, cultured and calm.

'I don't want to end up like you two! But it's not that simple. My friend Lori likes him too...' Flora flashed a weak smile.

'Ah, young love. Chance would be a fine thing, eh, Bea?' Alex said.

Bea nodded. 'Yes, indeed. It's been just over a year since Peter died.'

'Aye, you said. For me it's nearly seven since my Robert died and I'm still heartbroken. It's hard to get back out there.'

'Seven? I thought it was ten years?' Bea said, thinking back to their email exchange.

'No.' He shook his head. 'It was six years ago, coming up to seven. You don't forget that sort of anniversary, do you? The day, the minute, your world fell apart.'

Bea nodded sympathetically, annoyed with herself for obviously having got that wrong. She paused, then asked,

'Did he work here, at the Christmas Café?' An image flashed up in her head of Peter pottering about in the Reservoir Street Kitchen of a morning, keeping her company, reading the papers and drinking her profits in gulps of demitasse.

'No. He was an accountant, a lovely, quiet man. We lived upstairs.' He pointed towards the ceiling. 'That's why I stay. I see him sitting on the sofa and sense him around the place. It helps a little.' His smile slipped a little. 'I still talk to him. I'd like one more day with him, one more hour to talk to him. That'd be something.'

'Yes, I often think that too,' Bea replied, swallowing her emotion. 'How I would love one more day. But then I'm pretty sure I'd need another and another – so much to catch up on. Peter and I were great friends.'

'Us too. We were like chalk and cheese, but it worked. He had my back, y'know? Always had my best interests at heart and that felt so great. I wasn't always that discerning back in the day, so to find him was like winning the greatest prize.' He placed his hand on his chest. 'Oh, Bea, I treasured him! I really did.'

Flora stared wide-eyed at Alex.

'It sounds like you were lucky to have each other,' she soothed.

'We were, we really were.' He tutted and then clapped. 'God, I'm sorry, this is maudlin. There's me wittering on about how hard not speaking is, and yet for you it must be doubly hard, being single all of a sudden—'

'You mean at my age?' Bea interrupted. 'Embarking on later life all by myself? Yes, it is a bit scary. Unnerving, I suppose.'

'You don't seem unnerved. In fact, you seem pretty sorted to me.' He tilted his head to further survey her.

'Well, thank you. Yes, I am in lots of ways. But I can't help wondering how come so many of us end up alone at the very time we need someone most. Getting older is harder when you're on your own; a steady hand on the tiller would make all the difference.'

'That's exactly what Robert was for me.' Alex swallowed. 'Even though I'd only just turned thirty when I lost him.'

'You must feel cheated,' Bea said sadly, gazing into the distance. 'So young, so much you didn't get to do—'

'Gran knows about that too, don't you?' Flora interjected with typical bluntness, staring at Bea, unfazed at sharing her confidences with their new friend. 'She loved someone a long time ago but they didn't get very long together.'

Bea inhaled sharply and Alex looked shocked. 'Gosh, that all sounds rather intriguing. You talk about Peter with such fondness, I assumed he was the one.'

Bea considered how best to continue. 'Oh, Peter was wonderful, wonderful! And yes, we were very happy. Twenty-seven years of happiness. He was a truly great friend. He was very kind to my son and me, but there was no passionate, all-consuming love. I loved him, yes, but not body, mind and soul, not that kind of love.'

'Blimey, that's a bit of a shocker. Did he know how you felt?'

'Oh yes, we were always very open with each other. He knew I was fond of him, loved him, and I have no doubt that he loved me, but I believe that his capacity for love was limited by the amount I was able to give in return. It's one of those things that with hindsight I can see may have done us both a disservice. Maybe I stopped him from finding his soulmate and maybe he did the same for me.'

'Do you really believe in that, then?' Flora looked at her gran with eyes full of hope. 'That people have soulmates? Someone that you love in that way and they love you in that way right back?'

Bea smiled at her granddaughter. 'I know it exists. I glimpsed it once and it was wonderful, magical.' A voice filled her head. *'Please, take my scarf, Miss Beatrice...'* 'But the timing was all wrong and so that was that.'

'That's such a shame.' Alex seemed quite choked.

Bea smiled at this grossest of understatements. 'Yes, it was a great shame.'

'Forgive me if I'm being insensitive or rude...' Alex drew breath, hesitating almost. 'But if you knew that this potential soulmate existed, why didn't you go and find him when Peter died or why didn't you hook up with him at some point before Peter?'

'Because he wasn't free.' Bea spoke levelly.

'He wasn't in jail or anything like that.' Flora felt the need to clarify.

Bea yelped as Alex laughed. 'No! For goodness sake! Of course he wasn't in jail!' She tutted at the very suggestion. 'But he was trapped; he was with his equivalent of Peter. God, that sounds awful, but it's the truth.'

Alex sat up straight and cleared his throat. He seemed a little overcome by the situation. 'Goodness me, this has been quite a getting-to-know-you party!'

'I've loved meeting you today, Alex.'

'And I you. And you, adorable Miss Flora, Little Klitschko.'

'Do you know, Alex, I feel like I've known you all my life.' Bea spoke truthfully as he embraced her in a warm hug.

It had been a long day. As Bea and Flora climbed the steps up to The Balmoral, they turned to take one last look down the length of Princes Street. There was a hush in the air, almost of anticipation. And then one tiny white flake fell in front of Flora's eyes and landed on her gran's coat, disappearing the instant it hit the navy wool of her lapel. This was quickly followed by another and another.

'Oh my God!' Flora yelled as she ran back down the steps. 'Bea! Bea! It's snowing! It's actually snowing!' she shouted, twirling on the pavement with her arms outstretched.

Bea captured the moment and filed it away under her most precious of memories. She knew she would never forget the sight of her beautiful Aussie granddaughter standing there with her toffee-coloured hair glinting in the lamplight as tiny snowflakes landed on her nose and eyelashes.

'Come on! You have to come down here!' Flora called. 'It feels like Christmas!'

Bea trod the stairs and turned her face towards the sky. It was a lifetime since she'd last felt snow on her skin but she instantly recalled the unique sensation of the tiny crystals turning to water the second they hit her face. She closed her eyes and remembered standing in the back of her granny's garden in the snow. Her sister ran around her, crunching the flakes into tiny, hard balls that she threw at the wall. Bea had looked up then as she did now and thought the heavens were rushing down to meet her. It was blinding, exhilarating, disorientating. It was magic.

Bea didn't realise she was crying until Flora placed a concerned hand on her shoulder. How could she begin to explain that she was crying for her life that had passed so fast, in the blink of an eye? It felt like mere months ago that she had stood in the snow, a little girl with her whole life ahead of her, smiling and rosy-cheeked as her gran baked a pie for supper in the warm, welcoming kitchen. She longed to be that little girl again, just for one day. A whole day without having to carry the heartache, recriminations, regrets and grief that had shaped her, a whole day of thinking that the world was a wonderful place, because she had never seen its cruelty. A whole day that she would get to spend in the snow with her family, because they still loved her and she was still pure.

Second Chance Cafe

When they could stand the cold no more, Bea and Flora made their way in silence across the plush reception area to the hotel lift. Their room was invitingly snug and as darkness pulled its blind on the day the lights from the building and funfair drew their gaze. Bea turned off the lamps, giving a better view of the darkness beyond. Both were quiet, reflective, watching the flurries blur the view.

'I can't believe it's really snowing!' Flora was mesmerised. 'I think it's one of the most beautiful things I've ever seen.'

'Me too,' Bea agreed, having re-found her composure.

'I think Alex is great,' Flora enthused.

'He really is. And I've been thinking: I *would* like to,' Bea said decisively as she kicked off her shoes and unwound her scarf in the darkness.

'You would like to what?' Flora stared in her direction.

'Go and see Barnton Avenue West. I'd like to see where he lives. Alex got me thinking: I know what he means about one more conversation, one more glimpse. It's too late for him of course, poor thing. But not for me. I'd like to see where John lives, just once. Not to talk to, but just to see his world, Flora. Just to glimpse the house he has lived in for thirty-odd years. That would be wonderful.' She looked at her granddaughter.

'Shall we go tomorrow?' Flora walked towards her gran and kissed her on the cheek.

'Yes. Tomorrow.'

Fourteen

Bea sat up in bed and flicked through the channels on the television, finding nothing to grab her attention. She was on edge.

'What's the plan, Bea?' Flora called from the bathroom as she brushed her thick hair. 'I'm feeling a bit nervous. Aren't you worried that he might see you?'

Bea looked at the reflection of her granddaughter's back in the mirror on the dressing table. 'Not really, no,' she lied, hoping her calm facade might help them both.

Flora reached for her toothbrush and mouthwash. 'God, I would be! It might shock him, you suddenly appearing on the doorstep like a genie! We need to think about how to keep you out of sight – maybe a disguise, like I said before.' Her eyes twinkled at the prospect.

Bea considered this as she listened to the gargling sound that echoed around the room. She raised the corner of her grey wrap and applied it to the corner of her eye, dotting away a tear that threatened. 'I have absolutely no intention of appearing on his doorstep like a genie – not that it would matter if he did see me.'

'Of course it would matter! You're his long-lost love! I can't imagine not seeing Marcus forever and then ping! There he is on my front step. It would be a huge deal!'

Bea breathed deeply, pushed her hair behind her ears and raised a smile. 'It wouldn't matter, darling, because we don't even know if he has considered me in all these years, not really. And secondly, he wouldn't recognise me, I'm sure.' She touched her chin. 'I am nothing like the girl I was, obviously. And, most importantly, he is not going to see me. I shall make certain of it.'

Flora didn't reply but simply walked over and hugged her grandma tight.

The two breakfasted in near silence, each contemplating the mission they were about to embark on. Flora periodically checked her phone.

'Have you heard from your friends?' Bea couldn't help herself.

'Lori's not talking to me, she's mad that Mum and Dad know about the make-up.' Flora bit into her toast and marmalade.

'Why would she be mad about that? Is it hers? You never said that.'

Flora nodded as she chewed and swallowed. 'Please don't tell Mum and Dad. I kind of made out it was no big deal, letting her put it under my bed, but it was a really big deal. I couldn't sleep and every time there was a knock on the door I thought it was the police coming to arrest me.

It's been horrible, but Lori said it was just what mates do for each other.'

I bet she did. Bea gave a small smile and put her coffee cup back onto its slender saucer. 'That worries me a little, darling. I'm trying to keep an open mind as you're obviously anxious about your friendship, but to my mind, when someone asks you to do something in secret and doesn't let you tell your parents, or anyone in fact, then that smells a bit iffy, don't you think? What's she got to hide?'

'I know! But I don't have any other friends, I really don't. What am I supposed to do?' Flora countered. 'Just be on my own?'

Bea stared at her granddaughter. 'I don't know what the answer is, darling. I wish I did. But I know that Lori sounds like trouble and she's dragging you down with her.'

Flora sniffed as her tears pooled and toast crumbs stuck in her throat. 'She won't reply to my texts or answer my calls so it doesn't even matter now. I don't think she's my friend any more, which means I literally have no one! Because if she's not my friend then Katie won't be either and I won't get to see Marcus.'

'Oh, darling!' Bea placed her hand on her granddaughter's arm. 'Please don't cry.'

The two made their way out to the car park, seemingly the only people in the city impressed by the thin covering of snow; everyone else seemed to be calling it light slush. Bea turned the heating up in their little red bauble and let the blast of hot air thaw their toes. She punched the address into the satnav and pulled out into the slow-moving traffic. The Fiat didn't seem in any particular hurry to arrive at its destination, navigating the unfamiliar streets with caution and hesitating at speed bumps that a local driver might have approached with gusto.

As they tootled towards the A90, following signs for the Forth Road Bridge, Flora spotted a place name she recognised. 'Hey, look, Bea – Perth!' She tried out a smile. 'Didn't realise we'd driven that far – we're nearly home!'

Bea nodded, trying to let the light conversation calm her nerves. But the jovial atmosphere of the preceding day had disappeared. She glanced sideways at her granddaughter, who sat forward in the passenger seat, as excited as if she was watching a TV soap opera. Where she had previously found Flora's presence reassuring, now she wished that she was alone. This wasn't a game.

She peered through the windscreen as though she could see round the corner. Her neck muscles were taut, her breath shallow. She shook her hand from the steering wheel to arrange and rearrange the bangles on her wrist. Her chats with Flora about the past had until that morning felt like a diversion, fun almost, but now the enormity of the situation weighed down on her. She felt a keen sense of responsibility and for the first time wondered whether going to his neighbourhood was advisable. She slightly regretted having agreed to it.

Flora could sense the tension wafting from her gran.

With her eyes staring fixedly ahead, she reminded Flora of a cliff diver trying to conquer her last-minute nerves. 'You okay, Bea?' she asked.

Bea nodded and inhaled deeply, trying to slow her racing pulse. An image came into her mind, as she'd known it would. She had just given birth to Wyatt. He was brand new and crying loudly from a plastic bassinet on wheels, as though fully aware of how upset she was. She was in a crumpled heap on a plastic-covered mattress, sobbing. Her hair was stuck to her sweaty brow. She was wearing a cotton hospital gown that was unfastened at the back. As she stood, it fell away, revealing her breasts heavy with milk and a pouch of loose skin hanging down over her abdomen. Voices echoed around her, as though she was only semi-present. A young nurse tried to calm her. 'It's okay, Beatrice dear. It will be okay.' And her own voice, younger, shrill in its desperation to be heard, the words garbled through a torrent of tears. 'No, it won't, it won't be okay! I need John, I need him now! Please, help me find him! Help me, I can't do this on my own, please...' It was then that she'd felt the unmistakeable sensation of having failed her son. *I wanted the very best for you, but already I've failed. I'm sorry, Wyatt, I'm so very sorry...*

Bea laid her hand on her stomach, feeling her womb pulse at the memory, even now, after all those years. She coughed and sat up straight, flicking the indicator and turning into Whitehouse Road, passing the rather grand Royal Burgess Golfing Society before rounding the car into

Barnton Avenue West. It was a wide residential road and its properties occupied generous plots, many of them immaculately landscaped. There were flint-built Gothic mansions and ultra-modern glass-fronted boxes, and evidence of family life in many of the front gardens. One or two houses had dogs that yapped from behind electronic gates. The snow seemed to have settled better in this part of the city; it sat in thin piles on top of hoses coiled against stands by the front wall and was heaped around a small child's bike that had been tipped forlornly on its side. The Christmas decorations here were tasteful: there were ornate, handmade wreaths on the front-door knockers and colour-coordinated icicle lights. It was a classy neighbourhood.

'Nice houses, aren't they?' Flora said, breaking the silence that now seemed to have physical weight inside their little car.

Bea nodded, thinking that in a different life with a different ending it would have been post addressed to her that would have fallen onto the mat in one of these houses. It would be her key that opened the door to one of these grand hallways as she invited visitors to step inside, greeting them with hugs as they shrugged their arms out of their rain macs on a winter's day. *'How are you? Do come in. Would you like a cup of tea? John's in the garden…'*

'I like all the different designs,' Flora babbled. 'The old-fashioned ones and the modern ones. I bet they're all very pricey, eh?'

Bea nodded. Yes, they probably were.

The pavements were high and tarmacked, with dropped kerbs in front of each address to allow for easy access. Large modern lamp-posts were dotted along the road. Bea slowed the car as they approached the house in which, according to Flora's internet research, a Dr J. W. Brodie resided. A white minivan was parked opposite, half on the pavement; the large green logo on its side advertised the services of the landscape gardener who was at that very moment tending to the winter-flowering shrubs in a nearby back garden. Bea parked close behind it, using it as cover for their covert mission. She ratcheted the handbrake, unclipped her seatbelt and, despite the icy temperature, wound her window down and stuck her elbow out, trying to look nonchalant. She wanted any casual observer to think she was waiting for a friend and not spying on the home of her former lover.

They had a perfect view of the house opposite. A five-bar gate was wedged back against an immaculate high hedge and held in place by a large moss-covered boulder that sat on the gravel. The driveway, flanked by a variety of established trees, swept round in an arc, stopping in front of the imposing house. There was no car in the driveway, no activity apparent in or around the house. The exterior of the house was painted cream, with white sash windows and a grey shingle roof; the front door was pillar-box red, a colour that Bea associated with her English childhood, when everything from buses to phone boxes was a similarly vivid scarlet, making them pop out against the grey landscape. She looked to the right and smiled to see the snow-capped golf course that would have been visible from nearly every room in the house because of its elevated position. She remembered him trying and failing to explain his love of the sport. Unsurprisingly, the windows were closed on this very cold day and all indicators were that the occupants were out. Bea gave a sigh of relief and stared at the patch of grass at the front of the house. She thought of the games they might have played on it, football or rounders; she pictured a dad, mum and two children enjoying birthdays and homecomings in that very house, while she was caring for a son who shared the same blood on the other side of the world.

'Are you sure you're okay?' Flora asked again as Bea's hands fidgeted in her lap and rubbed at her temple.

Bea chewed her bottom lip with teeth that ground and snapped. She suddenly looked every one of her fifty-three years. 'I don't think anyone's at home, do you?' she said, gazing at the house. It was as if Flora hadn't spoken.

Flora shook her head, wondering how long they would sit and stare. What was the usual time limit in a situation like this and what exactly was her gran hoping for? 'We'll wait a bit longer, shall we?' she whispered.

Bea recognised the tone that she herself adopted when trying to make things better. 'I think we should probably go now, Flora. I've seen as much as I wanted to. Thank you for coming with me.' She smiled at her granddaughter, then immediately turned her attention back to the house.

Bea studied the windows and let her eyes linger over the door. She imagined her lover's hand on the doorknob, arriving home after a hard day's work, raising the blinds in the windows, sweeping the driveway, raking leaves, going about the business of life in that house. A life that excluded her. She pictured his wife, Margaret, welcoming their friends and family over the threshold for countless Christmases, arms spread wide on that very driveway, when through all those years the woman leaving footprints in the snow should have been *her*, creating memories that should have existed inside *her* head. And for the want of a different moment in time, it would have been. It was hard to accept that after all these years. Seeing the home he shared with another woman left her breathless, sadder than ever.

Flora tried to think of what to say next, what to suggest that might ease the tension. She was about to speak when suddenly the van in front started its engine and drove off. At the exact same moment, a silver saloon car swung into the road and turned sharply left into a driveway – not just any driveway, but the driveway of the house belonging to Dr J. W. Brodie.

Bea's heart raced as she turned the key and pumped the accelerator. The engine whirred but remained flat. Again she twisted the ignition and pumped the pedal. 'Come on, come on! Bloody car!' she muttered under her breath, hitting the steering wheel with the heel of her hand in frustration.

She looked across and could see three heads in the car. Two in the front and one in the back. She had only caught a flash of the driver, but it was unmistakeably a blonde-haired woman. She drew breath sharply and placed a trembling hand at the neck of her blouse, twisting it beneath her fingers. *Those people might know him.*

Flora felt her own heart miss a beat and for a second feared that her gran might be having a heart attack. Was the shock too much? But thankfully no, Bea exhaled and placed her hand over her mouth as her tears pooled. Flora handed her a paper napkin from her pocket and watched as she dabbed at her eyes and blew her nose. She instantly handed her another.

'We'll get out of here as soon as we can, Flora. The bloody car won't start!' Bea tried to keep the edge of panic from her voice.

Flora nodded and watched as the woman climbed from the driver's seat. She was in her mid to late thirties, naturally pretty, with strawberry blonde hair that fell to her shoulders.

Bea felt overwhelmed at the sight of her. She looked so much like Wyatt. There was no question about it: she had to be John's daughter.

The silver saloon was a couple of years old and covered in a thin layer of grime. There were a few dents in the boot and a bumper sticker that read 'Moira's Taxi'. Bea scanned the vehicle intently, gleaning what clues she could.

The back door of the car swung open and out lumbered

a tall boy in his mid teens, wearing jeans, high-top sneakers and a hoodie. He was preoccupied with the phone in his hand, punching both his thumbs into the keypad. He was broad in the shoulders, with toffee-coloured hair the same as Flora's and the large aquiline nose of his grandfather. This unexpected revelation was enough to cause fresh tears to spring. Bea turned to Flora, beaming through her tears. 'That's your cousin!' she said, then immediately trained her eyes back on the driveway.

A few seconds later, she tried the ignition again, forcing the key round until her fingers hurt, trying to apply brute strength in the hope it might make the engine start. 'Come on! Please!' She banged the steering wheel once more, but the engine merely wheezed and whirred, giving off an irritating grinding noise as she pumped the clutch and slammed the accelerator.

The two watched as the boy walked slowly to the back of the car and lifted the tailgate to reveal a mountain of grocery bags. Moira looked up briefly at the noisy Fiat stranded in the road. Bea could only stare back, frozen with fear and fascination.

And then, before Bea had time to fully prepare herself, a man climbed from the passenger seat. There he was, in full view, standing by the side of the car. Just like that. Dr John Wyatt Brodie, father of her son and the love of her life.

Bea felt the breath stop in her throat. She would have known him anywhere. She felt the familiar leap of longing deep down in the pit of her stomach, even now, at her age.

It was just as it had always been, an unconscious desire, and she felt it as keenly as she had when she'd stood on the ship's deck in the moonlight all those years ago. They were connected.

It was well over three decades since she'd seen him last. He had changed, aged of course, but also blossomed in the way that men in their late fifties can, when they finally get comfortable in their skin. He was smaller than Bea remembered, probably about six foot, a couple of inches shorter than Wyatt. Of medium build, not fat but not spare. His close-cropped russet hair was shot through with grey streaks. His skin was pale and clear, his eyes slightly more hooded than she remembered, but still beautiful and blue. He was wearing a white shirt under a navy V-necked sweater, a navy blazer, sand-coloured corduroy trousers and heavy, tan-coloured brogues. He looked smart, like he always had.

The boy stood by the back of the car, still gripped by his phone and unwilling to be the first to dive in and grab a bag, waiting for his mum to start the process. John walked to the front door and unlocked it, pushing it open with his foot. The boy now reached into the boot, pulled a packet of frozen peas from one of the bags and concealed it behind his back. As his mother bent over to retrieve the groceries, he snuck up and placed the peas against the back of her neck.

Moira yelped and jumped backwards. 'You horrid child!' she squealed as she attempted to grab the bag, which he held above his head and out of her reach. She laughed without restraint, a full, open-mouthed chuckle.

'Grab her arms, Gramps!' the boy shouted.

Bea was rapt.

John smiled at his grandson. 'No, I can't reach!' He laughed. 'Let's just get the shopping in, Cal. Your poor mum! It's cold enough without that.'

Bea strained to hear his soft Edinburgh accent, a voice that had filtered through her dreams ever since that night some thirty-five years ago. She hardly dared breathe, unable to take her eyes from him. She felt trapped, not wanting to be seen but unwilling to let him out of her sight.

Flora and Bea were so engrossed in the pantomime unfolding in front of them that they quite forgot they shouldn't really have been staring at this family going about their business. Suddenly and without warning, Moira, as if aware she was being watched, looked directly at the car and into the face of her father's former lover. She raised her hand in a wave and nodded her head as if to say, *'Boys, eh?'*

Bea gave a small wave back. It was a gesture she would replay in her mind countless times, her first interaction with John's daughter, the little girl who was waiting for her daddy while they had lain entwined on a beach at dawn. This was the little girl Bea had begged him to abandon. She had pleaded and cried until she thought her heart might burst. And he had been just as distraught, tearfully adamant that he would rather be with her than anywhere, that he loved her beyond measure. But on that warm early morning under the rising Antipodean sun, it was not about love. It was about duty. The comfort she had taken over the years from his words, knowing that given the choice he would have picked her, now left a guilty aftertaste. She hadn't planned on making contact; this was strange and scary, but also wonderful.

Moira spoke to her son, who, along with his grandpa, had begun to ferry the grocery bags up the path and into the house. Moira then turned towards the little Fiat and started heading their way.

'Oh shit!' Bea fumbled with the keys, accidentally pulling them from the ignition before trying to shove them once again into the little slot with trembling fingers.

'Hello!' Moira waved again as she approached, smiling openly and kindly. She bent down until she was inches from Bea.

'All okay? You ladies look a bit lost!' She spoke through the gap in the window, which Bea now wound down fully.

Bea was paralysed; it was left to Flora to say something, anything. Flora leant across. 'We're fine, thanks. The car's overheating or something. It won't start so we're just giving it a breather.'

'Oh no! I'm always having trouble with my car, things have a habit of backing into it, which is most unfortunate. The fence post over there and the parking barrier at the supermarket.' Moira gestured vaguely in the direction of the dented boot of her silver saloon. 'At least that's my story and I'm sticking to it!'

Bea smiled up at her.

'Have you come far?'

All the way from Australia, and more than a million miles in my mind, each one leading me back to your father, who I love! Who I have always loved!

'No, just the town centre,' Flora answered. That wasn't exactly a lie. 'We're staying at The Balmoral.'

'Oh, very nice!' Moira nodded and turned her head towards her son, who was keeping a watchful eye on the car with the two strangers in it. 'Callum! Come here.'

The twist of the boy's mouth and his sloping shoulders spoke volumes. He had other places to be, other things to do. He reluctantly stepped forward.

'Can you have a look at these ladies' car, love? It won't start.'

'Sure. Flip your bonnet,' he instructed.

Bea reached down beneath the steering wheel, eventually locating the relevant lever. Flora got out and stood by Callum's side. Bea could see their teenage tummies through the gap beneath the bonnet. Cousins. In another life those two might have bathed together, eaten ice cream together, side by side on her balcony.

'Are you okay, my love? Would you like a glass of water? You look a little pale. Do you feel okay? My dad's a doctor. I could go grab him? I know he wouldn't mind a bit.' This time Moira was addressing Bea directly; she had no option but to respond.

She looked up through the window. 'No! No.' She tried

to keep the edge of panic from her voice. 'But thank you very much. I'm fine. Just a bit jet-lagged, with the time difference.' Her voice quivered. *Please God, don't get your dad. He mustn't see me, he mustn't.*

'Are you from Australia?'

Bea nodded. 'Yes, Sydney. Just here for a holiday.'

'You must be mad! Isn't Sydney hot at this time of year?'

Bea nodded again.

'And you left that behind for this?' She waved towards the grey sky, which looked like it was threatening rain.

'It's beautiful here.'

'Aye, it is that. Let me just get you some water then. I'll be right back!'

And then, without a second thought, Moira patted her arm, patted Bea, the woman who had the power to bring sadness and devastation to her parents' world. The heat where Moira's fingers had touched her skin lingered like an invisible tattoo. She watched as Moira trotted up the path and into the house. She seemed happy; a happy daughter; a kind, happy woman.

Bea unclipped her seatbelt and got out of the car. She stood next to Callum, who checked the water reservoir at the side of the engine and proceeded to remove the oily dipstick. 'Do you have a cloth, a bit of rag, anything I can wipe some oil on?' he asked gruffly.

'Yup.' Flora stuck her head back inside the car to find just that.

Bea and Callum were alone for a few precious seconds.

'Are you a mechanic?' Bea had no idea why she asked him that.

'No!' He laughed. 'I'm only fifteen! But I've watched my dad enough times.'

'Oh! Is he a mechanic?' Bea stuttered the question at speed, feeling her cheeks flush as the breath caught in her throat. She shouldn't be prying; it wasn't her place. Each piece of information gleaned felt like something she was stealing from Margaret and that wasn't fair, she had taken enough from the poor woman.

'Actually, no, my dad's in the army and my grandad is a medic.'

'Here we go!' Moira stood next to her and handed her a tall glass of water. 'Oh look, you're shaking! Why don't you sit back in the car? And don't worry, our Cal will have you going in no time. Won't you, darlin'?'

Callum didn't answer but instead stood staring at the small wad of cotton wool that Flora had handed him from the depths of her rucksack. The item was instantly identifiable by the little piece of string that dangled from it.

'Yuck, gross!' Callum held it reluctantly in his palm.

'What?' Flora rolled her eyes. 'It's only a bit of cotton wool!'

Moira laughed into her palm. 'Oh, crumbs, your face, Cal! I'm afraid, coming from an army family and having only boys, things like that are a little out of our comfort zone! I'm always outnumbered.'

'I know what you mean. I have a boy too.' This Bea almost whispered. *Your brother, Wyatt, who looks just like you.*

Flora held her breath, waiting for her gran to say more, to reveal something that she might live to regret. But she needn't have worried.

'I'm afraid my granddaughter hasn't the first clue! Nothing is taboo.' Bea grinned.

'Oh, I think they're all like that nowadays,' Moira said kindly.

'I am *here*, you know. I can hear you!' Flora remonstrated, her hands on her hips. She was delighted to have finally found a use for the little piece of cotton wool she had been carrying in her bag for over a year.

'Don't you have anything else?' Callum asked, dreading what she might produce.

'No, just use that, it'll be right!'

Moira and Flora laughed at the boy's discomfort. Bea laughed too, but at so much more than just the boy who shied away from a tampon. She laughed at the sight and sound of the four of them standing there together, giggling and joking like they had so many times in her fantasies, related in ways they could not begin to imagine. It was incredible.

'Right, I better get going – I've got freezer stuff going off.' Moira turned to go. 'I'll leave you in Callum's capable hands.'

'No! Wait!' Bea was aware that she had shouted. All

three looked at her. It was a full second of silence before she spoke. 'You forgot your glass.' Bea handed it over. *I never wanted to hurt you or your mum. Never. I didn't know about you, not until it was too late. I loved him. I love him still.*

'Your oil is a bit low and you need a water top-up, that should fix it. You just flooded the engine and it is very cold.' Callum tried to sound like he knew what he was talking about. Bea noted his slightly bossy tone and felt sorry for him. He sounded like Flora. The two stood side by side, almost the same height and build, and with the same gloriously thick toffee-coloured hair.

'Righto. And thank you.' Bea released the supporting arm and let the bonnet slam shut. 'Thanks for looking at it for us.'

'No bother. Happy Christmas.' Callum waved as he pulled his phone from his pocket and trod the path towards the front door.

Bea imagined herself in the kitchen. *'All okay, Cal? Go and join Gramps in front of the fire.'* She smiled. 'Yes, Happy Christmas.'

She turned the key and the engine started. Breathing a long sigh of relief, she looked over towards the golf course and then back at John's home. It was time to leave this family alone to prepare for their Christmas.

Flora and Bea drove in silence, punctuated only by the sound of Bea's sobbing. Flora reached out and placed a hand on her grandma's shoulder. 'That was really weird!'

Bea nodded. It was.

'I was really nervous. I kept thinking of all the things I mustn't say and reminding myself not to say them.' Flora exhaled.

Bea ignored her granddaughter's burbled words, too busy processing the thoughts whirring through her brain. 'I saw him! I actually saw him!' She placed her hand on her stomach, trying to calm the nerves that threatened to make her vomit.

Flora nodded. 'Yes you did.'

'And they were a nice family, weren't they? Helping Moira with the groceries and being so kind to us. And Callum sorting out the car.'

'Yes.' Flora too imagined a different life, a life with Callum and Moira and the others in it, more like the sort of family she envied; she would have liked it. Maybe they could have hung out and then she wouldn't need stupid Lori. 'It would have been nice if we had a large family, wouldn't it, Bea? I'd have loved brothers and sisters and aunties and uncles and loads of cousins to mess around with, it would have been cool.'

'Yes, it would.' Bea swallowed.

Flora smiled. 'I didn't think we'd see them today, did you? Let alone get the chance to talk to them, but we did. I'd say mission accomplished, wouldn't you?'

Bea nodded again, suddenly overcome with emotion, leaving her unable to speak. They made the short journey back into town and ditched the car.

Without pre-planning or discussion, the two walked the length of Princes Street and once again wandered into the gardens that had become a feature of their trip. Flora plonked down on one of the wooden benches that lined the path and sat back in the seat, staring at the sky as she wrapped her arms around her trunk.

'I feel absolutely drained.' Bea was now more composed. 'Thank you for coming with me, Flora. I don't know what I would have done if you hadn't been there. You were so quick-thinking and smart.'

Flora ignored the compliment. 'Well, to be fair, without me you'd probably still be stuck in Surry Hills, hanging out with Kim and Tait!'

'Yes, quite probably.'

'It feels weird that I've met my dad's half-sister and seen his dad and he doesn't know anything about them.'

'I know. I will tell him. I will tell him everything. That's the right thing to do, isn't it? About time. Especially now that you know.'

Flora nodded. 'I didn't see John's wife.'

'No.' Bea hesitated. 'She could have been anywhere – shopping, inside. I dreaded her coming out too. God, that could have been awful.' She closed her eyes and placed her head in her hands as she breathed in the cold air.

'I'm loving this trip, Bea.'

'Me too. It's wonderful, a total roller-coaster of emotions. I haven't felt this alive in a very long time.'

'That whole thing back there was weird though, right?

Talking to Moira, seeing John. How did he look to you?'

Bea's tears flowed again without warning. 'I shan't forget a moment of it, not ever. His hair's greyer, of course, but the shape of him hasn't altered, not really, not to me. He looked beautiful and it took all my strength not to run to him.' She clenched her jaw and tried to muffle her sobs. 'It has changed things for me in the most dramatic way.'

'Changed them how?'

'For years I worried about his well-being, worried that our liaison might have muddied things for him. Had things worked out for his family, were they happy? Or had he died young, been injured? I know it sounds daft, but those thoughts have preoccupied me for the last thirty-odd years. It's been my own private torture, not to know the answers.'

'It must have driven you crazy.'

'It nearly did, more than once. But today, for the first time in all these years, I know I can stop worrying about him. He seemed happy. He looked wonderful, a beautiful man with his lovely family in his gorgeous home. I can *finally* stop worrying and that feels amazing! He wasn't damaged, he was happy!'

'Weren't you tempted to run up that driveway and talk to him?'

Bea shivered and tightened her coat over her lap. 'Of course I was, more than you can know. But what would have been the point, other than to satisfy my own need for contact? He is settled, content. There's an expression Peter used to use, "All you need is enough," and he has enough. He doesn't need me muddling things. I understand that, as painful as it is.'

'How do you know he's content?'

Bea laughed. 'Flora, people who are discontented are always in a terrible hurry. Whether it's to arrive at the next place, be awarded the next job or move to another house, they're always chasing something. All in the misguided belief that the next phase is where their happiness and contentment lies. He was in no rush to get out of the car, he joined in the larking around, helped with the groceries. I'd say he was content.'

Bea grinned at her granddaughter before closing her eyes, wishing that their life had turned out differently but acknowledging that this was for the best. She would go back to Sydney knowing that he was happy and wishing him and his wonderful family a happy Christmas and nothing but good things.

Flora sat up on the bench and bunched her knees under her chin; she held them in place by wrapping her arms around her shins. Bea looked at the knobbles of her spine that poked from the top of her fleecy hoodie. She sat forward and rubbed her granddaughter's back. 'I am glad you've been part of this adventure, Flora. I can't imagine having done any of it without you. We wanted to get closer and we certainly have, wouldn't you say?'

'Yes, I really would.' Flora paused. 'I've loved it. I feel better about everything. I want to go back to how things were with Mum and Dad. I feel sad when I think about them.'

'Why do you think that is?'

Flora shrugged and bit her fingernail. 'I think that maybe everyone was right. I've let people talk me into stuff and I know I'm smarter than that. But I didn't really want to be smart, I just wanted to be liked.'

'I can understand that, darling.'

'Seeing that family today, hearing what you and Dad went through, I realise how lucky we are and how we have to make the most of the family we do have. I don't want to make Mum and Dad worry about me.' Her tears gathered.

'You are smart, darling, and it will all be fine, just you wait and see.'

Flora nodded. 'I know. And I was right, you know – you are one cool gran.'

'Don't know about that, but I'm certainly one chilly gran. Can we go back to the hotel and get some tea?'

'Sure.' Flora stood and linked arms with her gran as they made their way along Princes Street towards The Balmoral.

Fifteen

Flora raced ahead, taking two steps at a time and charging into the revolving door. She needed the loo, so they arranged to meet in the restaurant for afternoon tea.

Bea stepped from the icy-cold day into the warm reception of their hotel. She was, as ever, taken aback by the grandeur of the building. Her eyes panned across her surroundings, taking in the ornate chandelier, sweeping staircase and grand piano. She smiled at the friendly staff that milled about until her eyes came to rest on someone familiar.

'Alex! This is a lovely surprise! Hope you haven't been waiting long. We've been in the park, getting numb bums and putting the world to rights.' She looked at him through narrowed eyes, slightly embarrassed, wondering if they had made arrangements that she'd forgotten about.

He stood and looked at her, his expression solemn. 'I need to talk to you, Bea.'

'Oh, gosh, yes of course. Is everything okay?'

'Shall we go and get some tea?' He led her by the elbow towards the restaurant.

Second Chance Cafe

Choosing a quiet table at the back of the room, the two sat opposite each other in near silence and ordered two cups of Earl Grey.

Bea was rather thrown by his sober demeanour and was wracking her brain to think how she might have offended him or what it was he might need. 'I must say, Alex, I'm a little unnerved. You look so serious!' She tried out a chuckle.

Just as she was trying to reconcile the man who'd previously been the life and soul of the party with this rather edgy character, Flora galloped into the room.

'Hi, Alex!'

'Hey, sweetie. I was just going to treat your gran to afternoon tea. Could I be really cheeky and ask if you'd mind giving us half an hour – if that's all right with you, Bea?'

'I guess.' She arranged her bangles, feeling a little confused, cornered. 'Go up to the room, Flora. You can watch a movie and you've got snacks up there. I shall be up in a wee while, or come down if you need anything or get bored. I'll be right here.'

'Okay.' Flora shrugged and made her way from the restaurant.

'What on earth is this all about?' Bea's tone was quite stern.

Alex ran his hand through his hair and exhaled slowly. 'I honestly don't know where to start, except to say that I think you're fabulous, Bea.' He smiled briefly at her.

'Oh God, this isn't a proposal, is it?' She laughed.

He carried on as though she hadn't made the joke. 'I miss Robert so much. The moment I saw him, I knew. I didn't know what I knew, but I knew *something* was happening, I knew he was going to be important in my life.'

'That's lovely, Alex. Sounds like you were lucky to have each other.' She wondered where this was going.

'We were. Thank you.' He smiled up at the waiter, who was arranging their teapots and cups. The silver strainers came with their own natty little saucers, and the slices of lemon had a dinky pitchfork to spear them with.

Bea poured her tea and watched as her companion did the same with shaking hands.

'When I came out to my family, it was tough. My dad was great. My mum... how can I put it, was grudgingly accepting, but it changed things between us. I think some of her veneer fell away. It's easy to offer unconditional love if it's never tested.'

Bea liked his phrasing. 'I guess that's true. I'm of the opinion that you love who you love and if you're loved back then that is the greatest gift in the world. That's all that really matters – the old saying is true, it really does make the world go around. I've lived in Sydney long enough to understand that love comes in many shapes and forms.'

'Oh God, you'd be one of those parents that was disappointingly understanding.' Alex smiled, showing a glint of yesterday's exuberance.

'Oh, I see! Not shocked enough. Yes, I get it, that wouldn't really help the sense of rebellion, would it?'

'Not even a little bit.' He sipped his tea. 'She told me I was giving up so much and I was too young to know my own mind. I half expected her to tell me that it was a phase.' He rolled his eyes.

'She was probably just having trouble digesting the news. And she did have a point.'

'In what way did she have a point?'

'Well, as a mother, we want our children's lives to be as easy as possible. We want them to flourish, be happy. And any route they take that might make those goals harder to achieve can be difficult for us to accept. It's not about your sexuality – who gives a fig about that? It's more about you leading a life that could expose you to others' prejudices. The thought of your kids suffering for a single second because of other people's ignorance or outmoded views, the idea that they might face hatred or opposition, well, that's hard. She was probably worried that your path might not always run smooth.'

'Whose life does?' Alex blinked.

'True.' She smiled, placing the delicate white china cup back in its saucer.

'My dad was incredible. He just hugged me and told me that he had loved me since the day I was born and would love me till the day he died and nothing would or could ever change that.'

'That's beautiful.'

'And then when I met Robert and told my dad how it felt, that just by glancing at him, I knew, he told me he understood because he had been through something similar.'

Bea nodded, slightly distracted, wondering if Flora was okay.

'He told me it had happened when he was married to my mum.'

'Oh, your poor mum!'

Alex stared at her. 'Yes. She never knew. My mum died a decade ago.'

'I'm very sorry to hear that.' She placed her hand on his arm and gave a gentle squeeze of condolence.

'I told my dad a year or so after she had passed that he should try and find happiness, find love. I shan't ever forget what he said to me. We were in the garden and he was cutting back the ivy, wearing gardening gloves and his old cricket hat. He said, "I found love once and it's lived in my heart ever since. I don't need to go looking for it, I carry it with me, in here," and he patted his two fingers on his chest in the rhythm of a heartbeat.' Alex paused. 'I thought he was talking about my mum, but it turned out he wasn't.' He held her eye. 'He was talking about a very brief but very deep love that he'd found when me and my sister were tiny and he was working away.'

Bea was finding it hard to breathe. She was able to take breaths in but couldn't exhale, not properly. She stared at Alex, whose emotion also threatened.

'I told him to go and find it, go and find her, the woman who had lived in his heart.'

Bea couldn't contain the tears that spilled from her. She swallowed, trying to get the words out. 'Why didn't he?' Her voice was small.

'He did. He did! He travelled to the other side of the world and he found her. He found her address and then found out she was married and then found out she had a son.'

Bea pushed the napkin into her face. *Oh God. Oh, John. I can't believe it, I can't...*

Alex reached for her hand across the table. 'He stayed for a few days, watching her coming and going. He just wanted to know she was happy, wanted to see where she lived. He didn't want to upset her life, not once he knew she was settled and married. He saw her smiling, laughing, and just as beautiful as he'd remembered. He watched her in Manly, he saw her playing in the sand with a little girl...'

My Flora, my little Flora.

'And then he saw her with her son, who looked so familiar to him his legs nearly gave way on the spot. He says he looked like my twin sister, Moira. Not a bit like me, Xander, Alexander.'

Bea couldn't speak. Her nose ran and her tears flowed. *This can't be happening. This can't be true.*

'He kept tabs on her: Beatrice Greenstock who used to be Beatrice Gerraty. He read snippets about her life wherever he could find them. Announcements in newspapers, stories about her business, anything he could devour at a distance. And then one day he saw that she had been widowed; her lovely husband who had made her laugh had died. He waited a year and he asked me to get in contact. He'd had the idea that I could tell her about the forum. And then he started emailing her.'

Bea looked up and sniffed back her tears. 'He started emailing me?'

'Yes. It was him you were chatting to, becoming friends and swapping facts about your life with. Not me. He sat glued to that screen day and night, waiting for contact from you. He's the walker, the one who can write about misty moors and tranquil lochs.' He smiled.

'Oh God! I can't breathe...' Bea pulled off her pashmina and rubbed her throat.

'He was working out how to proceed, how to come clean, when you announced you were coming over! He's been beside himself with joy and worry. And then today, quite out of the blue, Moira told him a story about a lady who was staying at The Balmoral and whose car had broken down, a lady who had come all the way from Australia...'

'I... I don't know what to say. I can't... I can't believe it! I can't believe it.' Bea was fighting for composure. 'I thought that would be it. I thought I would glimpse him and that would be enough. It was enough, to see him happy!'

'Don't be mad at us.'

She shook her head vigorously. 'I'm not... not mad, just overwhelmed, scared, happy, everything!'

'He's on his way, Bea.'

Second Chance Cafe

'What?' She sat up straight, squinting across the table, trying to understand.

'He's on his way right now to you. He'll meet you at the Christmas Café.'

'Oh my God! Oh my God!'

Alex took Bea's hand as they collected Flora from her room and made their way to the little teashop off the Royal Mile.

'So, what have I missed?' Flora asked, keen to be filled in on the details and slightly concerned by Bea's rather dazed expression.

'Oh, honey, you are going to need major updating!' Alex laughed as he whisked her round in a circle. The three of them were almost skipping, leaving footprints in the carpet of snow.

When they arrived, Alex let them in and flicked on the lamps while Flora bounced on the spot. 'Oh, Bea! He found you! He found you! Just imagine if you had stayed hidden, it would never have happened, but he found you!' She was lost in the romance, the prospect of their reunion.

'Come on, Flora, you and I can go upstairs and watch telly. Give them some privacy. The place is all yours, Bea.' Alex stooped to gather up a rather arrogant-looking cat, who eyed Bea dismissively before turning his head in the opposite direction. 'Yes, Professor Richards, this is the lady I was telling you about who isn't too fond of cats.'

'I'm sorry!' Bea gushed. 'It's not that I'm not fond of

cats, I just don't have one!' It wasn't clear if she was apologising to Alex or Professor Richards.

Alex stroked the cat's ears. 'Don't worry, Bea, he's not overly fond of you either, he told me.' He grinned. 'I'm so glad you aren't mad at me. I was worried that Little Klitschko might have got her boxing skills from you and that when you found out, I might get a good pummelling!' He gasped. 'I'm so happy for you, Bea. It's the most wonderful thing ever. It's like a fairy tale.' He turned in his lips, as if that might prevent his tears from welling up.

'I wanted to ask you, where did "McKay" come from?'

'It was my Robert's name,' he said quietly.

'Of course it was.' She paused. 'Is Moira okay?'

'She just wants Dad to be happy. That's all we both want.' He enveloped her in one of his warm hugs. 'Let me take your coat.' Alex eased her arms from the sleeves and ushered her towards the fire that was now roaring in the grate. 'You look lovely.' He stood back, admiring her snug jeans and loose, cream silk blouse.

'I didn't know what you'd want to eat, so I've prepared some snacks – cheese, oatcakes, homemade chutney, that kind of thing.' He fussed, lining up the salt and pepper and twisting the mini Christmas tree on their table, until everything looked just so. 'We'll be upstairs if you need anything. Anything at all. You just have to yell or bang on the ceiling and I'll be down quicker than you can say Jack Flash!' He waved a warning finger at her, as if she were sixteen and not in her fifties.

'Thank you, Alex. Thank you for everything.' She was touched by his kindness.

He winked at her before disappearing up the stairs with a gabbling Flora.

Bea studied the opened bottle of red wine, sat in one of the chairs in front of the fire and fastened then unfastened the top button of her blouse, overly concerned about not looking too formal but also not showing too much of her crêpey décolletage. She pushed her hair behind her ears, then let it fall forward again. Her heart hammered and her palms were damp. She felt as if she had just stopped running and was fighting for breath.

Exhaling slowly, she tried to calm herself. 'For goodness sake, Bea, he knows you're older. Just calm down!' She nodded as the voice in her head screamed, *He's on his way! John, your John is coming here, right now! Any minute and you'll see him again!* She nodded again, still trying to reconcile the fact that Alex was Xander. She felt confused and elated all at the same time.

Bea closed her eyes, hoping to clear her head and find a place of quiet contemplation, but no sooner had she taken a deep breath than she heard a gentle rapping on the door. She adjusted her bangles, practised her neutral face, stood and made her way across the room. She walked slowly, with one trembling hand over her mouth, trying to comprehend what was happening. Twisting the lock, she stepped back and opened the door.

There in front of her was a man so beautiful and

unexpected that the breath caught in her throat and her heart missed a beat. She felt her legs sway and her head swim; she placed a hand on her chest, worrying that she might faint. She wanted to move but couldn't figure out how. Her whole body shook and everything and everyone else disappeared. All she could see was the man standing in the street with the snow falling on his shoulders. *Look at you! You are real and you are here!* She walked forward until they were just a few feet apart.

'Oh, dear God!' he murmured. 'Beatrice...'

Bea nodded, slowly. 'John.' It was the first time in decades that she had addressed him for real, not just in her head.

They were overwhelmed, tongue-tied and rather awkward. There was no small talk; it would have felt ridiculous to discuss the weather and plans for Christmas when a volcano of emotions was rumbling inside each of them.

Bea stood back and let him pass. Both quickly sank into the chairs in front of the hearth, each stealing glances at the other's face, trying to relearn the features that time and experience had so altered.

'Did you recognise me?' she whispered. She spoke to her hands folded in her lap, wondering if he was looking at the map of crow's feet that had gathered at the corner of her eyes, the small pouch of skin beneath her chin, her grey hair.

'There was something today... It was just a glimpse, but it felt odd. Something didn't add up, but I couldn't figure out what. Then when Moira told me you were Australian it all fell into place.' He placed his hand on his heart. 'I felt you.'

His words sent a shiver to her core. *I have felt you too, all those nights apart, holding our newborn baby, watching him morph into the image of his daddy.* 'I didn't mean to barge in, John, or upset you or your family in any way. I don't want to cause you any embarrassment. I only meant to look at you. I never thought—'

'It's okay. It really is,' he interrupted. 'Margaret died ten years ago.' Saying her name aloud, he broke the taboo, brought the reason for their guilt into the open, answered the unasked. What had his email said? *I know what that feels like, we are in similar boats; for me it's been ten years.* Of course! He had forgotten to be Alex and had spoken the truth; ten years, his truth.

'Alex told me and I'm sorry.' Bea hated the flush of guilty joy that flooded through her.

He smiled sincerely at her condolences. 'When she passed, it changed things for me. I thought about you – I suppose I was finally free to do so. I wondered if I should try and get in contact, but I couldn't find the courage. So I did it by stealth. I guess I was worried about messing up your life, about interfering.'

Bea nodded quickly; his concerns echoed her own.

'I saw you, Bea, and I saw your son.' He stared at her, waiting for confirmation.

She simply gazed at him, speechless.

He twisted to face her in his chair. 'We need to talk,

properly talk.' His voice was soft but assertive. 'It doesn't have to be tonight. We have all the time in the world, we can take it slowly.'

She watched as he stood up, removed his coat and scarf and strode across the room to place them on a vacant chair. The temptation to jump up and cling to him for dear life was strong.

'Oh my word,' she gasped. 'I can't believe I'm here.' Every bit of her seemed to be trembling.

'My Beatrice.' John let his eyes rove over her face as they stared at each other, sitting in front of the fire inside the Christmas Café.

He lifted his hand and smoothed the tendrils of hair that had strayed over her cheek. 'It's really you, isn't it?' he said, and his eyes crinkled in a smile, the way they always had.

The touch of his hand against her face, skin to skin, sent a jolt right through her. 'Yes. It's me.'

Dr John Wyatt Brodie stood, taking a step across the creaking wooden floor of the cosy café. It was a single step, but it represented thousands of miles and many decades. He reached out and pulled her up towards him. Gingerly, Bea raised her arms and placed them across her lover's back, nestled in the space beneath his chin where she had always fitted so perfectly. They stood like that for a minute or so, savouring each other's presence, inhaling the scent of each other.

'I have over the years considered the fact that I might

have imagined you. Imagined the whole thing. I doubted that anyone could have the strength of feeling that I had for you.' His voice was soft.

Bea nodded. It was exactly the same for her.

'But here you are!' He stepped back so he could see her better, still holding the tops of her arms.

'Yes. Here I am.' She looked up at him. 'I got old!' She dropped her gaze to the floor.

'We both did. And not old – older. But it's still you and you are still…' He shook his head as if the truth was a surprise. 'Still so very beautiful.'

Bea swallowed the bubble of joy that was growing inside her. 'We've got wine.' She sat down at the table, wanting distance between them, unable to cope with the physical proximity and the overwhelming desire to lay her skin against his and never let go.

John sat down too and stretched his legs in front of him, crossing them at the ankles. 'Is Xander upstairs?'

'Yes.' She still couldn't quite make the connection between the man who she had come to think of as a friend and little Xander who had been in her thoughts for years.

'And where's Flora?'

She loved the way he pronounced her name. 'She's with him, no doubt taking over the remote control and the very large bag of popcorn.'

'How lovely to think of the two of them getting to know each other.'

'It is.'

'How long have I got you for?' John asked as the embers crackled.

'Tonight?' she said, wondering if he had to be somewhere.

'No!' He laughed. 'How long are you here in Edinburgh?'

'Oh! A good few days yet.' She didn't want to think about leaving, not already. This time it would be her travelling to the other side of the world.

'You have no idea what it felt like to get that email from you. Knowing you were on the other side of a keyboard sending messages to me!' He shook his head.

'Well, not to you exactly.' She smiled shyly, thinking of the confidences she had shared.

'I didn't know how to begin to come clean. I enjoyed our chats – it was fun, wasn't it?'

'Yes.' She had to admit. 'It was fun.' She decided not to tell John the extent of all her confusion, how she'd only recently realised that her e-penfriend was a man, and now it turned out he was someone else entirely. *It was you all along.* It was too much to digest just now.

John let his eyes travel over the pictures on the walls. 'I like it here. I like to reflect on all the Christmases that these other people have shared. Christmas was always a time I thought about you.' He studied the scenes and she wondered if, like her, he was thinking of all those they had spent apart.

'D'you remember how I asked you if it was only called the Christmas Café at this time of year, whether it changed its name at Easter, Valentine's and so forth?'

'I do! I thought that was a very good idea.' He laughed.

'Was it you writing back to me by then?' Bea asked.

'Yes. The first contact came from Alex, he wrote you the letter. I thought I'd be content for him to just read me your correspondence, but it wasn't enough, not for me. So I took over.'

The two sat in silence for a second or two, listening to the hiss and crackle of the logs on the fire.

'I can't believe we're here. I still don't know if you're real,' Bea murmured.

'I am.' He reached across the table and took her palm inside his. Their fingers trembled in sync as they each tried to absorb the reality of what was happening.

'I've dreamt of you for so long, I'm worried I might wake up,' she whispered.

'I have the same dream over and over. On our last night together, you fell asleep—'

'I didn't!'

'You did.' He nodded. 'Just for a few minutes. I held you as you slipped off to sleep. I watched your eyes flutter and your mouth twitch and I kissed you. Watching you sleep was the greatest privilege and I knew it was one I would never have the chance to repeat. That thought alone made my heart break. To this day I dream of you often: you lie in my arms and I hold you while you sleep. It's perfect. And then I wake up, feeling both very sad and very happy.'

'Oh, John! I used to imagine you'd died. It ripped me in two, but it was easier somehow to think of you as being dead, to think of you gone and unable to be with me rather than alive somewhere and choosing to remain hidden, like a thing in the shadows.'

'I never chose to remain hidden, Bea. But I couldn't bear to hurt you any more than I already had. To see you so distressed and knowing it was my doing, it has tortured me.' He swallowed. 'This isn't easy for me. I'm not used to sharing my thoughts so much – I rarely talk about my emotions like this.'

'It isn't easy for me either. I can taste the disloyalty, the guilt.' Bea licked her lips as if to rid her mouth of the sensation. 'I was married to a good, good man.'

John drew breath. 'I'm glad, Bea. So glad you could find love and happiness.'

I did love him. But not in the way I loved you. Bea tossed her hair to try and clear her head. 'His name was Peter. He passed away last year, just before Christmas.'

He squeezed her fingers in solace. 'Yes, I know. I have no right to feel jealous, but I still do.'

'When you left that morning...' Bea swallowed the tears that slipped down the back of her throat. She knew she had to broach the subject soon, otherwise it would sit like an obstacle between them. 'I thought I might die. I really did. I felt so broken, so bereft. It was a physical pain.'

'I have never felt such sadness,' John said, his voice choked. 'I hated myself. I hated myself for years. It was like I'd tricked you, but that couldn't have been further from what I'd intended.' He fixed his gaze on a spot on the table.

'I was twenty-three years old, thousands of miles from Scotland, doing my first job as a doctor, out there in the sunshine. Life seemed so full of possibilities. It was as though... as though I'd suddenly found myself. As though I was a different person and I was free. Free to be young and to start again.' He glanced up at her. 'I couldn't even admit to myself what was waiting for me back in Scotland, let alone tell you.'

'It must have changed things for you when you arrived home,' Bea ventured.

'Home,' John repeated, shaking his head. 'It didn't feel like home. It felt like prison at times. Margaret and I had always been friends, but the passion that you and I...' He hesitated. 'No, that's not fair. We continued as friends, raised the kids. Moira lives locally too. They're great kids.'

'I met Moira today,' she reminded him.

'Of course. Of course you did.' He patted the back of her hand. 'You broke my heart, Beatrice, clean broke it in two.'

'And you mine.'

'I'm a medical man, but I can tell you that it never quite heals.' He smiled at her.

Bea nodded. This, too, she knew to be true. 'I have danced with you a thousand times in my dreams. The thump, thump of our feet on the deck. You gave me your scarf...'

'I did.'

'I made it into a pillow and have it next to my cheek every night.'

'You smelt of roses.'

'It was rosewater. I borrowed it.'

'I can't smell their scent without feeling melancholy.'

'My hand seemed to fit inside yours, as if that was where it was meant to rest.'

'I've imagined it, lying there on so many cold nights.' He looked at her.

'And then the day you left...' Quite unexpectedly the breath caught in her throat and a wave of sadness engulfed her. Her tears sprang and her face crumpled. To her horror, John matched her tear for tear. Sliding off his chair, he knelt on the floor with his head on her lap and the two of them sobbed.

Bea ran her fingers through his hair and let her palm stroke his whiskered cheeks. 'John, my John! I raised your baby the best I could. I was so frightened, so alone.' She righted his head until he was looking up at her, reminding her of the twenty-three-year-old man who had left her at sunrise. 'He was a lovely child and he's a good man.'

'I knew it! I knew he was mine!' John's composure dissolved again. 'What did your parents say? They were so upright, judgemental. God, I can't imagine how they took the news.'

'They told me to leave Byron Bay, and so I did. I haven't seen them since, or Diane.'

'Oh, dear God!' He gripped her clothing and buried his face in her shirt. 'I knew he was my son. I saw him and I knew! It took all of my strength not to call out, to run to you! But I knew I couldn't. It wouldn't have been fair.'

'None of this is fair,' she murmured. 'I named him Wyatt and he looks just like his dad.'

'Wyatt! Does... does he know about me?' he croaked.

'No. Not yet. But he will. I couldn't risk telling him and him contacting you; it might have ruined your life. I didn't know your circumstances, didn't know about Margaret.'

'Oh, dear God!' John said again.

The two sat slumped together in silence for many minutes, digesting the truth, both replaying what had come next.

Eventually John straightened and stood in front of the fireplace. 'I can't live with secrets any more, Beatrice. Who knows what lies around the corner for us? But I can't live under the shadow of truths untold.'

Bea stood and slipped into his arms. She closed her eyes and let him hold her in the warm firelight of the Christmas Café. She might have been thousands of miles from where she lived, but she was home.

It was an hour later that the stairs above them creaked. Bea and John disentangled themselves and stood a respectable couple of feet apart, as nervous as teens. Bea was considering how to act when Flora's voice broke the silence.

'Shit! Wow!' She stared at them both from the doorway.

'This is Flora, my granddaughter.' Bea smiled at her beautiful toffee-haired girl. 'Your granddaughter too,' she said hesitantly, feeling the blush spread from her neck, suddenly conscious that Flora was part of John's story too; his flesh, his blood.

John nodded at her. 'Hello there, Flora.' He spoke her name with the lilting Scottish fluidity that it deserved.

Bea wondered if he'd noted Flora's colouring; if, like her, he'd seen similarities between Flora and his grandson, Callum.

'So, what have I missed?' Flora turned to her gran.

Bea laughed. 'Oh, Flora, too much to fill you in on right now!'

Alex came down the stairs. 'I'd tell her everything if I were you, Dad. She has a mean right hook.' He winked and strode over to his dad, who gripped him in a hug.

As Bea and Flora made their way back to their hotel, Bea was still feeling shaky, but Flora was very excited.

'He's very handsome close up!'

'Yes, he is.' Bea had to agree.

'Are you okay, Bea?' She linked arms with her gran.

'I think so.'

'I just met my grandpa!' Flora squealed.

'Yes, you did.' Bea grinned.

Flora came to a standstill in the street. 'Peter... Peter will always be my pappy, always,' she said, not wanting to offend her gran or tarnish the memory of her grandpa; her grandpa who had once given her her very own cigar.

'I know that, darling, and he knew it too. He loved you very much.'

Flora stared at her gran. 'You look like you've seen a ghost!'

'Not a ghost.' She swallowed. 'I've lived with a ghost for

the last thirty-odd years. This was a living, breathing man!' She grabbed her granddaughter and hugged her tight. 'I can't believe it! My John! I saw my John!'

'I'm happy for you, Bea.'

'Promise me, Flora, that when you're older you won't settle for a man that doesn't make you feel like your heart might burst with joy! I was so lucky to have John's love when I was young, and then Peter, my lovely husband, your lovely pappy, to care for me for most of my life. I was blessed. I want you to have that. Promise me you will never settle for less than you deserve.'

Flora nodded against her gran's shoulder and closed her eyes. 'I promise.'

Bea opened one eye and sat up straight in the bed. She took in the sash windows, printed wallpaper and tartan carpet and was beyond relieved to discover that she hadn't dreamt it – she was here in Edinburgh and last night she had sat with her hand inside John's! Like an excited teen the night before the prom, Bea screwed her eyes tightly shut, wriggled down the bed and with her muscles tense and fists clenched, she beat her heels on the mattress.

'What are you doing?' Flora raised her tousled head from the pillow.

'What am I doing?' Bea sat up and flung the covers back. 'I am living! I am feeling! And I am for the first time in a long time looking forward to my future!' She spun out of the bed, swirling and whirling like a dancer as she bumped into furniture and walls with her arms held high.

'You've gone nuts,' Flora concluded. She dropped her head back onto the pillow, pulled the sheet over her face and left her gran to go nuts alone while she caught up on some sleep.

Bea danced into the bathroom, slipped out of her cotton pyjamas and stepped into the deluge of water. Closing her eyes, she faced the showerhead, letting the warm stream run over her face and neck. She lathered her hair and soaped her body, humming as her thoughts wandered and her stomach churned with pure excitement.

Standing in front of the large mirror, she reached for the towel and stared at her body. It was something she rarely did, too busy rushing from shower to work or shower to bed. But today was different; she took the time, tried to imagine seeing her naked form from a stranger's perspective. Having been married for so long, she'd become very used to Peter's body and he to hers. Familiarity had covered them like a comfortable blanket and she'd rarely thought about how he perceived her physically. They were at ease in their nudity, not flaunting or courting it, but unconcerned about letting their dressing gowns slip, relaxed about cleaning their teeth while the other one dripped in the shower, neither of them blinking when holding the towel as the other slipped into their bathers. Passion had been replaced by friendship, desire by companionship and this, with the mutual respect they had always had for each other, had been the recipe for a lovely, loving life.

Second Chance Cafe

What Bea felt today, however, was different. Standing in close proximity to John the night before, she had been stunned to experience a surge of sexual energy she had all but forgotten was possible. It was as if smoking embers had been fanned back to life. They might have a combined age of one hundred and eleven, but this apparently was no barrier to the flames of longing that flared inside her. She pictured her body the last time it had been revealed to John, replaying that night as she always did, as though it were a movie, watching her young self from afar. This time, as she remembered their last cherished hours together, she ignored the emotion of it and concentrated on looking at her form. Her legs had been slender, her thighs and calves curved and well defined; her legs were straighter now, the knees more prominent, the skin a little loose. Her stomach, once milky white and flat, was now pouched with skin that was pulled with silvery stretch marks and at least one size too big. Her arms, though still muscly, had a slight wobble to them that no amount of walking could cure.

She had the body of a woman in her fifties – a great body, but much altered from the one John had once held against him in the dark of night. She felt a shiver of something like fear, but it was tempered by a particular kind of peace, resignation. She was a woman who had lived, loved and survived; that in itself made her beautiful. Bea thought back to her discussion with Kim. *'There isn't a switch that gets flicked at forty-seven that stops you thinking about, indulging in or desiring sex!'* She laughed at her reflection. 'You know what, Bea, if the best you get is doing crosswords and growing tomatoes with him by your side, there are worse ways to spend a life!'

'Who are you talking to do?' Flora called from the bedroom.

'Myself!' Bea answered.

'I knew you'd gone nuts! You'll be talking to your cats next, like Miss McKay!'

'Tell you what, Flora, if this is what being nuts feels like, long may it continue!'

Half an hour later, the two of them were sitting down to breakfast in the now familiar surroundings of The Balmoral's restaurant. Flora leant back in her chair as their friendly waitress brought them fresh orange juice and pots of tea.

'Are you going to get John a Christmas present?'

'I hadn't really given it any thought. What do you think he'd like? Money for Uggs?' Bea winked.

'Doubt it!' Flora scoffed. 'Old men don't really wear Uggs.'

'I've told you already, he is not old!' Bea raised her voice playfully.

'Not to you, maybe!' Flora countered, hesitating while she phrased her next question. 'Aren't you worried that you won't get on?'

Bea paused from pouring her tea and looked at her granddaughter. It was certainly a consideration. Had she romanticised their liaison so much over the years, applying a tragic *Romeo and Juliet*-style 'love denied' scenario that had clouded her view and skewed her memories? It was possible. But the John that had greeted her last night, who had held her hand across the table and wept as he recalled seeing his son for the first time... 'Not really, Flora. I mean, it's true, we don't really know each other, not properly, but I think we have a great foundation to build on.'

Flora pondered this as she chewed her toast. 'But what do you think you have in common? What interests do you share?' She thought about how she and Marcus both loved the sea, and how they both hated cheese.

Bea laughed. 'We share a child!'

'Good point!' Flora studied her gran. 'You look so happy.'

'I feel it.'

'Can I ask you something else?'

'Go for it.' Bea braced herself, knowing that Flora's questions could be blunt, offensive, random, or all three.

'How's it going to work? I mean, it's good you've found each other, but you live in Sydney and he lives in Edinburgh.'

'Truthfully, love? I haven't a clue. There's a lot of water needs to flow under the bridge before we start discussing that.'

'I know that, Bea, but will it be Sydney Harbour Bridge or the Forth Road Bridge? That's the question!'

'I don't know, love.'

'Can I ask you one last thing?'

'Sure.'

'What will happen if you properly meet Moira and she hates you, or when Dad finds out about John and meets him and hates him? I suppose what I'm saying is, what would you both do if all of your kids hated you both?'

Bea stared at her granddaughter. 'Eat your toast, Flora,' she said.

Sixteen

Bea settled back in her plane seat. Flora, like most of their fellow travellers, was sound asleep on this the final leg of their journey. She glanced at the Topping bag that protruded from the pouch of the seat in front of her, smiling as she recalled their wonderful day at St Andrews.

'Are you sure there's room for me in this?' John had sighed as Bea pulled up in the little red bauble.

'You'd be surprised, it's very roomy inside!' Bea said encouragingly.

'It's like the Tardis!' Flora added for good measure.

'Ah, well, I'm in good hands then – there's been a few Scottish Doctor Whos. Sylvester McCoy, David Tennant, Peter Capaldi.'

'Are you a Whovian?' Flora was impressed.

'Not really, I just do a lot of crosswords.'

'So do you, Bea, so that's one thing you have in common!' She smiled as her gran narrowed her eyes at her over the roof of the little Fiat.

In the end the trio had decided to switch to John's car, a comfy Land Rover whose extra ground clearance meant that Bea and Flora had the best view of the Scottish coast and countryside on the drive to St Andrews, John's old university town. As they left the Edinburgh suburbs, making their way along the A90 towards Queensferry, Bea repeatedly glanced to her right as if to make sure it really was John driving her on this chilly winter's day.

'And here we go, over the Forth Road Bridge!' John announced as they drove onto the high suspension bridge that spanned the Firth of Forth.

Flora ducked down, craning her neck to look up through the windows at the tall steel towers that seemed to reach up to the grey skies above. 'It's beautiful!'

'It is. I have a passion for bridges.' John spoke over his shoulder.

'Have you been over the Sydney Harbour Bridge?' Flora asked from the back seat.

'No. I'd like to though.' John glanced briefly at Bea.

'And which of those two bridges do you think would have the most water flowing under it?' Flora asked innocently.

'Goodness me, Flora, that's a bit scientific. I shall have to get back to you on that one.' He laughed.

Bea turned and shot her granddaughter a look.

St Andrews was beautiful. Snow was heaped on the rooftops and against the high kerbs of the well-kept streets, and the clusters of Georgian-fronted shops all had Christmas displays in their windows. Dappled panes of glass with frosting in the corners and twinkling lights around the edges gave the town a magical feel, and heather and tartan wreaths graced the front doors of many stone cottages. The famous Links golf course of the Royal and Ancient, the home of golf, looked immaculate even in the middle of winter, and the foaming white waves of the North Sea provided the perfect backdrop to the east. The whole place had the feel of a film set.

John guided the two of them around the ruins of St Andrews Cathedral and St Rule's tower and Bea drank in his knowledge, thrilled that he wanted to share this special place with them. He was proud to show them the impressive St Salvator's Hall, where he had lived for a couple of years before heading off to the other side of the world, where he would meet a girl...

The three made their way to Greyfriars Garden specifically to potter in Topping Books. It offered a warm welcome with its lingering aroma of fresh coffee, its blazing fire and of course books aplenty. Bea and Flora got lost among the aisles, mesmerised by the ornate spines and the number of topics covered. They were happiest of all among the cookery books, running their fingers over mouthwatering photographs of local dishes like Arbroath fisherman's soup with cheddar bannocks, and Hebridean spring lamb with crushed potatoes.

'What do you think, Flora? Would Mr Giraldi go for Arbroath fisherman's soup?'

'Well, not for breakfast, but yes, sure he would. He'd moan about it, but then he'd love it!'

Bea laughed at this accurate assessment of her lovely friend, wishing him well across the miles.

While John continued to browse the shelves, Bea and Flora popped out to explore the nearby shops. Returning half an hour later, Bea spied John at the counter, handing over his credit card and tucking a neatly wrapped book under his arm. He saw her out of the corner of his eye and his face broke into a smile. As she walked towards him, he watched her as if she was the only person in the shop, as if the other customers didn't exist and it was just the two of them. *I know you...*

Bea stood next to him as the transaction was completed. The girl behind the counter pulled John's card from the machine and thrust it towards Bea. 'Oh! Sorry, sir, I was just about to give your card to your wife!' She laughed and placed it in John's palm.

Bea couldn't help the tears that gathered, overwhelmed at being there with him, saddened by the thought of all the years that had slipped by without him.

John took her hand. 'Come on, Beatrice, there's no reason to be sad. Please don't cry.'

She buried her face in the sleeve of his coat and inhaled the glorious scent of him.

The trio slowly made their way back to the car.

'What's that you've got?' John pointed at the package under Bea's arm, which was wrapped in newspaper.

'Oh, I couldn't resist! It's a sampler I found in a glorious store called Rummage, just my kind of thing. I think it's beautiful!' Bea peeled the layers of newspaper from the picture.

John pulled a face as she turned it to face him. 'I think this is one of those times when the phrase "beauty is in the eye of the beholder" might apply! It's a little dusty!' He grimaced, wrinkling his nose and wiping his fingers on his scarf.

'Yes,' Bea agreed, 'but you have to look beyond the dust. Look at the original wooden frame. And how each word is perfectly embroidered in tiny cross-stitch. It must have taken forever! It's dated 1860 and it has a signature. Look!' She pointed to the bottom right-hand corner. 'It was done by Miss E. H. Arbuckle. I wonder who she was, what she did and where she lived?'

'I'm hoping she didn't sit in night after night making too many more of these!' John laughed and Flora chuckled too. 'Poor Miss E. H. Arbuckle, sitting in her room stitching pictures that no one in their right mind would hang in their hoose!' John boomed.

'I shall happily hang it in mine!' Bea shot back.

'Well, that tells us all we need to know, eh, Flora?' John winked at her.

Bea smiled at the thought of the sampler, now safely tucked inside her suitcase in the hold. She closed her eyes and prepared for sleep to take her over. Her thoughts drifted to their parting, which hadn't been nearly as painful as she'd anticipated. Having lived without him for all this time, wondering if he were alive and whether she would ever see him again, she was used to longing for him.

Knowing she would see him within the next few months, as they'd agreed, felt like no hardship by comparison. What was a few months?

John had smiled with relief at the prospect of finally being able to write to her from his heart without using Alex as his shield. 'I shall think of you every day and every night.' He had held her close and kissed her forehead.

'You will?' She'd beamed.

John had nodded. 'Just like I always have.'

Bea felt the flutter of joy in her stomach; the connection she had felt all these years was real. With a smile on her face, she tucked her green pillow under her cheek and fell into a deep sleep.

'You look different to how you did when we left,' Flora noted as Bea threw her rucksack over her shoulder and placed her sunglasses on her head. Peter used to call them the most expensive hairband in Sydney.

'I feel different,' Bea confirmed.

The two collected their baggage from the carousel at Kingsford-Smith Airport and stepped out into the blistering heat of the Australian midday sun.

'God it's hot!' Bea shook the front of her tunic.

'It's really hot!' Flora said, and they both laughed uncontrollably.

Wyatt waved from the Holden and flashed his lights. Bea walked towards her son as he popped the hatch and lifted her heavy bag.

'How was Bali?' she asked.

'Expensive and very hot,' Wyatt said. This again sent the two into fits of giggles. He raised his eyebrows as if he didn't get the joke, convinced nothing could be that funny.

'Daddy!' Flora flung her arms around her dad's trunk and hugged him tight.

Bea watched the smile spread across his face.

'Welcome home, Flora. Ready for Christmas?'

Flora nodded. 'I missed you, Dad. And Mum. And I'm sorry.' She let her tears tumble.

Wyatt held her close and smiled into her hair. 'It's a brand-new year soon. A good time for a new start, don't you think?'

'Yes I do. And I'll be fourteen! Can I get my ears pierced?' She grinned.

'We'll see.' Wyatt shook his head. They both knew a 'we'll see' was practically a yes.

'Do you want to come straight out to Manly, Mum, or do you need to go home first, unpack and then I'll collect you tomorrow?'

'Oh. Well, yes, collecting me tomorrow would be fine. Thank you, love. I'd like to see everyone at the Kitchen before we close for a few days.'

'No worries.' Wyatt gave a small smile.

'She's here! She's here!' Kim yelled as the Holden pulled up on Reservoir Street. Kim and Tait were hovering on the kerb, Kim jumping up and down and Tait beaming.

'Looks like you were missed.' Flora smiled at her gran. 'See you tomorrow.'

'You betcha.' Bea blew Flora a kiss, having made her promise on the plane home to let her tell Wyatt the news herself.

Her granddaughter's words of wisdom were still fresh in her mind. 'You need to tell Dad everything – about how you feel, about your life, about John, Alex, everything! Talk to him!'

It had taken Bea a second to formulate her reply. 'Yes, you're right, Flora, but it's tricky to know where or how to start. As it always is when things have been left unsaid for so long. Any topic carries a much bigger burden when it's been buried.'

'So dig it up, unbury it!' Flora had rolled her eyes, exasperated.

Bea chuckled at the recollection. 'Thanks for dropping me back, Wyatt.'

'No worries.' He smiled, looking so much like John it made her gulp.

Kim rushed forward. 'How was Mr McKay? Did he smell of cat pee and give you gifts that he'd knitted from their fur?'

'No, Kim! In fact quite the opposite. The charming Alex is suave, gorgeous, funny and gay.'

'See! I was right, I knew it was a sausage club!' Kim quipped.

Bea laughed. 'He's a lovely man and I'm his new best friend.'

'Do you know, I thought you had a bit of a glow about you!' Tait winked. 'Anything you want to share?'

'Oh, Tait, you'd be surprised!' Bea smiled at him. 'How have you guys been?'

'We've been busy, haven't we, Kimmy?'

'Yes we have. Busy, but in control. The books are up to date, orders are in, decks clear and looking forward to the New Year!' Kim nodded assertively.

'Well great, I should go away more often.' Bea was struck by Kim's polished delivery.

'Don't do that, Bea, I mean we coped, but we missed you!' Tait smiled as he hoisted his rucksack onto his back. Kim bent forward and whispered into her boss's ear, 'I did it Bea; I remembered that life is for the brave and I am chasing it! I'm a little way off grabbing it, but I'll get there.' She smiled.

'Good for you, darling girl!' Bea clapped. 'Mr Giraldi okay?'

'Yep. Complained that his muesli and honey wasn't up to scratch in your absence, but had it every day anyway, just to confirm the fact.' Tait sighed.

Bea laughed. 'Bless him! Look, you guys get yourselves off home and I'll see you both in a week.' She reached up and hugged first Kim and then Tait. 'Thank you both. I don't know what I would do without you. Your pressies are in your bank accounts.' Bea had, as ever, given them an over-generous bonus.

'You beauty, Bea!' Tait beamed.

Kim looked genuinely touched. 'Thank you.' She placed her arms around her boss's neck.

'I am so proud of you, Kim,' Bea whispered as she hugged her in return.

Bea waved them off in opposite directions and looked around her; it was great to be home. She dumped her bag and rummaged in the storeroom until she found a hammer and a nail. On an empty section of wall she hung the dusty sampler from St Andrews. She read the words that made her smile and wondered what Miss E. H. Arbuckle would have thought if she'd known that her beautiful work and beautiful message, embroidered over a hundred and fifty years ago, would end up in a café in Surry Hills, on the other side of the world.

Seventeen

'Who wants the last of the chocolate mousse?' Sarah held the bowl up high above the deck, like an auctioneer with one final lot. 'Come on, it's Christmas Day and this is Bea's world famous chocolate mousse!'

Bea noted the loving expression on Wyatt's face as he looked at his wife. They were clearly very happy together and Bea wondered why it had taken her so long to accept that simple fact. Could she have done more to welcome Sarah into their tiny family unit over the years? Made more effort to put her at her ease? She didn't like the answer that came back to her. For the first time she considered the part she'd played in distancing herself from her son and his wife. She'd kept so much from Wyatt; was it so surprising that communication was difficult?

'Bea, can I tempt you?' Sarah lifted the bowl higher, as if that might help sell it.

'I couldn't. I'm stuffed.' Bea smiled. 'The food was wonderful, Sarah. Thank you.'

'Oh, any time!' She smiled back. 'What about you, Flora? You've hardly eaten a thing.'

Flora had been quiet all day. Bea wondered if it was jet lag catching up with her.

'I'm good, Mum, but it was lovely.'

'Well, I don't know about anyone else, but I fancy a stroll on the prom.' Wyatt stood up from the table on their vast deck and looked out towards the ocean.

'Actually, Wyatt, I'll come with you.'

'Oh.' Wyatt glanced at his wife. Evidently, being saddled with his mother as he tried to clear his head and work off his Christmas lunch hadn't been part of the plan. 'Sure.' He gave a brief smile.

Flora gave her gran a secret thumbs-up.

Mother and son made their way from the house and on to the promenade, walking in silence side by side, slowing only to wave at friends and neighbours, wishing them a Merry Christmas and making a fuss of little ones trying out their new scooters and trikes along the walkway.

'Sarah's happy you're here, Mum. I know it means the world to her how you've talked Flora round. Things seem better now she's back. You were right, time away did her good.'

'I'm glad Sarah's pleased. I'd like to get closer to her too, like I did with Flora. It was lovely spending time with her in Scotland. Really lovely.' Bea began the conversation that she hoped would help dismantle the wall between them.

'She's a good kid.' He nodded out to sea.

'She really is. And you were quite right, this crowd she's got in with sounds like a motley bunch. But Flora's smart;

you have to trust her to do the right thing. She'll figure out what's what – she's nearly worked it out already. Although I think the soft spot she carries for Marcus might be a bit harder to tackle.'

'Marcus who she punched?' Wyatt was trying to keep up.

'Yep. The very same.'

'Blimey, that's a new one. I can only imagine what Sarah would have done if that had been my opener!' He grinned.

Bea noted how his shoulders dropped, losing their tension, as if he had expected a battle with her about the right way forward for Flora. 'I expect you just want her to find someone who makes her happy?'

Wyatt nodded. 'I do.'

'Sarah makes you happy, doesn't she?'

Wyatt looked at his mother. 'Yes. She always has.'

'I know. And that's all we ever really want for our kids.' Bea paused. 'Flora mentioned that you and Sarah argue about me sometimes...'

Wyatt glanced at her over his shoulder. 'We do.'

'What about, exactly?'

Wyatt was silent.

'I only ask because if I know what it is I'm doing that causes an issue, then I can try and put it right.'

'Why now?' he asked levelly.

Bea shrugged, a gesture she'd picked up from her granddaughter. 'Because it's never too late to put things right until it is.'

Wyatt sighed. 'Sarah thinks you don't like her.'

'That's not the case! I do like her.'

'Well, it feels like that to her, so it is the case!' he countered. 'She's always felt that you were in some way disappointed at my choice.'

Bea looked at her feet, feeling the uncomfortable grains of truth swirl then settle in her gut.

Wyatt continued. 'I've told her a million times that it's irrelevant what you or anyone else feels or doesn't feel. It's what she and I feel that counts, and we are strong and happy and if no one else wants to be a part of that, it's fine.'

'I do want to be a part of it, I always have.' Bea gulped down the tears that threatened.

'I don't think you even realise what you do half the time, how quickly you dismiss her.' He sighed.

'Dismiss her how?' Bea's voice was reedy, tense.

Wyatt slapped at his thigh as he tried to think of an example. 'I don't know... Take Christmas, for example. She always asks if there's anything in particular she can get you as a gift, she agonises over it, and you always say the same thing: "Good God, no! I've got far too much stuff." You deny her the pleasure of giving you a present every year. It just keeps her a little bit at arm's length.'

Bea was dumbfounded. 'I thought I was saving her the bother – I don't need presents!'

'I've told her not to chase it, but she does. She desperately wants your approval, hankers after crumbs of a compliment. Christ, she even tries to make your bloody chocolate mousse! I hate seeing her that way – it's so difficult for her, but she's determined to do the right thing, always puts everyone else first, that's her nature. And when you come over, she tends to drink a bit more than she should because she's nervous. I watch you eyeing her glass, but what you don't see is her throwing up with nerves before you arrive.'

'I had no idea.' Bea felt ashamed. She stared out at the horizon. 'I wish we had a bloody translator.'

'A what?'

'Doesn't matter. The point is, I want to fix it, Wyatt. I do.'

Wyatt only nodded. She knew him well enough to know that words meant little; it would be her actions that would make the difference.

'Did Flora tell you much about our trip?' Bea was trying to find a way to start the conversation she had been dreading for longer than she cared to remember.

'She said it was cold!' He smiled briefly, flashing his even, white teeth. 'Very cold! In fact that seemed to be her overriding impression.'

'We had quite an adventure.'

'Oh yeah? See the Loch Ness monster?' he asked, still walking slightly ahead, not looking at his mother.

'No, better than that.'

Wyatt picked up the pace. He wanted to walk in silence, clear his head, as was his habit.

'Wyatt, will you stand still for just a bloody second!' Bea spoke a little louder and sharper than she had intended.

Wyatt glanced round to see if anyone had heard, then stood by her side and looked out to sea. Surfers bobbed on the white-crested swells, wearing wetsuits and Santa hats, and sea diamonds twinkled in the distance.

Bea pinched her nose, conscious of the noise of her bangles as they rattled on her wrist. 'Come on, let's go down to the water.' Slipping out of her sandals, she walked back to the wide, shallow steps and trod them carefully until she felt the hot, soft sand underneath her toes.

Wyatt followed.

'When you were little, the water was like a magnet for you. Didn't matter what you were wearing or where we were heading, if you saw it, you'd run full tilt until you were submerged. I'd shout at you in the sternest voice I could muster: "Don't you dare go in that water!" Like it made any difference.'

Wyatt gave a small sniff of laughter, remembering doing exactly that.

'Used to frighten me half to death, but you were a natural, a little merman. I remember one day arriving at school with you all soggy. I'd done my best to dry you off, but you were sopping. Your teacher saw the funny side. You sat in the classroom in your pants until your shorts dried out.' Bea smiled at the happy, happy memories.

The two picked their way through the family groups and clusters of mates sipping cold tinnies and enjoying the day. Bea found a spot on the shoreline, set her bag down and plonked herself on the sand. Wyatt lowered himself next to her and sat with his knees raised and his elbows resting on his legs. A group of eight girls, all wearing bikinis, Santa hats and white beards, linked arms in the shallows for a group photo, the two on the end holding up bottles of champagne for the camera.

There were a few moments of silence while both Bea and Wyatt let the hypnotic rhythm of the ocean calm their emotions. The relentless roll of the white foam provided the perfect backdrop for Bea to share her news. She bit her lip and took a deep breath before delivering the words clearly and succinctly.

'I saw your dad.'

Wyatt turned his head and shoulders to face his mother and stared unblinkingly at her. 'You what? Sorry?'

Bea took another deep breath. 'I saw your dad,' she repeated, holding his gaze.

It was a while before he spoke. 'Is this some kind of a joke?' he asked.

Bea shook her head. 'No.'

Wyatt slumped forwards slightly, so that his legs were flat on the sand, his head bowed. A couple ran past them into the surf, heading out to sea hand in hand, splashing and laughing as they went. Wyatt waited for them to pass, trying to digest Bea's words.

'You saw my dad?'

'Yes.'

'You know who he is?' His tone was calm.

'Yes. I've always known,' she whispered.

'And you never said? You... you never thought it might be important?' Less calm now, he began inadvertently grinding his teeth.

'I didn't know what to do. I didn't know when would be the right time, and then the longer we didn't discuss it, the harder it became.'

'Holy shit.' Wyatt placed his hand on his chest. The two were silent for some seconds, both wondering how to proceed. 'Have you always been in contact with him?'

'No. No contact. I knew nothing about his life until this trip. When we met up, it was totally out of the blue. I'll tell you all about it.'

'I don't believe it!' Wyatt said. 'I feel quite numb. I feel sick.'

'I know it's a lot to take in.'

'*A lot to take in?* That's an understatement,' he snapped.

'I've never known what to do for the best. I wanted you and Peter to be close and I thought—'

'No, Mum, you didn't think!' Wyatt's voice went up an octave. 'You tried so hard to push Peter and me into a relationship, to make things easier for you, assuage your guilt, that we never had a chance to get close!'

'What are you talking about?' Bea stared at him. 'I only ever wanted what was right for you. Every decision I ever made was about what was right for you! Peter gave you a good life, he paid for your school—'

'Yes. Yes, he did. He was a good man. But you were like a gatekeeper, watching us all the time. It felt like an experiment. I didn't know how to play happy families, not with you over-analysing our every move. You should have just—'

'I should have just what?' Bea heard the crack in her voice.

'You should have just left us to get on with it. You didn't have to constantly coax, referee, make suggestions. You made it impossible for us to get to know each other; you made me feel like a guest when he was around. We were always on edge, everything going via you, afraid that we might not be living up to your dream.' Wyatt lifted his sunnies and wiped the sweat from his eyes.

Bea felt winded. 'I didn't know.'

Wyatt poked at the sand with his finger. 'I can't believe you knew who my dad was. I figured if you did, you would have told me. I've always felt like I had this big missing part – it's not like I had any contact with your family, and the other half of me was a complete mystery! And all this time—'

'It wasn't that straightforward.'

'Wasn't it? Why not? How could you not have wanted to put my mind at rest, stop the thoughts I had night after night, stop me feeling so crap and wondering where I came from, who he might be? And all the time you knew!'

'What did you think, Wyatt? That your dad could have been one of many?' She felt her lip tremble.

'Honestly? Yes! That crossed my mind, along with a million other scenarios, all just as unsavoury.'

'Christ, no wonder you judge me so harshly!'

'Who is he, Mum?' Wyatt removed his sunglasses and looked his mother in the eye. 'Who is he?'

'His name is John Brodie,' Bea whispered. 'A doctor. He's from Edinburgh and you look just like him.' Her tears broke their banks as she bowed her head and quietly cried, swiping at her eyes in embarrassment.

Wyatt placed his hands on his thighs and gulped deep intakes of air, like an athlete in preparation. 'Oh God! I don't believe it. Edinburgh! Did Flora meet him?'

Bea nodded. 'Yes.'

'Jesus H. Christ! Flora met him?'

'Yes. He's a wonderful man. We fell in love. Properly in love, but he was married and had to go home. As you know, I was very young. He truly broke my heart,' Bea stuttered through her tears, 'and I broke his. He never knew about you, I never told him and I didn't know he knew, not until this trip. I hadn't planned on meeting him, but I did. And honestly, Wyatt, it was as if time had stood still. The way I feel about him...' She shook her head.

'Did Peter know about him?'

'Yes.' Bea nodded. 'Peter knew everything. We had no secrets. He loved me regardless, and for that I will always be more than grateful.'

'Shit.' Wyatt rubbed at his chin and neck as if that might help his concentration. 'I don't know what to say.'

'I've only ever done what I thought was best for you, Wyatt. I need you to know that.'

'I do know that.'

This admission caused Bea's tears to fall again.

'Is he a medical doctor?'

'Yes.'

'Is he still married?' The questions were coming thick and fast now.

'No, his wife died about ten years ago.'

'Does he have other kids?'

Bea paused. 'Yes. You have a half-sister, Moira, and a half-brother, Xander; they are a couple of years older than you, twins.'

'Holy shit!' Wyatt sat back with his hands clasped behind his head and his elbows sticking out like wings. 'Do they know about me?' he asked, wide-eyed, looking so much like the child she had adored.

'They do. John's spoken to them. Xander has known for a while, Moira more recently. I found out that John came to Australia about nine years ago. He saw us, Peter and me, from afar, and he watched you with Flora.'

'Jesus Christ! That is insane!' Wyatt was finding it very hard to take in. 'Why didn't he speak to me? Why did he come all this way and not speak to me?'

'The same reason I didn't pursue him – he didn't want to create a big upset and he didn't know how much you knew or didn't know.'

'I knew very little, as it turns out,' he sniped, bending forward again as if he'd been punched.

'He asked me to give you this.' Bea reached into her

handbag and pulled out a paper bag with the word 'Topping' written on it.

Wyatt carefully took the gift into his hands and opened the bag, removing a slender book. '*The Collected Poems of Rudyard Kipling*,' he read out loud, then looked at her quizzically. 'Kipling was one of Peter's favourite authors...'

'Yes, he was,' Bea said. 'And one of John's too, as it happens. That's why I knew so many of the poems off by heart.'

Wyatt ran his fingers gently over the cover as though it was a precious object. He carefully opened the front jacket. Tucked inside it was a postcard showing the tumbledown ruins of St Andrews Cathedral.

'That's where he went to university – St Andrews,' Bea said, relieved that at last she could start filling in some of the blanks.

Wyatt turned the card over and saw for the first time the spidery handwriting of his father, in dark blue ink. He coughed and read the words aloud, oblivious to the surfies and swimmers frolicking in the Christmas Day sun.

'If you can wait and not be tired by waiting...
If you can lose, and start again at your beginnings...
Yours is the Earth and everything that's in it,
And – which is more – you'll be a man, my son.
Very best wishes, John Wyatt Brodie.'

Wyatt sniffed up his emotion and pushed his sunglasses firmly up his nose. 'You named me after him?'

'Yes.'

Second Chance Cafe

The two of them sat staring out to sea, trying to come to terms with the shift in their world.

'What do we do now, Mum?' Wyatt asked, sounding a little lost.

Bea stood up and wiped the sand from her bottom, straightened her tunic and pulled her shoulders back. Wyatt did likewise, clutching his Christmas present from his dad.

'We do what Peter taught us,' she said through her tears. 'We remember that life is for the brave and we make the bloody best of it – this is our one time around the block!'

Wyatt held her close, then kept his arm firmly around her shoulders as they strolled back to the house.

'Nice walk?' Sarah handed her mother-in-law a glass of chilled white wine as she stepped onto the deck.

'The best. And actually, Sarah, I wanted to give you your Christmas present.'

Sarah looked from her mother-in-law to her husband. 'But you already have – the spa voucher, that's very generous! I'll have a lovely day.'

'I'll come with you, Mum!' Flora generously offered. 'I can wear my new Uggs!'

'And take your new earplugs.' Bea winked as she stood and removed her bangles one by one. Carefully reading each inscription, she placed some in a small pile, before returning the other half to her arm. She picked up the first one from the stack and read the inside, 'To celebrate Wyatt's twenty-first! Milestone reached!' before handing it to Sarah.

And then another 'Your boy's wedding day! Let the bells ring out!' and so on, until Sarah was in receipt of six silver bracelets, each marked with a sentiment, a reminder of a significant event throughout her husband's life.

'I want you to have these, Sarah.'

'But... What? Why?' Sarah placed her hand on her chest. 'You love your bangles, Bea, they are part of you!'

'I do love them, but you are my daughter, we share this history and it's right that you should have some of them. I would get a lot of pleasure from seeing you wear them.' Bea handed the bundle to Sarah, who was clearly overcome.

'I don't know what to say!' Sarah blushed as her eyes brimmed with tears. 'I'm so touched!' She grinned at her husband. 'Look, Wyatt! Your mum gave me some of her bangles!' She held out her arm, jangling the bracelets on her wrist.

'So I see.' He smiled.

Epilogue

Bea opened one eye and smiled as she slipped from the bed. It was Christmas Day and for the first time in a couple of years she wasn't dreading it. In fact, quite the opposite. She felt a frisson of excitement as nerves made her stomach swirl. She scooped up her vintage silk kimono dressing gown from the end of her bed and tiptoed barefoot across the hallway to the kitchen.

The only sounds came from the birds chirping in the trees and the creak of the floorboards as she padded across them. She shrugged on her dressing gown, stretched, and pulled her hair into a ponytail.

'Ooh, the chocolate mousse!' she whispered as she filled the kettle, reminding herself to remove the monster cream creation from the freezer.

Bea's heart leapt with happiness. She cricked her neck to the left and right and smiled. She would be fifty-five soon. *Goodness me, where has all that time gone?* If time had taught her one thing, it was that the world felt better when she didn't carry regret and recrimination in her heart. It had been a momentous twelve months. She had given a lot of thought to her parents' behaviour and had tried to walk in their shoes, imagining their very real pain and disappointment when things hadn't turned out for their little girl in the way they had planned. It wasn't that she condoned their behaviour, far from it, but she had allowed herself to understand it. They were long dead now, she was sure, and she had finally been able to forgive them. Letting go of the hard nut of blame that had sat in her throat so long had lightened her spirit to a degree she couldn't have imagined. She felt healed.

Bea smiled as she recalled the extraordinary events of the previous December, picturing her trip to Scotland and culminating with the stroll with her son on Christmas Day; these events had changed her life forever. She took a deep breath and flicked the switch on the wall. The fairy lights twinkled on the modest Christmas tree in the corner. She touched her fingers to the dainty red and gold tartan bows that sat at the end of each branch. They looked magical.

'What are you doing at this ungodly hour?'

She turned towards the voice behind her and felt her breath catch in her throat; it was as ever a shock and a delight to feel the presence of the person she loved, the man she lived with, who had travelled to the other side of the world and never left, not this time.

'Just thinking how very lucky I am...'

'How lucky we are.'

'Yes.' She beamed. 'How lucky we are.'

John walked forward and pulled her towards him, cradling her head against his chest. 'I feel quite peaceful.'

She nodded against his bare chest. 'Me too. Although I don't know why – I have a million and one things to do!'

'Well, you'll have plenty of help. Want me to wake Flora?'

'No! She and Callum were out till goodness knows when. Let them sleep.'

'She's leading that poor boy astray! She keeps reminding me that she's very nearly fifteen, and God only knows what that means she'll be getting up to! Poor Callum is wide-eyed, not used to the Sydney high-life his cousin leads. He'll be exhausted after a month of this, be glad to get back to Scotland.' John chuckled.

'Ha! He is more than capable of leading himself astray, I can assure you!'

'You're a good gran.' He smiled.

'I try. Anyway, Kim and Tait have prepped nearly everything. I think I'm probably overstating my role – things are actually all under control.'

'Oh good. In that case, you can bring that tea back to bed and we can catch up on the news. Plus I'm struggling with a crossword clue in the local paper.' He took her hand inside his, where it seemed to fit perfectly, and led her towards the bedroom.

'What's the clue?' she asked.

'Copy of Baroque bronze, a famous Sydney Hospital landmark that is believed to bring good luck. Ten letters, ends with an "o".'

'Ah, that's our famous boar, Porcellino.' Bea smiled at Peter's photograph on the wall. He smiled back.

It was mid morning when Bea opened the door to the Reservoir Street Kitchen – or, as it was to be known for one day only, as denoted by the banner painted by Flora and Callum that hung on the wall, 'The Christmas Café!' The place looked amazing. Tait had done a great job of stringing the lights from girder to girder, and the vast tree with its abundance of red and gold tartan bows looked magnificent. The tables had been pushed together to form a large U shape and the white linen cloths were decorated with ornate centrepieces of candles, sprigs of Monterey pine, gold-painted pine cones, nuts and candy canes. Each place was set with an elaborate display of vintage china and a place name.

Bea cast her eyes over the settings. Mr Giraldi was of course sitting with his family: his son Giovanni would be there with his wife and boys, Claudia and Roberto were bringing their two kids, and Berta had travelled up from Melbourne. Tait and his parents were to sit in the centre, with Kim tucked in on Tait's left. Bea's sister Diane, her husband and their daughter Lou were next to Wyatt, Sarah and Flora. For Bea, the joy of having her sister back in her life was incomparable; this would be their first Christmas together in almost forty years. Bea ran her finger over Marcus' name card. Lovely, lovely Marcus, with his great grades and glowing future, who had, despite being on the receiving end of a well-placed right hook a year or so ago, forgiven Little Klitschko and was now well and truly besotted. The confident duo had ditched the unsavoury Lori and her big boobs. Alexander was going to be opposite Flora and she and John were to have Moira and her husband next to them, with Callum on the end.

Tait rushed through the door. 'Happy Christmas, Bea!' He waved as he hung his bag on a hook by the door. 'The place looks awesome!' He placed his hands on his hips and counted. 'How many for lunch now?'

'Twenty-seven.' Bea smiled.

'Just going to see if Kim and Mario need a hand.'

Bea followed him into the kitchen, where every square inch of counter-top was covered in bowls of sauces, platters of seafood, plates of salad, dishes of roasted meats resting under foil and beautiful patisserie that made her mouth water.

'Hey, guys, Merry Christmas! Need a hand with anything?' Tait asked as he gathered his long blond hair into a bun.

'Yes! Get over here and start wrapping these pigs in blankets and then you can whip some cream for the puds.' Kim issued the instructions assertively and blew her fringe from her forehead as she skewered the turkey breast to check on its progress. Bea laughed.

'Anything else, Miss Bossy Pants?' Tait quipped.

Kim looked up. 'I think that'll do for now, but if I think of anything else, I'll let you know.'

'Only me!' Alex called from the front entrance. He marched into the kitchen in his cut-offs and singlet, the ideal outfit for showing off his mahogany tan. 'I know we said no presents, but seeing as you're my best e-penfriend...' He winked and handed Bea a rectangle-shaped gift.

'Oh, Alex! You shouldn't have!' Bea tore at the red-foil wrapping to reveal a set of notelets. 'Thank you, darling. It's just what I wanted.'

'I rather liked you being my penfriend. This will encourage you to write to me more!'

'I will, darling.' She smiled.

'Plus you need to keep me informed about what the old fella is up to.'

'I will, Alex. He misses you, you know. So good to have you here. We need you to come back soon!'

'Why do we need him to come back soon? I've only just settled here and already the kids have followed me out! There's no escape.' John laughed as he stepped into the kitchen.

'You need me here because I make the best Christmas cake this side of Dundee!' Alex winked.

'I have no doubt you do.' John chuckled. 'Who's going to help me with these?' He held up a string of Chinese lanterns that he wanted dotted along the girders.

'Ah, they'll look lovely!' Bea beamed.

Bea looked at the happy faces around the table as John carried in the gigantic golden turkey to resounding applause. He set it down and stood poised with the carving knife in his hand. The wine had been flowing for a good hour and the atmosphere was buzzing.

'I think a wee toast is in order.' John lifted his glass and spoke to the assembled crowd. 'This is a very, very special celebration. Who would have thought, this time last year, that we would all be gathered here, as family, on this day of all days.'

Mr Giraldi sat up straight, beaming with pride at his brood and no doubt thinking of his beloved Angelica.

Bea smiled at her sister Diane, who winked at the woman she thought she had lost for good. 'Don't worry, Di, we've got Bird's Instant Whip with our Christmas pud!' She laughed.

'Banana flavour?' Di asked.

'Of course!' Bea assured her.

Sarah placed her arm around Flora's shoulders, enjoying the sound of the silver bangles that jangled on her wrist. She was so proud of her daughter and very much approved of her choice of boyfriend. Bea winked at her daughter-in-law, making a point of fingering the fabulous scarf at her neck that Sarah had given her for Christmas. She had to admit, Sarah had exceptionally good taste. Moira and Alex smiled at Bea, the woman who had made their dad happy in a way they had never seen before, bringing him much deserved joy in his twilight years.

John coughed and continued. 'I would like to propose a toast to us all; to the first but definitely not the last celebration at the Christmas Café, whose purpose it is to celebrate togetherness and the spirit of sharing and to give a warm welcome to strangers.' He raised his glass. 'Cheers!'

Shouts of 'Cheers' and 'Salute!' and 'The Christmas Café!' rang out around the room amid the whoops and yells.

'And finally,' he said firmly and slowly, 'I would like to give the last word today to a Miss E. H. Arbuckle, who I think phrases it better than I ever could.' He turned to the sampler that hung alongside the other pictures on Bea's café wall and read its words aloud. 'Find the courage to grow, the courage to leave, the courage to return, for only by being brave will you ever find your true happiness.'

'Hear hear!' shouted the voices from around the table.

It was a lunch that no one present that day would ever forget. The food, a combination of traditional Christmas fare, the best Aussie seafood and exquisite Italian puddings, made the most sumptuous feast. Everyone saved a small amount of space for Sarah's world famous chocolate mousse. Alex kept the crowd amused with his raucous anecdotes that sent giggles bouncing from the roof. Love and laughter were the glue that bound this very special family.

Bea looked at her man as he chatted to Diane, laughing no doubt at tales of Byron Bay, at how they had boarded a tall ship with no clue as to how that one short trip up to the Cape Byron lighthouse would change so many lives.

There was a knock on the door. 'We're closed!' came the

unanimous reply, not for the first time that day, followed by laughter.

'Ah, wait a minute, that'll be my guests!' John made a dash for the door. He looked back into the room. 'Clear the tables! Come on! Push them to the sides!'

Everyone got up and did as he instructed. Bea stood by the wall, not sure what was going on and, if truth be told, more than a little nervous.

John reappeared minutes later with four men in Irish costume: one held a concertina, another a fiddle, one had both a whistle and a flute and the fourth man held a bodhrán.

Bea placed her hand over her mouth, trying to calm her breathing and halt her tears.

The band took up position in the corner and started to play. The music was infectious, it was mere minutes before everyone took to the floor and the dancing began. Flora jumped up and grabbed her dad's wrist, swirling him around and around as the beat sped up. She shouted over to her gran, 'Now *this* is a proper party!' Bea beamed; it sure was. Wyatt threw caution to the wind and laughed as their feet stamped on the concrete floor. Bea had never seen him so relaxed. Marcus gallantly took Sarah's hand.

Kim ran over to Tait and grabbed him by the arm. 'I've thought of something else.'

'What do you mean?' Tait was curious.

Kim smiled. 'I told you I'd let you know if I thought of anything else, and I have.'

'What do you need?' Tait asked, expecting to be sent to the kitchen to fetch something.

'I need you to dance with me.' She placed her other hand around his waist.

'Really? You want to dance with me? That's great!' He beamed.

'She loves you, Tait, and she always has. Isn't that right, Kim?' Alex couldn't help himself.

'Yes. That's about the sum of it.' Kim looked up into the face of her surfer and nodded.

Tait pulled her towards him. 'You are kidding me! You are so out of my league!'

'That's what I said!' Flora shouted as she passed the couple. 'And no shenanigans, you two!'

'Oi!' Kim laughed but was quickly silenced by the kiss that Tait planted squarely on her mouth.

'I think you're fabulous,' Tait whispered, coming up for air.

'I'm funny too, really funny!' Kim laughed as they were pulled into the dancing throng.

Mr Giraldi tapped his cane in time to the music as his grandchildren danced around him in a circle. He cast his eyes skyward, knowing how much Angelica would have loved it.

John reached out his hand and took Bea's inside his. 'Reckon you remember how?' he asked, with a lick of fringe dangling in his eyes.

Bea nodded.

'Go easy on her, John, she isn't as young as she used to be!' Wyatt leant on his father's shoulder and whispered in his ear above the music.

'She is to me, son!' He smiled.

'You'd have liked Peter.' Wyatt felt it was right to mention the man who had raised him.

John turned to face his boy and looked him in the eye. 'Liked him? I love the man! He cared for the people most precious to me. I will forever be in his debt.'

Wyatt threw his arms around his dad and hugged him close. Those in close proximity clapped. Bea could hardly see through the fog of her tears.

John pulled her into the middle of the room and the two began to dance. With every step the years fell away until they were young and in love, with their whole lives ahead of them. Bea looked up into the face of the man she loved. His words filled her head like the sweetest music. 'I don't think there is anywhere else on the whole of God's earth that I would rather be.'

He held her close as they spun round, whispering into her ear, 'I waited for you, my love, and I was not tired by waiting. Happy Christmas, Beatrice.'

She closed her eyes and placed her hand on his chest, feeling the rhythm of his heart as it danced beneath her fingers. 'Happy Christmas, my John.'

About the Author

AMANDA PROWSE is a multi-million bestselling author who has published more than thirty novels and is one of the most prolific writers of contemporary fiction in the UK today.

Crowned 'the queen of family drama' by the *Daily Mail*, she writes about life's challenges – from heartbreak and loss to dysfunctional family dynamics – but also about the pockets of delight that can be found in our relationships with others, often when we need them most.

Amanda is known for her relatable characters, emotionally compelling plots, and the sense of connection that readers feel with her stories.

She is an ambassador for The Reading Agency and feels passionately about supporting other women, spending as much time as possible outdoors (preferably by the sea!) and her family.

Discover more
from Amanda Prowse

Short Stories from Amanda Prowse

Dive into the
How to Fall in Love Again series

Thanks for reading!

Want to receive exclusive author content, news on the latest Aria books and updates on offers and giveaways?

Follow us on X @AriaFiction and on Facebook and Instagram @HeadofZeus, and join our mailing list.